Construction

PAMELA JOHNSON

SCEPTRE

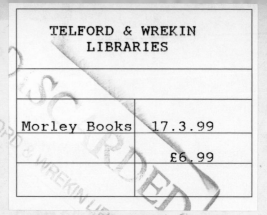
Copyright © 1998 Pamela Johnson

First published in 1998 by Hodder and Stoughton
A division of Hodder Headline PLC
First published in paperback in 1999 by Hodder and Stoughton
A Sceptre Paperback

The right of Pamela Johnson to be identified as the Author of
the Work has been asserted by her in accordance with the
Copyright, Designs and Patents Act 1988.

10 9 8 7 6 5 4 3 2 1

A CIP catalogue record for this book is available
from the British Library

ISBN 0 340 71798 X

Typeset by Palimpsest Book Production Limited,
Polmont, Stirlingshire
Printed and bound in Great Britain by
Mackays of Chatham PLC, Chatham, Kent

Hodder and Stoughton
A division of Hodder Headline PLC
338 Euston Road
London NW1 3BH

For David, Jacob and Isabelle

'The two kinds of space, intimate space and exterior space, keep encouraging each other, as it were, in their growth.'

The Poetics of Space, Gaston Bachelard

Contents

$\int$

An Open Fire

Amy can't sleep. She's given up trying to read but she's keeping the bedside lamp on. This new thought won't go away. It needs looking at. Two a.m. Her head is full of Conor and has been since he left three days ago. She doesn't have a photograph. She might have imagined him. If anything were to happen in Dublin what proof would she have of his existence?

She plumps up the pillows, lays one on top of the other in a pile. She still keeps four, two each side, even though she sleeps alone in the king-sized bed. She couldn't remove them at first; it would have been an admission that Greg was not coming back. Now she keeps them anyway, otherwise the bed looks lopsided. She sinks back into the soft heap.

This is a fine bedroom with its wide bay window and elegant fireplace; a white marble surround with tiles that form a picture of tall lilies in a blue urn. She could light a fire. A real open fire in the grate there. If she had what was needed she would do it now. She would light a fire for her and Conor. An open fire in August. It was hot again today but there's a chill in the night air. It's almost September when the air will change noticeably. In September they will all be back. Conor. The girls. Moss and his men to do the final 'snagging'. Fintan and Innes Quinn will make their inspection. The surveyor will issue the certificate of completion.

She will wait for the first frosty night and then light a fire here in the bedroom.

Will she remember how to do it? Newspaper, rolled into thin

tubes and tied in knots. She must fill the grate with these and then build a pyramid of coal. Fire lighters. She will buy a box of fire lighters to make sure it catches. She will spread a sheet of newspaper over the mouth of the fireplace to make it suck in the air.

'Crazy woman,' Conor will laugh. 'You'll burn the house down.'

Flames will lick around the coals breaking the blackness into orange, red and blue. She will put logs on the glowing embers. Damp, and still covered in bark, they will burn slowly. A gentle hiss through the night. In the morning the room will smell of woodsmoke.

She will light a fire when she's decided what to do.

Nothing stands still. Look at this house. Almost finished now, as if it had always been like this. Moss and his men were quick to rip it apart, turn it inside out. All that crumbling plaster and rotting wood. The house was worn out, injured. Putting it back together has taken longer. Now there are smooth walls, the freshness of new paint. Amy knows that behind these new walls and under the floorboards there are spaces that aren't normally seen. Spaces that she has become familiar with over the last few months. There is a gap around the new wooden floor downstairs; a margin which allows the wood to expand and contract. Her eyes scan the new ceiling. She can't tell where the steel girder is. She knows it's there, spanning the bay, holding up the weight of Imogen's new room. It's dissolved into the space between floor and ceiling.

Three days since she last saw Conor. He phoned from the airport to say he'd landed. He'll phone again when he knows better how Caitlin is. What can she be like? Will she have his hair, his eyes? Will Amy ever meet this woman? A female version of Conor.

Amy has Conor's number but she won't use it. They agreed, emergencies only. Wanting a photograph in the middle of the night does not count.

He will phone tomorrow.

Still, she would like to check the number. She goes up the short run of stairs from her bedroom to her workroom, feels her way in the dark to her desk and clicks on the reading lamp. Of course it's there, pinned to the noticeboard. Anyway, she knows it off by heart. If she punched those numbers now, would he answer? She would do it if she thought he would answer. To prove he exists.

She reaches for the bowl which sits at the other end of her desk.

Conor made this.

He took a flat disc of plywood, cut into it with a band saw, a fine power blade, a single continuous movement from the outer edge, round and round to the centre. He pulled the wooden spiral up to form this bowl. A trace of glue along the saw-line holds it in place. Nothing added, nothing taken away. But changed.

Amy runs her finger around the base of the bowl tracing the spiral upwards.

2

The Skeleton

'Can't you put something back, Moss?' Amy shivers in the March blast that slices through the hallway of this house where, soon, she must live. 'There's hardly a ceiling left in the place. Every time I come here there's less of it.'

'The worst is done.' Moss reaches to close the front door gently before the wind slams it shut. 'We don't want that broken. Lovely, isn't it?' They pause to admire the stained glass. A richness of red and blue petal shapes, framed by a row of bottle-green coils like boiled sweets. The play of light through colour lifts the gloom of the wide entrance hall. Amy notices how, from the inside, it is possible to see out through the glass. But from the outside you cannot see in. The irregular surface of the glass multiplies the movement of men outside.

'You're lucky you know. All original. It's a grand house, Amy.'

'It will be when you put it back together again.'

'What's this, you don't trust me, Amy?' Moss backs up his mock-hurt tone with his boyish smile, a tactic that's hard to resist, though Amy tries.

'Can I remind you, Moss, that I have to let the other house go in four weeks. Have to, Moss. The removal firm is booked. It's definite.' Amy says this to convince herself as much as to convince him.

What has she done?

'Trust me. Decorating the bedrooms starts next week. We're on schedule.' Moss leads her into what will be her front sitting room, currently the site office, and points to the flow-chart Sellotaped to the wall.

'You'll have bedrooms for the three of you, a temporary kitchen in the spare bedroom, one bathroom, your workroom. The upper levels. That's what we always said we'd do. That is what we will do. And your sitting room here will be ready too if I can get the site office set up down below.' Moss raises his eyebrows, holds them till he has her gaze, challenging her to doubt him now. He wins this one.

'Now,' he takes the pencil from behind his ear, 'have you your colour schemes? I've Liam on the phone every five minutes wanting to buy the paint.' Before Amy can answer there's a warble from Moss's black leather bomber jacket. He opens the front door, steps into the garden to improve reception.

Desmond, one of the labourers, wants the door open anyway. Amy puts down the carrier bag that she's been clutching. Desmond props the door wide, keeping it there with a brick while he brings in a new delivery of plasterboard. He fills the hall; there's barely room for Amy. She's in the way in her own house. She crouches to unpack the paint samples from the carrier, and huddles inside her coat. With the door open the hall is a chilly wind tunnel.

The floor is covered with sheets of board to protect the tiles; an Edwardian mosaic of terracotta, blue, ochre with a touch of black in the border. Like a band of mourning.

Without Greg. She's doing all this without Greg. On her own.

The ache of Greg is receding, it's nothing like the pain it was, but it can return. Maybe once they live here it won't creep up on her like this, freezing her to the spot. If she dwells on Greg the pain will grow. She can't let the ache take hold, so she makes herself think colour. She needs to find a place where she can pull up the protective layer of hardboard so that she can check the colours of the tiles against the paint. She finds a loose edge at the top of the stairs that go down below.

Below.

Best not to think about down there. Up here. Enough of up here for the three of them to be comfortable. That's what they are all aiming for now that the removal date is fixed. She nudges back the hardboard and lines up the sample pots along the skirting. Alice and Imogen have chosen these: a bright yellow, cornflower blue, cinnamon. All too strong. Something neutral. How can she choose colours for rooms she hasn't lived in? She doesn't want schemes. What she needs is to cover up the scars of the building work; a clean slate on which to rearrange her life. Perhaps she'll give Liam one colour that could go through the whole house as a backdrop. Something like this soft grey. She paints a patch above and below the dado rail while Moss argues delivery dates and quantities of ballast. How much of that stuff can they need? It keeps coming. Lorry-loads of it.

Amy's not sure that she knew what ballast was a month ago when the estate agent rang to say that, at last, Durham Road was hers. Would she like to collect the keys? After the complications of legal and financial to-ing and fro-ing, she had walked into Crompton & Platt's office simply to be given three keys on a plain ring.

'Is that all?' she had wanted to say.

As she'd pulled up outside the house she'd felt like an intruder. It didn't seem right that she could let herself in when it was only hours since the last tenant left. She sat in the car and stared. It reminded her of the houses Alice and Imogen drew when they were small. A door in the middle with a generous bay window on either side. Untended rhododendrons and hydrangeas needed cutting back so they would flower again and let the light into the main rooms. The roof was steep: grey slate with two rows of red chimneys. The square garden was sliced in two with a straight path of cracked concrete from the door to the gate. In all her adult life she has never had a front gate. This one wasn't up to much, giddy on its hinges, rotting posts. Most of the woodwork was in a bad state.

'We'll get Keane for the joinery. Not the cheapest, but he's the best.' Moss had reassured her at their first planning meeting that everything was possible if she had the money. Amy had money. Scads of it. Imogen's word. So much money that she could afford to stay in her old house for eight weeks while the heavy part of the refurbishment was done. On the drawing board this appeared to be a neat plan. She imagined that she would be moving into a house that was almost finished. Here she is, half-way through the eight weeks with less of a house than when she bought it. Of course, there was still going to be months more work when she moved in, she knew that. But the difficult bit, the digging out of the basement down below, could be sealed off. The men would enter through the front cellar door. The two parts of the house – site and home – would be kept separate. Amy would simply get on with life in the upper part of the house. There would be no living with the builders, she'd decided. She would hardly know they were there. She would have civilised meetings with Moss to discuss progress. If things weren't running smoothly she would call in Fintan or Innes Quinn. Once she'd made the decision to move, she allowed herself to believe that she would slip effortlessly from her old life into her new one. It had to be done. Life, at what she was beginning to think of as her 'old house', was cramped. It wasn't just the small kitchen and the fact that the girls had to share a bedroom.

Greg's absence wouldn't leave.

All those doors he'd stripped to the bare wood, the shelves he'd built in the alcoves, sagging now with the weight of books. These traces of him weren't a comfort, as she'd once thought they might be. As long as they stayed at Salisbury Road they would be stuck in the past. Waiting for something that was never coming back. The new house at Durham Road had space for a future.

The money was much more than she'd imagined. Amy wanted to spend it. She didn't want amounts the size of a telephone number in her bank account. She didn't want to think about managing investments, at the mercy of a financial adviser. She'd kept something for the girls for later, enough for a small income but the rest, she was determined, would be converted into something solid.

The Durham Road house is big. Amy is making it bigger. She's putting life into the dead spaces in the loft and the cellar.

Room for them to expand.

Room to get away from each other. Amy and the girls, in some respects, are closer, huddled together in the intimacy of grief, but after three years it's beginning to feel too close for comfort. They need to ease apart. They need the space of this new house to accommodate their loss, each to go on living in her own way.

It will be all right. This is what she wants. Isn't it?

'Why couldn't you have bought something ready to move into with all that money?' Liz has said to Amy, more than once. Too many people still treat Amy with kid gloves, but not Liz.

'Because I want to make it mine. Ours.'

'Jesus, Mary . . .'

'Fuckin' . . .'

'Christ . . .'

A bunch of mud-smeared men and Moss burst through the doorway as the heavens open. Hail beats the front path, bounces two feet high, drowning out the rumble of the concrete mixer.

'Crazy March weather.' Desmond ducks inside, flicks his damp ponytail. They all huddle in the doorway, watching the squall. How can she think about colours with this going on? It's overcast, the light is bad. She will come back tomorrow. She'd like to get home in time to return Muriel's call.

'Keane's around somewhere, Amy. I need to get you two together,' says Moss. 'You've not met Keane, have you?' Amy can't say for certain whether she has or hasn't met Keane. She meets someone new each day, a stream of sub-contractors all wanting her to make a decision. They come and go. It's Moss she pays attention to. Moss juggles the contracts.

'Your kitchen. Had any more thoughts?' Moss doesn't like to stand around wasting time. If things come to a halt in one direction he finds another way of keeping up progress on the programme of work.

'I'll be with you in a minute,' says Amy. She screws the tops back on the sample paint pots.

Decisions. She made *the* decision to move here. One decision leads rapidly to another, they multiply like splitting cells. There is pleasure in each individual choice she makes. Each one is a step towards their new life, but decisions don't come in a steady stream with a space in between to savour the last one before facing the next. They pile up and collide. *Something ready to move into*. Liz has a point.

The day she took possession, Amy had wandered from room to room trying on the idea of this new home, seeing if it would fit. The house was scruffy, neglected, with washbasins in every room and a communal kitchen. Hardly livable in. No central heating.

No time for second thoughts.

The next day the Quinns' sign went up in her front garden. Moss and a team of labourers swarmed through like an invasion. They tugged at the old lino, tore into the plaster, prised up the floorboards. Things that Amy believed were permanent, unalterable, were dismantled before the morning break.

'Let's see if everything is as it seems,' said Innes Quinn the elder of the two brothers. He was there to refine the specification. 'There's always more to be done than you think when you disturb a place of this age,' he had warned. 'A job this size can be unpredictable.' Immaculate in grey flannel trousers and a navy blazer, he made notes on his clipboard. He wore a hard-hat: white, with a green Q above the peak. He offered one to Amy.

'This is a building site now. A live site. Run according to current health and safety regulations.' Would Innes Quinn look as smart at the end of a day? Dust appeared not to settle on him.

On they went, tearing rooms apart, looking for dry rot, subsidence, checking out the old gas piping. Amy reminded Innes Quinn that she'd had a survey done.

'Not worth the paper it's written on,' he said.

They skinned her house back to bare brick and timbers, picking at the flesh of its staid, worn-out body. Sinks, carpets, window frames were dispatched to the skip. Within a day her new home was a skeleton. A bare structure. A building site.

HARD HATS MUST BE WORN ON THIS SITE, says the notice in blue felt-tip pen, that Moss has pinned to the front door. A door which is hardly ever closed now as men come and go, strangers swarming through her house.

'Will you be using all of them?' A new voice cuts in. Not a voice she knows.

'Grimmet. Sweep,' he says, anticipating her question. He shakes hailstones from his cap.

Another decision.

Would she ever go to the trouble of lighting open fires? Think of the dirt. Would there be anywhere left to store coal once she's modernised the cellar? She wouldn't be lighting them for the heat. Comfort. A fire would make these large rooms more cosy. It needn't be a chore. It was rare to find so many fireplaces intact, some cast iron, some marble. All boarded up and unused.

'All of them then?' Grimmet's tone says, hurry up, make up your mind.

'All of them,' says Amy. 'They've not been swept for twenty years.' She's glad sweeping chimneys is a one-off, half-day job. She wouldn't like to meet Grimmet on a daily basis. He wants to push on. The job is bigger than he thought. He sends his assistant back to the van for more brushes and bags. They both wear the same navy blue overalls. Grimmet's cold eyes peep out from his blackened face. He makes it clear that he doesn't want to be watched by Amy. Still, she follows them up the house, curious to see how it's done. Up in the top bedroom, the one with the sloping roof, the one she's claimed for her workroom, Grimmet notices her peer around the door. He turns to face her, holds out a sharp, white skeleton, one of several he's extracted from the chimney. A bird, bone clean, dry like a museum exhibit or a child's model. The soot shakes easily from it, revealing its distinct structure. Clarity in the midst of dense black, like precise thought. A decision made.

She will leave now. Muriel said to call after lunch. If her message means a project with the museum Amy will have to consider it, no matter how bad the timing.

'Amy?' Moss's voice booms up the stairs above the din of the power saw and the thud thud thud of hammering.

'Up here, Moss.' He won't let her go now.

'Keane's up in the loft there. Come and see how it's going. You can maybe have a word about your kitchen.' Moss is determined to get more from Amy before she leaves. He steadies the ladder that reaches from the top landing up into the roof timbers.

'I'll be glad when I can come up here without using this.' She hates the last bit where she must swing her leg up onto the joists, then haul her other leg up. She could easily fall. Amy steadies herself astride two joists. Between her feet she has a view through the entire house. A frail, vulnerable skeleton which needs fleshing out. With the ceilings removed she can see straight through the bedroom below, the sitting room below that and into the cellar. She could fall right down there. A cold blast brings with it the smell of damp earth, wet clay and new plaster. There must be a dozen men working here today. She sticks her head through the space cut for the skylight. Three roofers are hunched under a blue tarpaulin on the scaffolding platform waiting for the squall to pass.

'Why don't you come out and have a proper look,' teases Dermot. 'It's safe enough. You'll have a grand view from here. We'll have your felting on by this evening if this clears.' She ducks back in. They've done so much since she was last up here. New timbers mark out the framework of the two new rooms. Imogen's bedroom and, across the landing, a bathroom. Clean yellow bones of wood, a ribcage breathing life into this once dark, musty space. Two more men cut plywood sheets, fitting them like a jigsaw to make a floor. She hasn't seen them before. Keane's men.

'Keane. Over here.' Moss shouts above the screech of a saw through plywood. Keane, both hands stretched above his head, doesn't take his eyes off the yellow steel tape flexed above him. He makes a mark on the wall with a pencil, scribbles figures on a notepad.

The man is busy, and so is she.

'Keane, come and meet our client.'

Keane concentrates on his calculations.

'Look, Moss,' says Amy, 'I've had it for today. I'll see him later in the week.' She must go. Her mind is elsewhere now, curious about what Muriel has to say.

Keane scribbles again on his pad, then releases the steel tape. It coils back in on itself. Amy turns to leave, bracing herself for the ladder.

'Sorry about that.' Keane has a gentle voice. A pleasant sound which falls easily into the quiet between bouts of sawing. 'I want to get these windows right.' He extends a hand and warm smile.

'Mrs Beardsley,' he says, 'pleased to meet you at last.' A mix of formality and kindness that she's come to expect of the men Moss brings on site.

'Amy. It's Amy.' Keane is a relief after Grimmet. Grimmet wasn't Irish, that's what made him seem even odder.

'Conor. Conor Keane. Can I have a word with you about this

window?' He offers her his arm for support as she takes the joists awkwardly. He leads her to the far wall that is mostly a void covered in flapping blue plastic.

'I'd like to take the sill lower. I could make two box sashes to match the room below, in proportion. You want this all to look meant don't you?' A gust lifts the blue plastic sheet, it sounds like a giant bird taking off.

'I'm sure that will be fine.'

It wasn't a good idea coming up here, she is beyond all this.

'That's always been the plan,' she makes an effort, 'to match the original windows.' If this man has the solution, why doesn't he make the decision himself? She has enough questions queuing up in her head.

'Yes, but to get the right proportions your sill needs to be lower.' It's only a matter of a few centimetres, he explains, but he wouldn't take the risk of making that decision himself without consulting the client.

'I'll be guided by you.' What's the odd centimetre in all of this?

'He's an artist is Keane,' Moss laughs. 'Perfectionist.' What has this to do with her? For a split second it happens. Surely Greg will . . . On her own. Everything is down to her. They are asking her because she told them to do this. She has asked them to rip it apart and make it new.

'The kitchen, then,' says Amy. One thing at a time.

'I've a scale drawing of the space below.' says Keane. 'If I'm to make your kitchen, and keep up with Moss here, I need to know what you want sooner rather than later.' Isn't that what they all say. And if she stalls, the hold-ups in the programme become her responsibility.

'Delivery dates.' Fintan Quinn had warned her. 'No use asking for the latest stainless steel, precision-made German kitchen if there's a six-month wait.'

'Let's keep it simple,' says Amy.

A fierce gust sucks the plastic sheet, right out this time, so it almost flies away. Amy loses her balance and grabs Keane's arm. For a second it feels as though they will both fall through to the bedroom below. They steady each other until they're firm on the joists again.

'Here, stand on this,' Keane lays a sheet of plywood down. 'Not the best place to talk. Let's make an appointment. I've photos of other work I've done. You give me an idea what you want, I'll draw it for you. We'll take it from there.'

She swings her legs back over the joists onto the ladder and down to the floor below.

'Don't worry Amy,' Moss calls after her. 'We've everyone doing double shifts.'

As she moves back down the house she loses count of them. The trades are tripping over each other: roofers, electricians, plumbers, joiners, bricklayers, plasterers. In the main bedroom, her bedroom, three men are tacking up plasterboard to form a ceiling, hammering the flat heads of galvanised nails. They stand on platforms that fill the floor so she can't get into the room. On hand are buckets of flesh-pink liquid that they will skim over the boards. When the plaster sets hard, all it will need is a coat of paint, if she could choose the colour.

On the ground floor the plumber, the electrician and the man installing the burglar alarm, shadow one another, channelling highways of pipes and wires between timbers. How would she describe that space? Is it beneath the floor, or above the ceiling? Soon she'll never see it again. It will disappear and she'll be left with the flick of a switch, the turn of a tap.

Down below, a mud-stained man in a hard hat looks as if he's at the coalface. Crouching in the cellar, he vibrates to his pneumatic drill, cracking the old concrete floor, breaking through to sticky clay. He must dig deep enough to create a space where she can stand full height.

Back up in the hall she returns to the paint samples. The sun is bright now that the hail has stopped. The light is stronger. She sits on the stairs to make a list for Moss. She will meet the girls halfway. Warm creams and yellows for the north-facing front rooms; cool shades of green for the sunny south-facing back rooms and the pale grey throughout on the woodwork. Alice and Imogen can have whatever they like in their own rooms.

'A lot to consider,' says Conor Keane as he picks his way past her.

'Yes.'

'Hard to imagine a home when it's in this state. See you soon, then.' She watches him go. He exchanges a word with Desmond as he slides into his car.

3

Woman In A Boat

Why is she shaking? It starts as she turns into Salisbury Road. So familiar is this corridor of solid, Edwardian brick. Why, then, is she shaking? She clutches the steering wheel, presses her back into the seat, steadies her arms. She gasps. Small, irregular intakes of breath build to a larger sob.

Why?

Amy knows about crying. She's had to learn. *The tears need to come, Amy*. Dr Hampton has told her. *Let them come. We can talk later*. Amy has learned to read her tears.

Not Greg.

She's not crying for Greg. This doesn't feel like Greg. *It's a process, Amy*. And hasn't she followed it through? Each battering and bewildering stage. *Give yourself time, Amy*. Two years, more, she had spent in what she thinks of as the glass case. In the world and yet not. She had watched other people getting on with life. They didn't have the weight to carry. They weren't trapped inside the glass. How disturbing to see people laugh. She once overhead two women on the Underground grumbling about their husbands. They didn't know yet what it would be like.

Sometimes the weight had become so heavy that it developed a physical presence. As if, hung in a sling around her neck, she carried a boulder; its weight pressing in on her breasts, dragging down her shoulders, so she could barely raise her head. It seemed so unfair, such a tall order that, though she had the boulder to contend with, she must carry on living in the normal way. She could allow her own work to slide but she still had to wake up in the morning to produce food for the girls, to encourage them to go to school when they too wanted to stay in bed. Sometimes, after they had left, she didn't go near her desk. Instead, she would load the washing machine simply to watch the movement through the porthole. It soothed her to see the suds gathering. She felt a mild ripple of relief as the water changed from clear to grey. A problem solving itself. It was a comfort to see the dirt moved on, swilled away, before she became aware again of the weight of the boulder.

I can't do it. A shriek. Always inside her head. Mustn't alarm the girls. In Dr Hampton's dark room, sitting next to the stuffed bird in a glass case, she would cry. Sometimes for the whole fifty minutes. Afterwards the boulder would feel lighter, as if the tears had eroded it. If the weight became too much before her next appointment, she would leave her body to it. Her mind would slope off. She was physically present yet somewhere else at the same time. She could see her hands butter toast or fold the washing, but, in her head, she was out, looking for Greg. She conjured him up till she could see him. Greg sorting through contact sheets, his eye to the magnifying glass, the chinagraph ready to circle the images he would print, a cross through those he would reject. Greg at the light box, checking transparencies. Greg so alive. A call to his editor, 'is the flat-plan fixed, Mike?' Greg infecting others with his enthusiasm, 'three spreads, Mike, I promise you it's knock-out stuff.' Of course Greg has not gone for good. He's on a shoot, he's been delayed. He's had to reshoot. 'Hair in the fucking gate,' he hated things to go wrong. Greg with a fine brush, cleaning his lenses. It didn't happen often. A hair in the gate, a reshoot. He will come back. Greg at the end of a day opening a bottle of red wine, pouring a glass for Amy. And when Amy could no longer bear the sight of Greg so vivid in her mind's eye, she turned her attention to what she must tell him, when he came back. *Write it down, Amy. You could write a letter to Greg. Keep a notebook.* Once she had begun, she couldn't stop. When she was writing she didn't notice the boulder quite so much. It was getting lighter. It wasn't gone, but it was light enough for her not to think about it all the time. She found herself able to do everyday things again. Small things like reading the newspaper. One Friday evening as she skimmed the classified section of the local paper she had seen the advert for Durham Road.

HUGE POTENTIAL. NO CHAIN
Edwardian, double-fronted. All original features.
Currently arranged as bedsits.
Easy potential to reinstate as family home.
Vision and loving care required.
Priced accordingly.

It was in a road about half a mile away. She and Greg had often walked along there when the girls were younger; a short cut to the park. A road of rambling houses that she and Greg would admire, then dismiss because they couldn't face the building work. Amy hadn't realised that she'd wanted to leave Salisbury Road until she read the advert. *Huge potential. No chain*, became her mantra, words to keep away the boulder. Soon the house became her main preoccupation. She didn't notice the boulder. It appeared to have gone, though she still felt the sensation of being trapped behind glass. She couldn't entirely trust that she was fully out there in the world again, joining in with the rest. Then one day, not long after her offer on Durham Road had been accepted, everything around her had a marvellous clarity. She noticed how the garden had thrived despite her neglect. The camellia was alive with plump buds. It was like looking through the windows when they've just been cleaned. There is the same familiar view, nothing is different, but everything is clearer.

She wipes her cheek with the back of her hand. Her eyes are blurred with tears. She is thankful for the privacy of the car. What state of lunacy has allowed her to think that upheaval on this scale will behave itself? Here she is, owner of two houses, neither of which she can call home. Durham Road is a building site. Salisbury Road is a chaos of cupboards being turned out. Boxes are piled in each room waiting for her to decide what must go to storage, what must go with them. Each empty box is an accusation that she can't answer. Here, in the car, is the only safe and constant place. She knows where she is behind the wheel.

In control.

Maybe she will drive on, crying like this, till the tears stop. It doesn't matter how many flow-charts Innes Quinn makes, no amount of planning can allay these doubts.

Doubt.

That's what it is. Doubt that has welled up and can wait no longer. She pushes away more tears. She's nearly home but she doesn't want to get out of the car, her lifeboat in this swelling sea of doubt that's crashing around her. If she ploughs on for long enough and far enough maybe she will reach calmer water. And while she's gone, maybe her old house will pack itself up and the new house will be built with no more decisions required of her. Let Moss or the Quinns decide on tiles, floors, and the position of walls. She will arrive on removal day to find it finished. Set up with her things, ready and waiting for her to start again. Get a grip, Amy. It's foolish to drive in this state.

Amy pulls hard on the hand brake and sits for a while to compose herself. She shifts the tile samples off the passenger seat. There are tissues here somewhere.

It's not only the doubt. She's cross too because, damn it, until last week she was enjoying working on the house. It was wonderful to feel that kind of energy again. To be alive and present in the moment as she lived it. Not thinking about the past. Her mind and body synchronised, engaged in each task in the present, inching her way towards a future. She was surprised to find that choosing doorknobs and window catches could induce a sense of excitement. A doorknob chosen was a handle on the future. And through the tears she laughs at this thought. A door marked 'future', all she has to do is choose the right shiny, brass knob that will open it.

She has made progress. Her life is flowing on again. She must not lose her nerve now. Understandable that things pile up at this stage. Moss is putting the pressure on to be ready for the move. It will be easier once they live at Durham Road. And she hasn't slept all week. She rifles through her bag for tissues, and finds her notebook.

It's because of the dream, the dream shook me. Thought I was done with this. Not for weeks, not since I bought Durham Road. It's too much. Maybe say no to Muriel. Decisions. I could see Dr Hampton again. It's the dream, can't get it out of my mind. Packing cases neatly stacked in the removal van. The van turns the corner into Durham Road too fast and over it goes, cartons everywhere, books, papers, clothes, furniture, flying up in the air. Where will it land? Things flung so high they go on and on, into orbit. Clothes fly and dance then fall, piling up in a heap. Some things fall and break, Greg's CD collection, his cameras. Moss's men picking up the bits, tossing them into the skip. 'Got to keep the road clear,' Desmond leering. 'More ballast on its way.' Me trying to salvage things but everything I pick up slips from my hands. Cold, slippery surfaces, scaly, like fish. I can't hold on. Moss is laughing. Not in a good humoured way. Not his harmless flirting, more menacing. A house full of menacing men who can't distinguish between what is mine and what is rubbish for the skip. Me in the road begging them to stop. 'Stop,' a huge effort to form the word. A massive sound inside me, filling my head, throat, deep down inside. The whole of me an echo chamber but nothing, nothing comes out. Woke in a sweat. Four a.m. Worst time. Couldn't get back to sleep. See Hampton for pills?

She puts the notebook back in her bag. She's quieter now. A few short sniffs as she reaches round to the back seat. The tissues are there under the folder Conor Keane left when he came round last week. In it are photographs of kitchens he's designed and colour samples. She hasn't had time to look at them.

Amy slumps into the green leather armchair; its worn arms extend a welcome. Her front room is, as yet, untouched by the upheaval, the only room in the house that is still intact. Along the sofa, she lines up the boards that are stuck with tile samples. A row of stiff-backed visitors who she would rather not entertain. Tiles for the bathrooms. What about that border pattern of fish, the blue would look strong against a pure white tile. What is it about fish that attracts? She looks around the walls hung with paintings and prints. There are fish in three of them. The pictures will have to come down soon. She's not trusting them to storage. Liz will keep them in her spare room. 'Yes, please,' she'd offered eagerly. 'I'll have the art.'

Each one has to be taken down, the corners protected by card. She could start now. Amy reaches out and takes the two bottom corners of the frame in her hands. It's the largest painting, the first one she and Greg bought together. *Man and Woman in a Boat.*

They had both been drawn to the energy; a charge captured on paper in fast, bold brush work. A dream-like scene where the sky is a backdrop of crimson, stippled with the hottest pink. A solid orange sun sits above the couple in the boat. Amy eases the picture upwards, slides the wire off the hooks. It is heavier than she thought. She rests a moment, letting the wall take its weight. The boat is small, too small for the two of them. It could capsize. The man and the woman are absorbed by something beyond the boat, not in the picture. They stare out. A still, steady gaze. The woman is at the bow, standing, leaning over the side. The boat dips in her direction. He sits behind her. His body tilts, ever so slightly, over the stern. Is this a gesture of fear? That's how it seems some days. Other times, Amy is sure, the man is in control; the tilt backwards is a confident move, to stabilise the boat. Today, the boat could capsize. Amy steadies the picture. Slowly, she lets it slide to the floor.

In between the man and the woman, there are fat silvery fish in the boat. A tail fin hangs over the side. The woman catches another one with her bare hands. She has it by the tail. Can she hold on to it? Amy rests the picture against the wall. She crouches to examine the surface of the paint. Her nose almost touches the glass. She sees the join. She has forgotten that the picture is two pieces of paper joined. The woman is on the left, the man is on the right. Amy stands back and considers each side of the picture. Two pictures. She could take them apart and reframe them as separate pieces. She could put the man away. *Woman In A Boat.* Woman on her own, clutching the tail of a fish, with the boat tipping forward. There would be nothing in the frame to show whether the boat would right itself.

Amy takes down a few of the smaller prints and stacks them against the painting. Maybe she should phone Liz, arrange a time to take these over. She needn't do it yet. Three more weeks. She slumps back into the chair to see the ghosts of these pictures. A grey line describes exactly where each one hung. There are holes in the plaster where the hooks sat. *Here, Amy?* Greg holding up the picture, a pencil ready to mark the spot. *Are you sure?* He has the hammer ready to hit the nail. Now, she is dismantling their home. Willingly pulling it to pieces. She is throwing things away, giving things away. Greg's leather jacket to Oxfam. What's left must either go into storage until the house is finished, or come with them.

'Bring only what you really need.' Moss reminds her, daily. She's not sure where anything is anymore. It will be months before she sees most of her possessions again. If she can live without stuff for six months does she need it anyway?

A cup of tea.

As she waits for the kettle to boil she lays his photographs out on the kitchen table. Conor Keane is an artist, a craftsman, as Moss keeps telling her. In these glimpses of other people's houses Conor Keane's joinery sits, quietly, comfortably. Kitchens, cupboards, shelves. Some are in the natural wood: pine, oak, ash. Others are painted in muted tones: mulberry, a sage green. There is no strain to assert a presence. Why not let him get on with it?

She opens the back door and sits on the step with a mug of tea between her hands, thankful for the sudden mild weather. She dreads the thought of moving in the rain. The air is still edged with a trace of winter, but in the shelter of the doorway she enjoys the warmth of the strengthening sun. This is the best time in the garden. The parade of bulbs is almost finished, snowdrops, crocuses, daffodils and now the black-throated tulips. Their orange cups are widening, the petals will soon fall. She'll be gone before the blue fuzz of forget-me-not is out. The magnolia is ready. A few more days of sun like this and its fat brown cigar buds will unroll to the freshest pink. The first summer frock shaken early from its winter store. The camellia, in its shady spot by the shed, is heavy with red blooms that will burst for weeks, shedding petals along the path. She will dig it up, take it to the new house. Greg bought it for her, seven, eight years ago? No particular reason. 'I know how you like to keep the colour coming.' It can't be a good time to do it though, not now it's in flower. She must be careful how she digs it up. If she takes a big enough rootball and gets it quickly into the ground at Durham Road it should survive. The noise of the telephone pulls her back into the house.

Liz. Let it be Liz. A good long chat with Liz will clear the thickets in her head.

A man's voice. Irish. Not Moss. Not a Quinn.

'I've more drawings for you.'

Conor Keane. She hadn't expected to hear from him so soon.

'Have you had any thoughts?'

'I have your folder here on the table in front of me.' Amy's been caught not doing her homework.

'Did the photos help?' Why is she even considering other kitchens. Let him do it. A decision made.

'I could drop by. I've a sample of the beech floor. Would the morning suit – around nine thirty?'

'Nine thirty, then,' says Amy.

She'd been irritated by his pedantic questions about the windows in the loft, but when they met last week it was his attention to detail that impressed her.

'Think how those high cupboards will work day to day,' he'd pointed out. 'Do you want to be forever up and down a step ladder?' His designs were thoughtful, uncluttered.

'These cast iron handles lie well next to the glazed panels on the cupboards.' He had a sample. 'Adds texture.' The weight of it felt good in her hand. After an hour he'd said that he had a much better idea of what she wanted. He'd do more drawings.

'Elevations. To give you a better idea of the finished thing.' He'd left the photographs and a colour chart. He'll be here tomorrow with her kitchen worked out.

Amy holds up Keane's colour chart.

'I have them mixed to order.' What he gave her was a strip of brown paper. Strong brown wrapping paper. The strip is broken by a ladder of colours. Opaque, subtle tones. 'Gives a good sense of how the paint sits on the wood.' He must have made these himself. She sees him painting large sheets of brown paper with long stripes of colour. Maybe several would hang around his workshop waiting to dry. He would then cut them into strips to give to clients like her. A phrase of her mother's comes to mind.

'He's not your normal run.'

4

An Awkward Space

'Imogen, Alice.' Amy loops the chain of the plug around the tap. Her voice is lost beneath the suck and gurgle of bath water. 'Can you get that?' She will not be moved from her pocket of peace. It can only be the postman at this time. She hugs the warm towel around herself and settles into the wicker chair.

Her morning ritual is like a meditation, and she needs it after another bad night. When Greg died she would sit like this indefinitely, unconvinced that choosing clothes for the day was worth the effort. Sometimes she had crawled back into bed clutching the towel around her, slept a sad, disturbed sleep, waking in the afternoon, cold. There were days when this was her only sleep. Back in the land of the living, the daily ritual is a litmus test that shows how she's doing. For five or ten minutes after her bath she allows the warm pile of the towel to blot the water while she enjoys the steamy warmth of the bathroom, gathering herself together for the day. No more than ten minutes or she'll be sunk. She still finds it hard, some days, to put on clothes. There's a moment of relief once she's dressed. She's made it. Clothed, she's better able to withstand the lethargy of grief that has a way of creeping up. Where are the girls? Amy's only just sat down, she needs time to rub oil into her damp, neglected skin. As she sat in bed at six this morning, hugging herself out of the nightmare, she pulled back the duvet and noticed her legs were dusty with dead skin. She won't let the dream back in, yet, but she can do something about her skin.

'Answer the door. Imogen. Alice. One of you.' It could be the man to read the meter. Wasn't he supposed to come the day she moved? She needs to think about what to wear. Her leggings hang from the towel rail where she left them last night. They sag at the knees, a tired version of herself. Same old leggings. Same old sweater. A skirt perhaps? She has no tights without snags. She hasn't bought clothes since, since when?

'Imogen, Alice.' Maybe after she's seen Conor Keane she'll go up to town.

Conor Keane. He's early.

She throws off the towel, pulls on her kimono, stuffs her damp feet into her slippers.

'All right, I'm going.' Imogen, her Doc Martened feet clomping down the stairs, collides with Amy.

'What kept you?'

'I was doing my eye-liner.'

'If it's Conor Keane show him into the kitchen. Offer him tea or coffee. He's early. What am I going to wear?'

He'll have to wait. She must find something, anything but those leggings. What can she pull on quickly to look halfway decent. No time for make-up, maybe a smudge of lipstick. Odd that he would call this early. It's barely eight.

'Nine thirty then.' He was quite definite. She can hear the distinctive, softness of his voice. 'Nine thirty then.' It would be odd to call so early without phoning first. The black wool skirt, the red sweater, black tights and never mind about the snags.

'It's Craig, Mum,' says Imogen, walking in on Amy as she flings open drawers. 'What's the panic, anyway?'

'No panic, I thought it was Conor Keane for the meeting that's all. No panic.' Relief and irritation in equal portions. How many times has she told Craig to phone before he comes? He always turns up unannounced. Can't he read the sold sign. Why would she want her windows cleaned when they belong to someone else.

'When you off then?'

'Another week. Look Craig . . .' No time is right for the window cleaner, having someone in the house, never quite sure where they are, moving from room to room, listening for the rumble of a sash window. Amy can't think with someone like Craig in the house. She'd better get used to it, there were fifteen men at Durham Road yesterday.

'Give you this, can I, for the new people. Helps if you recommend, know what I mean?' He hands Amy a photocopied slip with his phone number. INSIDE AND OUT – REASONABLE RATES.

'What number Durham are you then? I do a few in Durham.'

'It will be a while. There aren't any windows in the back of the house.'

'A big job then? Used to do roofing. Did a roof in Durham once. Big houses.'

'Yes, a big house. Bigger than I thought.'

'Alice, Imogen, where were you? The last thing I need is to stand on the doorstep chatting to Craig.'

'Tell him to push off Mum.'

'Imogen. Do you need to wear eye-liner to school?'

'Mum, do we need to have this conversation?'

'It would have been helpful if one of you'd dealt with it. I was hardly out of the bath.'

'It's all right for you to fuss about how you look but not me?'

'I was having a bath.'

'He'd only ask for you anyway,' Alice reasons. 'Don't answer the door.'

'It might have been Conor Keane.'

Imogen giggles.

'What's the joke?' But Amy is talking to their backs as they head for the kitchen. She follows them. Might as well have breakfast now she's down. Lately she's avoided being in the kitchen in the morning with the girls. It's an awkward space. None of them is at their best at breakfast, each silently claims an area of table. Or, worse, Imogen paces between the chair and the door, never quite managing to sit down. Each, unreasonably, feels something bordering on resentment at the presence of the others. Not much is said. Mornings exaggerate the inadequacy of the space. Never an ideal space, too narrow. The old pine table and four chairs all but fill it. When Amy and Greg had first moved in they were snug in the cosiness of the breakfast room. Sundays, before the girls, seemed so long ago: Greg scrambling eggs, grilling kippers, always happy to make another pot of coffee. Two or three newspapers spread out. Always the ones that had used his pictures and the others to see what the competition was doing. He would buy them late on Saturday night at King's Cross on their way home from the cinema or a party. And when he'd compared all the colour supplements he would throw crusts to the birds. They had time, then, to watch the birds swoop and peck. The bay window over the garden created an illusion of more space than there was; a space that became tighter and tighter as it filled up with their lives. First a high chair, then a box of toys in the corner, a second high chair, paint boxes and jars of dirty water left on the windowsill. Amy would mentally knock down the side wall, rebuild it a few feet out, but they never got around to it. Now the space is full of books and folders, Imogen's magazines stacked up in the corner. Alice is spread out over most of the table sorting her English folder, the work she didn't finish last night.

'Coffee?' says Amy, in a bid for family unity. 'I'll make a big pot.'

'I'm OK.' Imogen takes a low-fat yoghurt from the fridge. She selects the shiniest crisp green apple from a bowl by the cooker. How can she bear the tartness so early in the morning? Imogen leans against the fridge, but thinks better of it, and, for once decides to sit at the table.

'Come on Ali, move over.' Imogen makes more than she needs of squeezing her lean self around Alice, to reach the far end. Imogen insists on sitting at the window end. Greg's seat. Amy would always ask him to go in first, so that his large frame had the most space. If he sat on either side, no one could get around him. Both girls have inherited Greg's height. With Imogen, this has emerged into an elegant slenderness; for Alice, as yet, it's a gawky skinniness. Imogen has her father's colouring too; the near black hair, the creamy, pale skin. Imogen turns the chair sideways in order to look out of the window as she takes slow, deliberate scoops of yoghurt. Her sleek curtain of hair falls, shutting out her mother and her sister.

'You'll need more than that,' says Amy unable to stop herself. 'Something warm.'

'I'm OK.'

'At least have some coffee.'

'It's bad for you.'

'Alice, you'd better clear that now, before something gets spilled on it.' All the bother of doing Durham Road must be worth it not to have to shoe-horn themselves around one another in a morning.

'Have you made a start on your room?' Amy keeps the tone light, mildly inquisitive.

'Plenty of time yet, Mum.' Alice reassures. There's an eagerness to please in her clear blue eyes.

'Yeah, a week.' Imogen spoons the last of her yoghurt. 'Can't we do it at the weekend? I was going to Maxine's tonight.'

'I'll need you for other things at the weekend. To move the pictures over to Liz's while she has her brother's van.'

'Tomorrow then.'

'It will take longer than you think.'

'But Mum . . .'

'You have to decide what to take with you, what to put into storage. You can't take everything. You won't like it if I do it for you. Anyway, I can't do all this alone.' It's the strongest Amy can manage, not wanting to give in, not wanting a row, not wanting the move to become a battleground. Alice pulls back the mass of her wavy hair, winding it tight into a scrunch. She stuffs her papers into her bag, leans across to peck Amy on the cheek.

'It's all right Mum, we'll get it done, tomorrow, won't we Im?' A slight movement of Imogen's left shoulder implies agreement and then she too is gone. As the front door slams Amy's shoulders relax. She pours a second cup of coffee, and in the quietness the dream comes back, she can't shake it. *Dreams are valuable, Amy. If you write them out, they won't haunt you. Let them go.* Quarter to nine. Conor Keane will be here soon. She might as well show him in here, let him see what she doesn't want at Durham Road. No tight seating. Enough room to lean back in your chair and have someone walk behind you. Amy gathers up cups and plates, quickly washes and wipes them and wipes down the table, straightens a pile of books left by Alice, pushes in the chairs. One at the centre of each side of the table. She sits down again. It's no use, she has to do it now. She'll feel better. Best not to think too much, just write quickly, how it felt, the images. It will take a moment, then she can let it go.

A road. Me driving. Mountains on my left. A steep drop down to the sea on my right. Driving steady. Calm. I was calm. A gully forms in the solid mountain range to the left. It fills with water. Builds up to a surge, a river flooding. Massive water poised to deluge the road. Although I see the flooding river, I feel perfectly safe. Although it looks as if it is about to flood the road ahead, I know I can drive past before it spills. This rising flood is no threat. It's happening behind me now. I'm filled with relief. Relief surges through my body. I can't believe my luck. But then I notice that the water is not contained by the gully. It's spreading the length of the mountain range. Water brims over the ridge of the entire mountain range. The length of the road, as far as I can see, will be flooded. Ahead of me and behind me, at any moment. There's no way I can drive fast enough to beat it. The swell of water is enormous. Beyond comprehension. Beyond survival. Any second now, any second I'll be gone. But I wake. Why do we never let the disaster happen?

Back in the bathroom Amy screws the top onto the bottle of oil. *Rub into moist skin after bath or shower*, the instructions say. Her skin is bone dry by now. She scoops up the leggings, no time to think about what to wear, she pulls them on. Her knees easing into the familiar shapes they have moulded in each leg. After she's moved, when the warmer weather comes, she will choose new clothes. In the bedroom she catches sight of herself in the long mirror. Her legs, shaded black by the leggings, look much the same as they always have: slim calves, perhaps a touch heavy on the thighs. Her arms and shoulders are firm and smooth, unchanged. Though she is not tall, shorter now than both Imogen and Alice, her slender limbs have always made her seem light, giving her a sense of height. The slackness and thickening in the middle of her body surprises her. Even if she breathes in she cannot quite smooth out the ripples gathering around her waist. It is as if a new, older version of Amy is encroaching on the younger one. Secretly, silently beneath her sweater, it has been spreading from the centre, inching its way upwards and downwards. She hasn't the height to carry these extra pounds and, at forty-two, they won't go away without some effort. She will start swimming again, maybe.

Amy rummages in her drawer, pulls out a black polo neck, too sombre. This is better. She settles on a tunic length, soft, red. Her hair sparks with static as her head emerges from the neck. She has left the dark brown waves to grow, brushing it back from her face, letting it fall where it will. It's almost shoulder length. The colour seems flat. She will make an appointment, a cut and some colour, maybe. There's a winter greyness, too, about her skin, she needs the sun to lift the colour. She dusts blusher on each cheek. That will have to do for now.

Conor Keane looks different. It's the jacket. Tweed, greyish. A dark green shirt. No tie. He has a black portfolio under one arm, his other hand is sunk in the jacket pocket as if searching for something, a gentle rummaging. He lays his portfolio on the table as he pulls back one of the side chairs.

'You'll be more comfortable there.'

Amy indicates the end seat. Imogen's seat. Greg's seat.

'There will be so much more space in your new kitchen.'

He's not a big man, but he seems to fill the end of the table. 'This has always been an awkward space.' Yet his hands are slender. He slips one into his pocket again. A pipe smoker, maybe. It's as if he's secretly filling the bowl with tobacco. 'And it gets worse as the girls get bigger.' Now the jacket comes off as he spreads out and reaches for the drawings. 'Let me take that.' As she does so, she brushes Conor Keane's arm. There is a fraction of silence, an awkwardness, broken as she takes his jacket into the hall to hang it up. A distinct smell. Sharp, but pleasant. A blend of wood, mothballs and the raw human scent of this man. No tobacco. Not a smoker.

Keane has spread out his scale drawings. He talks her through each of the elevations, introducing the room he has imagined for her.

'I've gone ahead as if you've gutted that space,' he explains. In his imagination he has pulled out the fire surround, the original cupboards and dresser.

'Those original features are not worth saving in my opinion. Too far gone. They set such a limit on what you can do.' If she keeps them and makes that area the dining space then she won't gain much, he tells her. 'You won't have substantially much more

31 •

room than you have here.' This working out of awkward spaces has been muddled in her head, but Conor Keane, at the stroke of a pen, has removed the chimney breast, 'It will mean another steel reinforcement.' He's checked this with Innes Quinn. He has torn out the cupboards and the half-broken dresser. 'You could keep those doors, some of the wood. I could maybe recycle them elsewhere in the house, but they're not going to give you the space you need.' Then he produces another version of her kitchen/dining room. 'Just a thought, you might want to consider.' With his gentle, easy voice, he explains how he's taken down the wall between the present kitchen and scullery, ripped out all features in the current dining room and knocked the wall down between the two areas. 'See how it makes a ballroom of a space.' And if she puts the dining room where the kitchen is now she'll have a grand room with a full view of the garden, and, tucked around the corner, is a space perfect for any kitchen she cares to design.

'A floor like this,' he says, producing a piece of solid beech, 'could go through the whole area.' And on he goes creating the heart of her new home with his drawings and samples and careful explanations. By 11 o'clock she senses that Conor Keane ought to be on his way though he doesn't say so. He's happy enough to talk about variations on the design, give examples of the costings. She asks to see the samples of etched glass again, the ones she might choose for the cupboard doors.

'I'll fetch your jacket.' Amy's aware of him watching her as she turns a piece of beech around in her hand. 'Could you leave this with me?' He shakes himself into his jacket. His right hand goes straight for the pocket and fumbles. If not a pipe then what? She could ask him. She wants to know.

'Would you like a coffee?' Is that her voice, did she say that? He mustn't go. Not yet. He might not like coffee. It's bad for you, Imogen says. He will have work to do, other clients to see. It's the lack of sleep, she's not herself. He looks uncomfortable. She will make an appointment with Dr Hampton. Why did she ask him to stay for coffee when he's so clearly ready to go? She wills the words back into her mouth. He can only say no.

'I'd love a coffee.'

5

Mirrorwork

'Too small is better than too big,' says Imogen. She sorts through her cupboard, making piles of grubby bras, snagged tights and shrunken T-shirts. Alice looks at herself sideways in the long mirror.

'Katie Morgan has them specially built. Imagine that Ali. Thirty-eight, double G. They have to *build* them for her.' Imogen knows that she's told Alice about Katie Morgan many times before; every time Alice starts whinging about her flat chest, in fact. But each time, Imogen tells it as if it's a new discovery. She lingers over the details. How Katie goes to an old woman in Stamford Hill who has a moustache; she takes Katie into a dusty cubicle at the back of her shop and does all kinds of weird measurements. How it takes ages, with Katie naked from the waist up, as the woman measures each one in every possible direction: across, round, top to bottom, side to side. She writes each dimension on a chart, accurate to the last millimetre. The shop window is full of corsets. Katie Morgan doesn't need a corset. She has narrow hips, top heavy.

'You'd think she'd topple over. And one's bigger than the other,' says Imogen. 'I've shared a changing room with Katie at the swimming pool. I'm telling you, her bras are the size of a hammock. Each cup is big enough to put your head in. Gross.'

'People have operations,' says Alice. She pushes her shoulders back, adjusts herself to exactly the right angle for maximum effect.

'Katie's having an operation when she's eighteen,' says Imogen.

'The doctor said to wait till they'd stopped growing. Imagine that, Katie could get even *bigger*. You've got three more years to go before you can be sure that's all you're getting. Come on, let's finish this.'

At Durham Road Imogen will have her own room. No more sharing with her younger sister. She could have had her own room here but they couldn't agree who would keep this big front bedroom, who would take the small room at the back. Imogen, at seventeen, could have put in a strong bid for the larger space, evicting Alice. Anyway, mum likes to keep a room for visitors. Even if Alice had gone to the back room she would have had to return each time Gran came to stay, or when Liz drank too much and stayed over. The possibility of making dad's darkroom into a bedroom again wasn't ever mentioned. Anyway, there was plenty of room for both of them in the big square room at the front of the house. It could be chilly in winter, but in summer she and Alice would lie on top of their duvets on a hot night, talking as it grew dark. She would miss that, not having Ali to talk to in the dark. Her new room was in the roof, the wall sloped at one side but Moss's men had opened up the other side, squared it off. Two new windows overlooked rooftops and the sunny garden. A bright, warm room. She might persuade mum to buy her a TV. She could make it like her own flat, and Conor Keane has designed a cupboard to fit the space where the roof slopes. It's divided into shelves and drawers simply for Imogen's things.

'If you're chucking those trainers,' says Alice, 'I'll have them.'

'What for? You've got new trainers?'

Alice says nothing. She takes the trainers and puts them to one side with a couple of old sweatshirts, a heap of tights and a pillow.

'What are you doing Ali? This is the Oxfam pile.'

'I know.'

'So why start another one?'

'These are for somewhere else.'

'Somewhere? Don't you mean *someone?*'

'Leave it out, Imogen.'

'Esther?'

'Maybe.'

'I bet you're saving those for Esther, aren't you?'

'What's it to you?'

'You're going to give all that to Esther.'

'What if I am?'

'You're mad. You can't give her your pillow.'

'Mum's bought new ones.'

'She'll only pee on them or spill booze.'

'Look, Imogen, you know nothing about Esther.'

'So you're still sneaking off to see her then?'

'Sneaking?'

'Yeah, sneaking. Does mum know?'

'These are things we don't need. Mum couldn't care less where they go, as long as we have a clear out.'

'She won't like it.'

'I do not *sneak* off to see Esther. We talk sometimes.'

'She smells.'

'So would you if you slept in a doorway.'

'Well do it quietly. Mum's twitchy enough at the moment.'

'She's stressed-out with the move, Imogen. Instead of getting at me, you could do a bit more for Mum.' An uneasy silence as they add to the piles around the floor.

'You're not throwing that out.' Imogen grabs a T-shirt from Alice's chucking-out pile. 'You're so busy thinking about Esther.'

'Oh, sorry,' Alice slumps on to the bed, picking her fingernails.

'How could you Ali. Imagine if that had gone to Oxfam. How could you?'

'I'm sorry. OK? I said I'm sorry.'

'Besides anything else Ali, it's an antique you know, cost a bomb at Camden Lock.'

As she folds the rescued T-shirt Imogen notices how worn it is. Twenty years old at least. She's seen photos of Mum wearing it when it was deep, cornflower blue. Now it's paler, faded like it's been in the sun. Someone offered to buy it off her at a party. Imogen's friends look for things like this in jumble sales. Imogen wriggles into the T-shirt, sliding it over her 'body'. She'll wear it, that way it won't get lost. It's cut to hug the breasts, taper into the waist then flare out again. The bottom edge is shaped like a half moon. The neck is scooped low, long sleeves open like bells at the wrists. The front is encrusted with tiny round mirrors held in pockets of fabric. It's covered in embroidery; red and white flowers, stitched by hand. Most of the mirrors still sparkle but on some, brown speckles dull their surface.

After Dad died Imogen had found Mum crying as she tried to clear his things. Everything reminded Mum of something. She was crying over the mirrorwork T-shirt that she'd found amongst a pile of Dad's stuff. Mum tried to tell Imogen about the time Dad had bought it for her one summer evening in Brighton before they were married, but she was too upset. She couldn't bear to keep it, she couldn't throw it out either. How could it hurt so much to think of him buying the T-shirt, that's what Mum had said. How could she guard against the hurt when it came like this without warning? The strangest things could set it off. Imogen had cried too as they sat together on the bed. Imogen had asked Mum if she could wear the T-shirt, which seemed to make her happy. Imogen let Alice wear it too. Sometimes. It was special. Imogen would wear it on her first date with Nick Baxter, if he *ever* asked her out. She knows he wants to. If he doesn't ask her soon she will ask him.

Not long after Imogen had found Mum crying over the T-shirt, they'd all gone to Brighton for a day out. It was the Easter after Dad died. They'd hired deck chairs and Mum sat staring at the horizon. The beach was a large shelf of pebbles. They sat on the edge with their backs to the hull of a boat. Mum had brought sandwiches. The sun was hot and they rolled up their sleeves. Imogen took off her shoes and socks, dug her toes into the pebbles, the sea breeze tingling in her nose, fresh as mint. As they ate, Mum started to tell the story of her and Dad that time in Brighton. But it was like Imogen and Alice weren't there, it was as if she was telling it to herself.

He'd picked her up one Friday evening from the museum.

'Where are we going?' she'd said, when she saw they were heading south through Brixton.

'Wait and see.'

He was doing a recce of the piers for an assignment that could lead to a book, he thought. Definitely a Sunday supplement in June, though he knew he could make more of it. At the entrance to Palace Pier there were people selling things, a man with hair to his waist, just back from India. You couldn't get these T-shirts in London yet, he said. Mum loved the way the mirrors sat in the pockets of fabrics. She chose the blue.

'Lovely with your eyes,' the stall man had said. Then Dad said they should walk up the beach and watch the sunset. When they reached where the boats were, Mum had squatted behind one of them to take off her blouse and put on the new T-shirt. She went quiet then, like she didn't want to tell anymore of the story. She started to pack up the picnic and said that they should walk to the end of the pier. As they passed the pier entrance Mum froze, like she was afraid she would fall, her feet astride two planks of the pier's deck. They could hear the hiss of the waves, see the spray through the gaps. Imogen helped her to a bench. Her face was quite grey. None of them knew what to do next. Imogen was afraid. Alice picked her nails and they all huddled together on the bench.

'Why did you have to go?' Mum said, to no one. Her body was tense next to Imogen's. Then she turned to the girls. 'I can't believe it you know, I can't believe that he's really not here anymore.' Imogen held her mother's arm and stared at the sea between the planks as it swirled and hit the steel legs of the pier. There was a weird noise like distant applause as the sea churned the pebbles, dumping them onto the beach. Alice suggested that they go back to where they had been. They sat with their backs to the boat on the shelf of pebbles and watched the sun go down behind the domes of the pier until the glass glowed orange. It was as if they were looking at one of Dad's pictures, from the book he did, *The Great British Seaside*.

'Do you think they did it, there on the beach?' says Imogen. 'Mum and Dad. That time when he bought her the T-shirt.'

'Oh Imogen, do you have to?'

'They did it on the beach, I bet they did.'

'Is that all you can think about?'

'Don't tell me you've never thought about it?'

'It must be strange not having Dad in bed anymore, sleeping alone.'

'Not for much longer.'

'What do you mean?'

'You know.'

'What, Mum marry again?'

'I didn't say *marry*.'

'What, Mum get a boyfriend?'

'Hardly a boy.'

'She's started wearing make-up again.'

'So?'

'She's bought a new lipstick.'

'So?'

'Rocket Red. I saw the box in the bathroom bin.'

'So, she bought a new lipstick.'

'Mum always wears those yucky pinks. This was Rocket Red. And mascara. She never bothers with eye make-up.'

'Oh, so what. She's doing lots of new things. This move for instance. I'm taking these to Esther now, OK?'

'Don't tell Mum.'

'Look, I'm not telling her, and I'm not *not* telling her. I'm taking them because there is nothing wrong with doing it. I can decide that for myself. I don't need permission.'

'I'm telling you, it's more than the move that's stressing Mum out.'

6

Sawdust

Conor sorts the bits from the spindle moulder. Every bench, the length of the workshop, littered with tools and clamps. The floor is ankle deep in shavings. The lid has been left off a new drum of glue; with that skin on it now the whole lot will have to go. How can he do every damn job himself? This is what happens when he's out to a client. Gerry's supposed to supervise this place. He's responsible. He mustn't let the lads go until they've cleared up. It's part of the job.

'A matter of safety.' Conor hears himself explaining again and again. No use them grabbing their jackets and off at five. Maybe Gerry's not up to the job. Maybe Conor is expecting too much of Gerry. The Durham Road contract is putting pressure on everyone. If Gerry can't rise to the responsibility, Conor will have to consider taking on another man. He'll have Gerry in first thing on Monday. No, he'll have them all in, make them aware of the situation.

Conor doesn't bother going into the glassed-off area that is his office. He won't settle to the drawing-board in this frame of mind. There'll be no concentrating on the Durham Road designs until he's cleared the worst of it.

What bothers him most is that it's not about appearances. 'Keane's worse than my Ma for giving out about the mess,' he'd overheard one of the new trainees.

Christ, it's about safety. The workshop's a risky place.

'A man could lose his hand, a finger easily. You know that, Gerry. There're enough risks around here without making more of them.' And if the lads are careless with equipment, next thing, it will show in their work. Sooner rather than later the way of working shows up in the end product. The likes of the Quinn brothers come to Keane Joinery because they know they'll get quality and on time. Conor can't afford to let the Quinns down.

He puts the last of the bits in its marked place on the wall, rows of jagged-toothed discs like heavy metal Catherine wheels.

In too much of a hurry to get down to the pub. Wages on a Friday night and the weekend ahead with not a thought for their work. Conor doesn't like the twinge of envy. He wouldn't like to think he begrudged the men their time off, but here he is again on a Saturday. All the men see is him drawing, planning, out to clients. Not real work, they think. It's a pity they can't see responsibility. If only they could see it the way he feels it, clinging to him. Where do the lads suppose the orders come from? The Quinns are top-of-the-league now doing up the big houses, everything restored, quality finish. That one by the Heath was featured in a magazine. If Conor's work got that kind of publicity the cabinet-making side would take off. A contractor the size of the Quinns needs reliable suppliers. Conor can produce everything for a job like Durham Road: copies of the original window frames and doors, newel posts and bannisters. And now he's got the contract for the kitchen and other furniture in the bedrooms. Amy likes his designs. This is how he wants the business to develop. He doesn't want to be reproducing nineteenth-century pattern-book stuff the rest of his working days. Which is why he'll be here well into the afternoon, not until lunchtime as he'd promised Maureen. She'll give out to him about how he never sees the children.

The bag on the extractor system is full to bursting. Christ. He's invested thousands installing the system to make this a fit place to work. Fat silver tubes, like giant caterpillars, feed into each of the power saws, sucking up dust as it spins off the wood. Each tube joins a main pipe that runs along the ceiling. At the far end of the workshop, the pipe turns downwards, spewing the sawdust into a clear plastic sack that's held firmly in a hoop. The whole operation is supposed to be airtight. Even so, the sawdust gets everywhere. A fine film clings to the walls. It settles in piles in the corners under the benches. Even with the system working efficiently, the place is never rid of it. Another morning's work on those saws and the sack will burst. Well, he's not shifting it; that's a two-man job. Gerry can come in early on Monday. He gathers up clamps, six or more left lying around. He hangs them on the wall in a row, they regard him, gaping blue jaws laughing at him.

It's down to him in the end. He should have got back here by five yesterday, but the visit to Durham Road had taken longer than he thought. He hadn't expected the client to be there, but since she was it made sense to talk through the possibilities for the new hardwood floor. And then she had revisions for the inside of the daughter's bedroom cupboard.

'A good sign, don't you think, the smell?' Conor had said as they stood in the bright new room, considering the space. Her eyes had looked puzzled, her dark brows drawn in.

'The fresh plaster. When a house starts smelling of fresh plaster you know you're near the end.'

'You're forgetting the basement, aren't you?' Didn't matter how much any of them reassured her, she was tense, over-anxious about the move. Understandable. 'It might be nearing the end up here, but they've hardly begun in the basement. I can't bear to think about what goes on down there.'

The daughter had drawn up her own version of how the inside of the cupboard should go and Amy wanted Conor to take this into account before he got too far on with the design.

'If I give her what she wants, maybe she'll put things away,' Amy had laughed. She looked different with the tension gone from her face for a moment. Lively eyes when she laughed. A clear greyish blue with fine lines that clustered around them as her face eased into a smile. He'd say younger than himself. Thirty-seven, thirty-eight, maybe. There's no grey in her dark, wavy hair and her neck is smooth. Quite something to find that she knows Luke's work. Amy recognised the box, which Conor keeps in his pocket, as an early piece. She has an eye for things.

He must finish the drawings for the daughter's bedroom. If he delivers them to Amy today, the work can start Monday, they'll have it finished in time for the move. She'll appreciate that.

Not often he gets a client who's so interested in the way he works. Usually all they want is the end product and to a price.

Amy Beardsley noticed what he was doing with the kitchen, how the simplicity of it depended on the way he'd worked out the proportions of the parts to the whole. She recognised that it was designed, that it hadn't simply happened. There was a correspondence between each door, each inset panel, glazed or solid, the drawer fronts, all these related to the outside dimensions of the cupboards. He'd considered the proportions already in existence in the house, the height of the ceiling and the dimensions of that large sash window that would dominate the kitchen. Easy to talk to, she was, and she enjoyed discussing the things most clients take for granted. A rare thing to have a client that wants to work with you. He was glad he'd stayed for coffee that time at her old house. Not something he did as a rule, sit around talking beyond the job, but she'd brought up the subject of Shaker design and he was off then, telling her about the research he'd started at college. And hadn't he enjoyed her surprise, the brows raised.

'Way ahead of their time in many ways,' he'd said, and gone on far too long about economical production runs and fitness to purpose.

'The celibacy was a bit of a mistake,' she'd laughed. 'Did you go along with that too?' The minute it was out, her neck turned red as her sweater. She'd gone off to find a book, a scholarly tome from the Whitney that must have been recent, he hadn't come across it before.

'I've four children.' Why had he done that? Drawn attention back to the remark that she clearly regretted.

'A design fault, don't you think?' he'd blundered on. 'The celibacy. Doomed to die out.' She ignored him.

'Four years ago,' she said, confirming the publication date. She said she knew it was around then because Greg had used it to research the project he never completed. A photographic record of all existing Shaker houses and their contents. It would have been a stunning book. She'd planned an exhibition, to coincide with publication. They didn't often work together but this was an area where they could overlap. They were about to spend the summer there, in America, when it happened.

'A heart attack,' she said quietly. He hadn't asked, hadn't wanted to pry, but the question was hanging there between them.

'Almost three years ago.'

'I'm sorry.' Inadequate, but what else could he say and he got the impression that she didn't want to dwell on it, didn't want to say anymore. He'd fiddled awkwardly with Luke's box in his pocket, brought it out and turned it around in his hands, and her face had lit up.

'Can I see that?' Her arm stretched towards him. 'That looks so like Luke Marsden's work.' She was eager to hear more. When had Conor known Luke, was it before the alcoholism took over? And she'd offered another cup of coffee. It wouldn't take long to make a fresh pot, she'd said, already filling the kettle.

Conor fills the office kettle having done what he can in the workshop. There's only a jar of cheap instant, it's like gravy browning, bitter and not tasting of coffee, but he needs something inside him to get down to these drawings. Amy had made fresh coffee and they talked till he was late for his next appointment. He hadn't meant to leave abruptly but he was late. Talking about Luke had led back to Judy. He hadn't thought of Judy in a long while. That part of his life was history, best forgotten. But he would like to talk to Amy again. It makes a change. He reaches for the Durham Road file, finds the notes and sketches for the dormer bedroom cupboards. They're fresh in his mind from yesterday. He will finish them and drop round to Salisbury Road on his way home. He ignores the phone. The answer machine clicks into action.

'Conor are you there, are you?' Maureen waits, gives Conor a chance to pick up the receiver. Maura squeals in the background.

'Will you stop it now. I'm trying to talk to your Dad. Wait now.' But there's a click as she hangs up. He'll phone her right back, almost finished. Before he has a chance, the mobile goes.

'Ah good, you're on your way then,' says Maureen, more cheerful than she had sounded on the answer machine.

'I'm still here. At the workshop.'

'Conor, you let me talk to that machine?'

'I was going to ring you straight back. Look, I've almost finished here but I need to deliver the drawings to the client today.'

'Conor, I need you here by three. I've to take Clare to her

dancing class and Maura's in no mood to be dragged out in the car again. She needs her nap.'

'I'm sorry, Maureen. This is the biggest single contract I've ever had. A whole house. All the cabinet-making too. There'll be long hours while this is going on. I can't afford to give it less than one hundred per cent Maureen. Four. I'll possibly be back by four. OK?'

'Sooner if you can, Conor.'

'I'll do what I can.'

'By the way, Caitlin phoned. She was giving nothing away to me, of course, but she sounded upset.'

'Upset about what?'

'She didn't say.'

'When did she ring?'

'Not an hour ago. She said nothing really, but she did make something of not hearing from you in a while. It seemed to me that she expects you to call back today. She's at the cottage.'

The number for Caitlin's Dublin flat is in his head, but he will need to check the cottage number in his address book.

'Hello, there. How're you doing?'

'Conor, I'm so glad you've called. Her saintliness told you then?'

'Told me what?'

'That I'd rung. I'm surprised she did that much. I got the impression I'd no right to claim a moment of my brother's attention.'

'I'm very busy. Big contract. It's tough on Maureen.'

'All work, Conor.'

'I know, I know.'

'I was thinking, you know, about how I wish we'd made something of our birthday last year. We should have made an effort, done something. I was thinking it would be nice to plan a big get-together, over here. For no particular reason. What do you think?'

'Caitlin, this is not like you. You don't do anything for no particular reason. What's brought this on?'

'It would be nice. Think about it.'

'So what's wrong?'

'Wrong?'

'What's making my strong, self-sufficient sister sentimental all of a sudden?'

'Oh, you know, time passing, and all.'

'Am I talking to the same person who last year thought that forty was insignificant, that age was a state of mind?'

'I should know better than try to keep anything from you.'

'What is it?'

'Probably nothing.'

'Tell me what nothing is.'

'You remember I told you a couple of months ago when I couldn't pee? It's happened again.' She'd laughed about it then. How she woke in the night next to a new lover, desperate to go but couldn't. She'd sat on the loo at 3.00 a.m. running the taps, trying to visualise fountains. It had taken her half an hour, pacing around, drinking water, but she'd managed in the end. Now it had happened three or four times and it was getting harder each time. And it didn't seem so funny. Stress, she thought. She'd had a busy term, she was under pressure to finish the book. Tension, she thought. But now she wasn't so sure.

'Look, see the doctor, first thing on Monday, Caitlin. You might be right that it's stress and all, but for God's sake find out.' She must be worried to be ringing him about it.

'Promise me, you'll check it out, will you?'

'I promise. And you promise me you'll think about getting over here sooner rather than later.'

She's right, they need a break. When this contract is finished, they will go over. For once, Caitlin and Maureen will be in agreement.

He doesn't like the sound of this; it's not like Caitlin, she's not one to hold things in. If she's stressed she lets the world know. It's an unpleasant feeling, a full bladder and not able to piss. He remembers the time in Gran's barn, rain drumming on the tin roof. The rain didn't stop that summer, he and Caitlin, playing in the barn, because Gran said they were under her feet in the house. Gran hung her washing to dry in the barn; floral aprons upside down, the strings dangling to the floor, and a row of her voluminous knickers. Caitlin unpegged a pair, tried them on. So big, they came up to her armpits and they laughed so much that they needed the toilet. Caitlin squatted down right there in the barn.

'Caitlin, not in here.'

'It'll soak into the ground.' She didn't think twice. Conor, not wanting to take the risk, saying he'd wait, but bursting and wishing he could be more like Caitlin. When Caitlin set her mind to do something, she did it. The sight of her squatting there and the steam rising from the stream between her legs had made him have to go. As the flow started Gran appeared. Of course, it would be him that got caught and held responsible. Not Caitlin.

He didn't like the sound of it. Caitlin was not one to hold back.

Conor reaches for his client book. He dusts the sawdust off its black cover and flicks the pages until he finds Amy's number.

7

A Live Floor

'Your floor will float.' Conor's Cork accent is buoyant in Amy's head as she makes her way to the restaurant in the basement for her lunch with Liz. Conor Keane talks about wood as if it had a life. When she meets him this afternoon she will ask him to explain the floor, once more, simply for the pleasure of hearing him speak.

The meeting with Muriel had gone better than Amy expected.

'Good to see you looking so well,' Muriel had said. 'Think about it. We'll talk again once you've moved.' She didn't want a commitment straightaway. Amy would have time to consider if she could take on an exhibition while doing the house. Muriel was checking her out. Is she up to taking on a big project; is she reliable again? After Greg died Amy had pulled out of an exhibition she'd been working on with Muriel and hasn't taken sole responsibility for anything since. Muriel has fed Amy small bits of projects, but this is the first time she's suggested anything on this scale.

Amy is early. Liz is always late, so Amy claims a table for two. Since this place was smartened up it's popular at lunchtime, the queue is already building up. Amy considers the 'specials', chalked on the blackboard: cream of broccoli soup, poached salmon, mushroom brochette. When Amy and Liz were trainees it was more like a school canteen; steamed cod and mash on a good day. Then, the smell of cabbage and dishcloths lingered on the Formica table tops, and tea the colour of treacle dribbled from a huge chrome urn. Now, there are colourful salads in glass bowls, tables are stripped wood and tea is served in individual pots: Earl Grey, Lapsang Souchong, Orange Pekoe. Quite a lot more has changed at the museum since Amy worked here. When she arrived at the staff entrance this morning for her appointment with Muriel, a man in a wooden sentry box wanted to know her business before directing her to reception where her name was ticked off a list. She was handed a visitor's pass in a plastic wallet with a clip. Amy had pinned it to the lapel of her jacket.

'It must be visible at all times,' said the receptionist through her microphone behind bullet-proof glass. The woman had telephoned Muriel's office to announce Amy. Amy could imagine Muriel setting off to meet her. It would take some time because her office was on the other side of the building, quite a walk. There were seven miles of gallery alone here, probably as much again of corridor. Amy had sat on the bench at the foot of the grand stone staircase waiting for Muriel to make her entrance. *Fruit cake*, Liz calls her. *A good egg, Muriel's a good egg*, had been Greg's view. Food describes Muriel well; her steadily expanding form is carried beneath bold, flowing garments. A swirling print of purple and turquoise had billowed above the grey of the stone as Muriel descended.

'Amy, so lovely to see you.' Amy had followed the swirling colour back up the stairs and along vaulted corridors, past mahogany cases of books and objects. Muriel's keys rattled as she walked. If Amy had followed a career within the museum she too would have a bunch of keys the size of Muriel's. Amy hadn't wanted to be a storekeeper of objects by the dead. She wanted to work with living artists, to be involved with why and how things were being made now.

'What are you doing with yourself?' asked Muriel, offering coffee across her leather-covered desk, the sun streaming in through a large window that overlooked the courtyard. 'You look so well.' Muriel brought Amy up to date on the proposals for the new wing.

'All hinges on the Lottery bid, of course,' said Muriel, 'but the private money is there to match it, so we're optimistic.' The new wing would be for special exhibitions of work by living artists.

'As you know, dear, I'm an historian to my fingertips – extending people's understanding of the made world of the past in order

that they may shape and value the made world of the future.'
Amy has heard Muriel's policy statement many times before. In
anticipation of the new wing and the new emphasis on living
artists, the plan is to mount a series of exhibitions that bring
exciting contemporary work into the museum.

'What I would like you to consider, Amy, is a show that
has its own ideas about today's world, but one from which
connections can be made to the historic collection. Dialogues
between objects.'

Amy was relieved that she didn't have to make a decision
today, she was happy to allow Muriel to enthuse as only Muriel
could.

'I take care of the past. You bring me the made world of today
and between us we'll make the connections. The common thread
of course, dear – I don't have to tell you – is the curiosity about
materials. Why do human beings *make* things? *Homo faber.* Man
(and woman) has always made things beyond need. Why? That
is what we are both about.'

I wish I had more time to make the things that matter to me. Amy
would like to know more about what Conor Keane would make
if he had more time.

'You are in touch with the new work. I want you to surprise
the public, show how young talent continues to find new ways
of working with clay, cloth, wood. I don't mind the odd wacky
piece, but if the idea behind the show is that objects tell us about
ourselves – three-dimensional narratives or poems, as it were –
then bring me the thoughtful lyric rather than the advertising
jingle or soundbite.'

'Look, Muriel, this sounds exciting and I would love . . .'

'Don't say anything now. Think about it. I can give you a
week or two. Then, if you're interested, I can pay you for initial
research. You'll need to put together a proposal for the next
committee meeting which is in July. If we get the full funding,
the real work begins in September, that's roughly the timing.'

'I'm moving house next week.'

'As I said, mull it over, let the ideas start to come. We'll talk
again once you've moved.'

'Working for Muriel already?' Liz lands in the seat opposite, flicks her hair away from her eyes. Amy looks up from her note pad, the list of questions she is making for Moss and Conor Keane is not quite complete.

'No, this is house stuff,' says Amy. How she would love to take scissors to Liz's fringe. Liz cares so much about what she wears, but once she's had the expensive haircut she never keeps up with the six-week trim. As a keeper of textiles, clothes for Liz are less about fashion, more to do with the feel of the cloth, or some quirky detail. Today, over a black crêpe de Chine skirt cut on the bias, she wears an antique cream silk shirt and a waistcoat made from cloth embroidered in a traditional Bengali way, depicting birds, flowers and mythical creatures.

'No major projects till the house is finished. What happened to that resolution?'

'I haven't committed myself. Anyway, I need something to distract me from tiles and floors.'

They join the queue for the salads, shuffle around the table filled with large bowls. Amy can't decide between fennel and cauliflower, or cherry tomatoes with mangetouts and coriander, or pasta swirls with olives and red peppers. An American woman is creating a bottleneck wondering if there are nuts in the couscous. Amy taps her halted feet on the cool, tiled floor.

Harsh, ceramic. Don't you think? Wood gives you a live floor.

'Wine?'

'Sorry?'

'Are you here?' says Liz. 'Would you like some wine?' She waves a half bottle of red before Amy.

'No, better not. I've got a site meeting later.'

'Hardwood or ceramic tiles, what do you think? For the kitchen,' Amy asks, biting into a chunk of granary bread.

'I thought it wasn't built yet? Aren't they still knocking it down or digging it out?'

'Things have to be ordered. They need to know what the finish will be, it determines the levels they build to.'

'Getting technical, Amy. I see you're bringing a curatorial thoroughness to this house.'

'I want to get it right.'

'It's your home, not an exhibition.'

'I know, but I'm only going to do it once. I might as well do it properly.'

'And frazzle yourself in the process?'

'It's a bit like putting together an exhibition. There's the research, the selecting, then bringing things in on schedule, coordinating the different skills.'

'This is a new perspective on having the builders in.'

'It's good to be working with people who know their stuff. You know, I had this image of the builder: one man with a ladder, a rickety van and ill-fitting jeans.'

'Plumber's bum, you mean,' says Liz. She tells Liz about the Quinn brothers, Fintan and Innes, in their smart jackets and handmade shoes. They manage the site from a distance, popping in without warning to see if Moss has things running smoothly, checking the programme of works. The Quinns bring in all the best contractors. People like Conor Keane.

'And you're going to be living on this "site", as of next week. You, your teenaged daughters and all those hunky Irishmen, day in day out for the next six months.'

'It's not like that,' says Amy. 'So what do you think then, wood or ceramic?' It's the heart of the house. The great, light, airy space that will emerge from the rubble. A space to sit, eat and chat around the table. Conor Keane says that wood will give the place warmth, it will be kind under foot. A live floor. It will give under her tread. Ceramic is harsh, unyielding.

'Your floor will float,' Amy tries to imply Conor's accent, as she recounts his explanation. She tells Liz how helpful he has been turning up on Friday afternoon with samples of oak and beech.

'Solid beech, I'd recommend,' he'd said.

'It all sounds very expensive,' says Liz. 'What's wrong with vinyl?' Conor had described how he would lay the planks, each tongue fitting the other's groove, raised so that the floor would give.

'Is he good looking too?' Liz laughs.

'It's not like that.' Amy's relieved to have people who know what they are doing. Conor Keane is a craftsman, an artist, he has a passion for wood. Though he hardly has the time now, he used to make things, sculpture, large bowls. He used to know

Luke Marsden; has an early piece by him. One of the tiny boxes. He keeps it in his pocket.

'He takes such care over the details,' says Amy, telling Liz how Conor will leave a gap all the way round where the floor ends and the wall begins. He'll allow for the movement. Wood is unstable.

'Well,' says Liz. 'Talking, as we were, about the properties of materials. Did you know that Lycra has three times more restraining power than elastic and yet it is one third of the weight? Revolutionised the corset industry.'

'The book? Liz, you've got the contract? Why didn't you say so earlier?'

'I've signed at last.' Liz's book on the history of underwear would be a definitive work.

'Great. That's wonderful news. Liz, I'm so pleased. We must have a drink on this. You should have shut me up. Look, I'm dying to know more, but really, I must go now or I'll be late. I must choose this floor.'

'Sounds to me as if you've decided already.'

Gliding down the escalator Amy notices the girl ahead of her. She's about the same age as Imogen. She has a ring, an earring Amy supposes, through her top lip. Amy shivers. It must have hurt; it can't be like piercing an ear. The flesh on the lip is thicker than an ear lobe. The girl wears a tight Lycra skirt that skims her bum with three times the power of elastic, though there is little to restrain.

What would be worse: if Imogen came home with a ring through her lip or a boy that Amy didn't like? *All those hunky Irishmen.* How could this girl kiss with a ring in her lip? Wouldn't it hurt to smile? Conor Keane has well-defined lips when his mouth is closed, when he's thoughtful. When he smiles, it's with a wide generous mouth.

8

A Perfect Match

'Keane's on his way. He phoned just now. Sends apologies.' Moss appears up the steps from the dungeon, from what will be the kitchen, to greet Amy in the hallway.

'Taking shape now, isn't it?' he says, nodding to indicate the lining paper on the walls right the way up the stairs.

'I'm having this boarded up tomorrow,' he says pointing back down the stairwell. The door into the basement is off its hinges, through it, Amy glimpses two stacks of bricks. One stack is sharp-edged Accrington red, the other is crumbly yellow London stock. They were delivered a while ago and they haven't budged.

'No progress down there?'

'I'm waiting on you. Kitchen plans, a decision?'

'Almost there.'

'Don't worry, you want it to be right. We've had to slow up below anyway to finish up here, ready for your move. Sealed off, that door will be, Amy. You'll be comfortable enough up here.'

Amy has no reason to doubt Moss. He is doing what he can. This is to be her home in a week. How could she have agreed to live amongst chaos on this scale? Better not to think about the whole of it. There will be enough rooms ready for her and the girls to seal themselves off. That's the beauty of this house, the way it's laid out on levels rather than floors. Amy will live, at first, in the upper levels. She will create a pocket of order. It will be all right.

The Durham Road house is on a hill, it doesn't have whole floors. Instead, there are levels with stairs and half-landings zig-zagging between them, like a squared-off spiral. She is adding another level with the stairs up to the loft space.

There are three different ground levels. The hall, where Amy stands now, comes straight in from the front garden at street level. Down the stairs and through the door that Moss is going to seal off, there will be the kitchen and dining room with French windows onto the garden. Down another short run of steps from the kitchen comes the cellar. This is the bit that will take time. 'Tons of clay to be dug out to achieve your head height. Labour intensive,' Innes Quinn had explained when he showed Amy the first set of figures. Barrow after barrow of thick, sticky clay. Moss's men must dig down half a metre. This cellar floor will be the lowest level, making space for a storeroom, a utility room, a toilet and a large room for the girls. A den, a sitting room, whatever they care to call it, where they can blast their music, sit and talk late into the night, have parties. There will be French windows in there too, opening onto a small, sunken patio that is a drop down from the garden. Three different ground levels, three different ways of entering or leaving the house.

The two lower ground floor levels will be a building site through the summer and into the autumn. 'Snagging' and 'cleaning', the last items on the programme of works, will take the schedule into September.

'There will be slippage,' warned Innes Quinn, a fair man and a realist. 'Can't be helped. Late deliveries. The unexpected.' It's only the second week of April. Think of the slippage that might accumulate through the summer. Who knows when they will hand back the basement as part of her home. Best not to think so far ahead.

'The two halves of the house will be separate once you move in. I've put a lock on the front cellar door, and I'll have the site telephone run down there.'

'You make it sound so easy.'

'You'll hardly notice us. You've a minute now, while Keane comes. Will I show you how far we've got? Come on, let's do the tour.'

Moss likes doing 'the tour', proud of the progress he and the men are making. They are working from the top downwards, so Moss likes to take her up to the top of the house and walk down again through each level, right down to the dungeon. Things get progressively worse as they go, from the smell of fresh paint at the top, they descend to the rawness of newly-dug, clay in the cellar.

'I've a surprise for you up there.' Moss is more pleased with himself than usual today. Amy follows him to the top of the house, to Imogen's bedroom that is emerging in the transformed loft space. A bright, light room where there had been only the heavy roof timbers, years of grime and pigeons nesting in the darkness.

'See,' Moss smiles. 'The ladder is gone. You have your staircase. Keane's men did a good job. Looks like it's always been there, doesn't it?' Amy's hand glides along the smoothness of the hardwood rail.

'He's matched it well. You'll never tell it from the old one. Liam's men will stain it, bring it to a finish like the original. Lovely piece of wood.' Unstained, the wood is a matt, dusky red like terracotta. Stained, it will go deeper, nut brown with a dull shine, the colour of a conker. The colour of Conor Keane's hair, a rich, reddish brown thick with curls.

In Imogen's room the first coat of paint is on. A livid purple. The colour she chose. She will have to live with it. The window frames, which Conor was so anxious to get right, like the handrail, seem always to have been part of the house. A perfect match. They look like old sash windows. But Amy knows that each panel of glass is a double-glazed unit, made to look like an ordinary pane.

'You'll need it up here,' Conor Keane had explained. 'Otherwise you'll have a cold spot. Condensation. Tricky things these loft spaces.' He has a way of holding her attention with information, such as this, that she never would have thought could interest her. It is the eyes. Dark brown, so dark that the pupil is barely visible.

As they walk down a level from Imogen's room, to what will be Amy's workroom, the dry rasp of Liam's men filing and sanding the woodwork gets louder. Their work leaves a fine film of dust on everything. Her black suede shoes are turning grey. Down again to the level with the main bathroom and a small bedroom. Amy has no plans for this spare room once the house is finished.

For now, it will be her temporary kitchen. Here, she will cook, eat, do the washing until the autumn. Moss has installed a sink unit in one corner and further along are pipes for the washing machine.

'I've an old base unit in the lock-up,' says Moss. 'It would give you a work surface and some storage.' Through the noise of the sanding comes a sound which makes Amy's stomach churn; a sensation as if she's in a lift that is going down quickly, before she's ready, before she's realised that it's moving. A warm sound.

'Will I bring it for you, then?'

Bring what? What is she supposed to say to Moss? What is he talking about? Her concentration is drawn entirely to the sound. It's coming closer. Changing, it swells to a rich laugh. Conor Keane banters with one of the decorators.

'Sorry I'm late,' he says, as he joins them.

'Drawings are one thing, but you need to consider the actual space. Even in this state,' says Conor. They stand amongst the clutter and dust of her half-gutted basement. He lays out the drawing and explains how, if Moss and the lads knock down that wall, remove that door, she will have a generous, L-shaped space where kitchen and dining areas could blend, seamlessly.

'Take out that wall. Gut this room back to the brick and start again. Make this the kitchen.'

Just like that. Move walls. Build new ones. Make one room where now there are three. Simple as taking a rubber to a pencil mark on a sheet of paper. She only has to give the word.

She's standing in what was a breakfast room in its Edwardian heyday. Now it's all grease and grime. A fire surround is littered with old jam jars, a cracked mug, a broken clock. It had been a communal eating area in this house of bedsits which she has been foolish enough to buy. For years this room has belonged to no one in particular. The cupboards in the alcoves are thick with grease and muck. Moss can't wait for her to give the word, and off to the skip they will go.

'Not worth saving,' says Conor, and he takes Amy through the drawings to see how it might be. He's careful, encouraging. She projects his neat black lines onto the rough, old plaster, tries to imagine how it will look in three-dimensions. She leans over the drawings, her head bent towards Conor's head. Concentrate. She sees rectangles and squares. She knows that these represent cupboards, drawers, a work surface, but she's having trouble making sense.

The shapes slide away as the scent floods in.

Unbidden. A surge. She is swollen with it. She's tired, that's all. Not used to working closely with so many men. Keane squats before her, extending his steel tape this way, then that, as he checks measurements. He's had his hair cut since they last met. It has that fresh-cut look, a sharp line around the ears and the nape. On top, thick, loose curls, the colour of hardwood. She could slide her fingers into those curls, bury her nose in them. Smell him. A raw human scent tinged with wood shavings. He's taken off his jacket. She recalls the trace of camphor that underlay the other smells the day he came to her old house and she hung his jacket in the hall. Mrs Keane, Maureen, puts mothballs in the wardrobe. A good housekeeper. 'My wife, Maureen . . .' Amy can't recall what it was Conor said about his wife. Something in relation to kitchen lay-out? She can't recall Maureen's preference for work surfaces. She had fastened onto the phrase: *my wife, Maureen.*

'You see how much space we'd create by losing those?'

Amy can't take her eyes off his back. The olive green cotton of his shirt tightens against his body as he reaches, stretches. He is not a tall man – five eight, five nine – but he seems to have a long body. A fine back. He reaches again. She studies the contours of muscle in his shoulders and upper arms. She would like to reach out, run her hand the length of his back. Liz warned her the stress would get to her in the end. *All those hunky Irishmen.*

'Plenty of room here for your sink.' Reaching and stretching, his jeans tight around his bum. She must concentrate hard if she's not to lay her hand on his shoulder. What could be easier as he squats there, measuring, right in front of her. She need only move her hand inches. She needs to put her hand on his shoulder to stop herself from falling over. The force of this energy makes it hard to stand up.

She cannot distinguish his individual words. She knows that Conor is speaking in sentences. Logically. He is explaining, imparting information. Concentrate. He must surely feel this surge of energy. 'I see,' says Amy. She nods and sees nothing at all but the stretch of his back. She needs to put her hand on his shoulder, to check that he is real. Her hand would rest on his shoulder. Lightly at first. Light enough to engage his attention. Then, she might squeeze it or stroke his neck, trace her finger round the newly cut hairline. He would stand up, hold her, absorb the energy. Restore her balance.

Pull yourself together.

The change, the upheaval. A symptom of stress. The physicality of it. The power these people have to take hold of her world and change it with their own bare hands.

An early night. More swimming. She must get out of here. Invent an appointment. But she doesn't want to go. She wants to stay, held in this force field, drawn towards Conor Keane's back.

'I see,' she says again, a signal from the automatic pilot that takes care of her outward appearance. It's all right. He can't possibly see. Emit the right signals. Indicate she's heard, she understands. The floating is an illusion. Rising and dipping, rocking on the gentle undulations of his voice. His voice. It surrounds her, enters deep. His voice is more than vibrations on her eardrum, sending messages to her brain; it reaches further, down to her belly. She really must put her hand on his shoulder in order to steady herself.

'Sorry. I'm going too fast, am I?' says Keane, raising himself to standing, so that Amy must lift her head and catch his eye. She thrusts her hands into her pockets. A deep breath. She will drown.

'You OK?'

'Tired.'

'Well, I think I've covered everything. It's up to you now, Amy. Do you want me to go over it again?'

'Thanks. No. I must go.'

'Will I give you a lift?' Amy hardly knows what to do with the words that fall quietly from Conor Keane's mouth.

'I'll walk. It's only ten minutes. Thanks.'

'I'm going past the end of your road. It's no trouble.'

'Thanks.'

* * *

'You're getting there then?' Moss calls after Amy as she walks through the front gate with Conor.

'Mmm. Much better idea. I'll have a decision soon.' It's hard to hear him over the concrete mixer. Desmond shovels more ballast into its gaping mouth. He smiles at Amy; a smile that says he's noticed that she's leaving with Keane. Something about her must show that inside she is liquid. Churning.

'Good man, Keane,' Moss shouts. 'Talk to you later.'

Amy slides into the passenger seat. Heart thumping, a knocking at the temples. Shortness of breath. Don't speak. She couldn't say a word. As she turns to clip her seat belt she notices how Keane, though he isn't a big man, seems to fill the space of the driver's seat. Only inches between them, his jeans tight on his thighs; taut muscle against the softness of worn denim. His freckled hand reaches to shift the gear stick.

'A week now and you'll be in there.' A nod. A smile. No words, they would only come out as gasps. Keane's attention is on the right turn he must make at the end of Durham Road. Amy closes her eyes and makes an effort to slow down her breathing. She will have to speak. By the time they reach Salisbury Road. She will have to say, at least, 'Thank you' and 'Goodbye'. She ought to say something about the kitchen. There is no doubt in her mind, she will hand it over to him.

'It will be easier once you're living on site. Speed up the decisions. Quinn's men move fast once they know what you want.'

'Yes,' her voice sounds a little quiet, but normal enough.

'I hope that was some help. No pressure now, but if you do want me to make the kitchen I'm going to need six weeks, the way the order books are at the moment.'

Speak slowly. Say as little as possible.

'OK.'

Outside her house in Salisbury Road, Conor says he'll leave her to get on with the move. He'll be on site with other things. He offers her a card with his workshop number. Keane Joinery. And a mobile number.

'Call me,' he says, kindly. 'Anytime.' She slips the card into her jacket pocket, leaves her hand in there feeling the edges of the card.

'Good luck with the move,' he says. She must get out now. He turns towards her with a smile and a look. And there it is. The eyes. A layer gone. The protective layer between client and contractor. That smile, that look. She could be imagining it. She holds the image of that smile, the turn of the head, the warmth in the eyes. She fixes it. She will examine it later.

'Thanks for the lift.'

9

The Red Camellia

'Take your time,' says the one with the droopy moustache. Amy can only rush. The house must be cleared by lunchtime. The new people are due around two o'clock. She runs upstairs to her study to check labels again. What about the box of exhibition catalogues? Has she used the right colour, made it clear that it's going into storage? They are taking things away so quickly. She doesn't know what's gone and what's still here. Everything is labelled, it can't get lost. Colour-coded. Blue means going to Durham Road. Not many items have a white label overwritten in blue: bedroom furniture, a sofa, a coffee table, a small table at which they can eat, four dining chairs. So little. Will it be enough? There are cartons packed with bed linen, towels, crockery, a few books. Larger cartons, with hanging rails, contain clothes.

Things for storage are marked in red. There are many more of these. Amy has used extra white labels to list the contents of each rigid cardboard carton supplied by the removal firm. MAKE THE RIGHT MOVE is printed on each one in large letters underneath the name and telephone number of the company. Everything except furniture has been fitted and folded into one of these uniform rectangles. There's no telling what is where. Amy has given each box a number which cross-refers to an inventory that she keeps in a ring binder. A cataloguing system of museum standards. It will make things easier when it all comes back. The listing and cataloguing reassures. It keeps her mind off other things: whether or not to phone Conor Keane. *Call me, anytime.*

'You sure about this?' Droopy moustache places a carton at her feet, points to her neat red writing, 'only it says books. Don't feel right. Weight's all wrong.' He opens the carton that should contain, according to its label, guidebooks.

'Thought so,' he says. Amy uncovers tightly packed tablecloths and napkins. How could that have happened? If that's wrong the whole list could be out. Maybe it's just this one.

'I shouldn't worry, love. We count them into the container. It's locked till you give the OK for us to count them out again. Final total. That's all you need. Save yourself the worry.' He seals the carton and stacks it onto another. 'Like I said. Slow down. It's the rushing that takes the time.' He bends at the knees and with a sure, strong back lifts the two cartons together. So much, with so little effort. He knows how to use his body to bear the weight without strain. She has no inclination to reach out and touch the back of the removal man. She is as close to him as she was to Conor Keane when he bent and stretched, measuring with his steel ruler. It's not the back of any old male, then, that can disturb her. She has not seen Conor Keane for a week; not since the day she registered his firm, straight back.

'You've enough on this next few days with the move,' he had said as they sat in his car. 'It will be easier once you're living on site.'

On site. Home, from this afternoon. Will he be there? Perhaps, when she sees him, he will appear to her as the joiner. An expert. One of several that she must engage in order to remake her house. Perhaps he won't fill her with his scent. Perhaps he won't have that soft, unprotected look in his eye. Perhaps he won't hold her gaze so that she has no chance of shielding her own unprotected eyes. She is both eager and in no rush at all to see him again. *It's the rushing that takes the time.*

There really is nothing for her to do. Storage or Durham Road, that's all the removal men need from her, and to make cups of tea. Nothing to do, yet she must be here, idle amidst the activity.

It's getter hotter. More like May or June than mid-April. Amy peels off her sweatshirt. Droopy moustache is down to a white singlet. He has tattoos the length of his arm. I LOVE YOU says the scroll inside the red heart on his right shoulder. Who is that for? One person who he loves without doubt, so much that he declares it, indelibly, in his flesh? Or is it there because that is where a woman would lay her head, kiss his neck and read, I LOVE YOU. He need never say it. If Amy had laid her head on Conor Keane's shoulder what would he have said? What would she have said? It's opening up again. The space that Conor Keane inhabits. It's getting bigger. Each time she opens it, she finds more in there. Scenes multiply.

Call me, any time. She can hear the tone. She sees him offering her the card. She had held it in her pocket. Its sharp edge left a mark along her fingers. There must be something she can do to keep these thoughts at bay. She hasn't checked the garden. Do they know that the bench has to go?

'We've done the shed. Bench goes last. You could sunbathe,' says Roy, the boss.

The sun is full of heat already. She stretches her arms along the back of the bench, head turned upwards, eyes closed. *Call me, anytime. Whatever you decide, Amy, I can make it for you.* She decides to run her hand down Conor's back. What will he make of that? Will he respond? Will he be embarrassed? Will he remain calm but understanding. He will protect her. She's an important client.

That look.

No mistaking the change in his eyes. Amy plays the version where she knows it to be real, a reciprocal gesture: *I feel the same way too, Amy.* And when he looks like that at her again, she will respond. *MAKE THE RIGHT MOVE.* But in comes the version she doesn't like at all. The look again, only this time Amy sees that he is saying: *I've noticed how you are. I understand. I won't humiliate you.* Peeling back the protective layer in order to protect her, a vulnerable, important client.

Business, that's all.

She cannot rule out this version, it fits as well as any other. She cannot be sure which is true. So much space filling up with Conor Keane. She could get lost in there. She shakes her head, opens her eyes. This summer, she will not sit here on this bench with the honeysuckle above her head, its scent startling, as it always had been, when she sat out here on a warm July night with Greg. She looks around the garden and sees Greg lazing in a deck chair, checking proofs. Imogen and Alice, toddlers on the swing, the grass is still worn where their feet caught the ground as they got bigger and bigger. By the end of the day it will all belong to someone else. Not her house, not her garden, but the setting for other people's lives. She walks the length of the path to the shed which Roy and his men have emptied. Cobwebs in the corners, the dust and grime on the window, are all that is left. Through the streaky blur of the pane she sees blooms still coming on the red camellia. The heaviest heads are bowed with their own dense weight. Petals are scattered on the soil and on the cracked concrete of the path. She's forgotten the camellia. How did that happen? She was going to dig it up. Dig right into the soil, carefully ease out the whole root ball. She had a tub that would take it; gone now with the contents of the shed. Too late. How would it look if the new people arrived to find a freshly dug hole in the flower bed. There was a clause in the contract about shrubs. The camellia is no longer hers. If she digs it up she will be stealing. Stealing a present from her husband. It's too late. She has sold it.

The new people are a kind young couple with a toddler and a baby. He's an obstetrician. A caring professional. He would understand that Amy needs the camellia. She runs to the kitchen where droopy moustache is packing sharp knives. He wraps each one in sheets of blue paper that feel like cloth.

'Have you packed the scissors?'

'Don't know, love. Don't really take it in. Wrap it, box it.'

'That drawer.' Amy can't get through for the stacked cartons.

'Not done that yet.' His tattooed arm reaches to open it. 'Scissors. Here you are, love.'

Back in the garden, Amy squeezes the blades around the woody stem of the camellia. A cutting might work. Too tough. She needs secateurs. Gone, with the contents of the shed. She finds a thin spindly branch which yields more easily to the sawing action of the scissor blades. She will wrap it in damp tissues. It's worth a try.

'Kettle gone yet?' She hears Roy at the kitchen door. It's time she made another pot of tea. She can't object, they need to drink in this heat. They started at 7.30. A couple of hours later she made the first pot and they drank where they stood, hardly stopping, slaking their thirsts, before carrying on. Now, at 11.30, the sweat is gathering on Roy's brow, his hairline is damp. They need a break.

Amy is glad of something to do. She takes the tray of mugs out to where the men gather around the van. They sit on the ramp that leads to its vast interior like tribesmen at the entrance to a cool cave. Back in the house Amy wanders around. The sitting room is empty, there is nowhere to sit. All that remains is the cream telephone on the red carpet.

Call me, any time.

If he had been there when she had called, maybe she wouldn't be making so much of this. If she'd heard his voice, had a chance to speak. If. It gets her nowhere. She will clean each room as they finish. It can't take long to vacuum an empty space.

'Almost clear in the bedrooms,' says droopy moustache as he hands Amy a tray of empty mugs, his tattooed heart damp with sweat. I LOVE YOU. 'Except for the double bed. Tricky, Roy's still working it out.' With awkward, bulky things there is a discussion first. A route planned. Roy choreographs the moves, negotiating the turns from landing to stairs. He positions the men to bear the weight equally. Shifting the heaviest items appears effortless. Like doing a steady fifty miles an hour on the motorway, Roy and his men conserve energy. Now, for the first time, Roy is ruffled. The solid pine bed cannot be persuaded to turn the corner from the landing and down the stairs.

'I seem to remember we did have trouble bringing it in,' says Amy trying to recall what it was they did eighteen years ago to solve the problem. The bed had been specially made to accommodate Greg's six feet two inches. It was wider than average too. She sees Greg at the top of the stairs talking to the man who had made it. They agreed to take the slats out so that they could negotiate the newel post.

'We'll not be moving from here in a hurry.' Greg laughed later as he sprawled on the bed. He pulled Amy down next to him, folding her into his large, lean body. He kissed her, his hands gliding under her sweater. Afterwards, sticky in each other's arms, Greg laughed again, *official launching*. Amy had sailed into a deep sleep. Later, she had worked it out. That was the start of Imogen.

'You OK?' says Roy. 'Steady on.'

'It's the heat.' Amy sits on the stairs while the dizziness passes. The sight of Conor Keane's thigh, tight against his worn jeans, or the stretch of his back in the olive-green shirt can induce a longing as exquisite as Greg's touch that day on the new bed.

'Out the window, then,' says Roy. 'Can't spend anymore time on it.' In the bedroom Roy swiftly removes the sash window frame. He lays a blanket on the windowsill. He and two others lay the bed on its side, a man at each end and one in the middle. At a signal from Roy they lift it onto the sill. Down below, droopy moustache is ready to receive the bed. Gently they lower it, the rope takes the strain against the windowsill. In no time the bed is standing, all four legs, on the pavement, alongside the ironing board waiting to be swallowed up by the van. It seems no size at all.

She will check the girls' room. The cupboards in each alcove are empty, the doors swing open. Yesterday she wouldn't have been allowed to look in them. Once she had filled these shelves with nappies, tiny vests and socks. She had folded and stacked cardigans, sweaters, T-shirts. But for the last few years, certainly since Greg had died, going into their cupboards was off limits. And lately, coming into the room was by invitation only, especially if Imogen had anything to do with it. But last night they had let her in. Amy had sat on Alice's bed, like she used to do when they were smaller, to read stories.

'Do you remember how you always used to say goodbye to your room when we went on holiday?' Amy had said.

'Leave it out,' Imogen groaned, and slid under her duvet. 'Don't get soppy.'

Last night her daughters had slept in here. Now there were only dents in the pale green carpet that showed where the beds had stood. Alice and Imogen were ready to go. They showed no reluctance. All they talked about was what they would do to their rooms at the new house.

They had gone off to school this morning with no hesitation. Imogen, stuffing files into her bag, had looked up briefly and, in a parody of her younger self, said, 'bye bye little house,' mock waving. Then, swinging her bag over her shoulder, 'stay cool, Mum,' and she was gone. Alice had lingered.

'Will you be all right? I could stay off if you wanted.'

'There's nothing to do.'

'You sure?'

'Off you go, thanks.'

'I'll come straight home and help you unpack.' Straight home. She didn't say, I'll see you at Durham Road. Or, I'll see you on site. Straight home.

'All clear in the front room,' shouts Roy. Amy bundles the Hoover downstairs. It keeps her busy.

Call me, anytime.

How many times in the last week has she punched the telephone number for Conor Keane. She knows it off by heart. The office number, the mobile number. She can recite them. How many times had she punched the number then hung up before it connected? Could she trust herself to speak to him. Even on the telephone he would detect her disturbance. A crackle on the line, maybe. She is surrounded by a field of energy shimmering, like heat rising from a hot road in summer. It could be detected on a telephone, surely.

She aims the aerosol of polish along the empty bookshelves. A frothy white line. She does the same as she dusts the mantel and the windowsills. A fresh, anonymous supermarket smell: 'Spring Bouquet'. She Hoovers into the corners that have been hidden for years. She doesn't want to leave a trace; not their dust, nor the fine flakes of skin and strands of hair that fall, unnoticed, and settle. She digs the nozzle into the dents left by the sofa's wheels, raising the carpet's pile, rubbing out the map of their lives.

She had punched Conor's number, hands shaking, cross with herself. Like a teenager. A grown woman. Legitimate business. There were good reasons to phone him. And it had been his suggestion. He gave her his card.

Call me, anytime.

She had made a list of questions. Queries on the drawing, costings, materials, colour. Genuine, necessary questions. She had written a script so that when he came on the line she wouldn't dry up. She had rehearsed a business-like tone. Client to contractor . . . *to go ahead with the kitchen . . . the drawings marked Durham A . . . a full costing . . . appliances?*

'Good morning. Keane Joinery.' Irish, but not Conor Keane.

There was no mistaking the gravelly softness of Conor Keane's voice. She had known immediately that this was not him.

'Keane's out till four. Will I take a message?'

'I'll call back.'

'Who may I say has called?'

'I'll call back.'

'Have you the mobile number? You'll maybe get him on that before four.' Relief, that she hadn't been put to the test. Disappointment too. Having got that far she had wanted to go on. And though she knew precisely what his mobile number was, she had taken out his card, run her finger along the figures. A quick business-like call. He was to go ahead with the kitchen, she was confirming this so that he, Conor Keane, could liaise with Moss. A responsible call, paying attention to the programme of works. She had punched the mobile number. Silence. She was about to redial. A noise, like a radio warming up; airwaves opening to take her voice. Surprise as a woman spoke: *the cell phone you are calling is switched off. Please try again later. The cell phone you are calling is switched off. Please try again later.* Since then, she hasn't tried again. She's lost her nerve.

Amy drags the Hoover into the kitchen. Not thinking, she almost puts it away in the broom cupboard.

'We're done now,' Roy wipes the back of his hand across his forehead. 'We'll grab a bite to eat. See you at Durham say, twoish?'

Alone in the empty kitchen Amy is not sure what to do. Lock up, take the keys to the estate agent. Simple. The kitchen still looks too small even though it is empty. She regards the space where the table had been, where Conor Keane had drunk coffee.

Call me, anytime.

She had called. He had not been there.

'The door was open,' a tentative voice, a young man with an apologetic look stands in her empty kitchen. 'We're early. Sorry,' says Dr King. And he mumbles about solicitors, and completion. If she wouldn't mind, with such young children, they'd like to get started. Their removal people had made good time on the motorway. So, if she doesn't mind, since she seems to be ready anyway. And he is thanking her, thanking her, for leaving it so clean. Amy fights back the tears. This reasonable young man standing in her kitchen, no *his* kitchen, is saying that he would like her to go.

'Would you like a hand with that?' says Dr King, reaching to pick up the vacuum cleaner.

'No. Thanks. I think I've left something upstairs.' It's all she can think to do, to claim a moment on her own. In the girls' room the tears come. It wasn't meant to be like this. She wanted to walk round the house, and close each door. To leave slowly, quietly. To say goodbye. Already the Kings' removal men are unloading the van. Amy's car is in the way.

'I'm sorry,' Mrs King appears, puts an arm on Amy's shoulder. The tears flood. Five, maybe six months pregnant; a third child. Amy's house filling up with a new family. Amy wants to wish them well, but there's anger now, because they've caught her out, robbed her of her last moments here. She can't say goodbye. *Goodbye little house.*

'Good luck,' she manages.

Bundling the vacuum cleaner onto the back seat of her car she feels like a contract cleaner leaving a job. She checks the mirror before she pulls out, sees the removal men carrying the Kings' bed through her front door.

As she turns the corner out of Salisbury Road, she remembers the camellia cutting. It is where she left it; on the kitchen windowsill.

A Hole in the Floor

A clear sky. Not even the vapour trail of an aeroplane. Amy, almost at her new home, slows down, glances upwards at the pure blue blankness of the April sky.

The Kings did her a favour coming early. She simply had to leave. She feels better now that she's eaten. She had been light-headed with hunger. At the wine bar she had cancelled the glass of white wine as soon as she'd ordered it. One would lead to another and she would fall asleep. At a quiet corner table she had eaten houmous and pitta, mopping up the grainy paste with the warm strips of bread. A Greek taverna. Goodge Street. Friday nights, before the girls were born. She and Greg would share dishes of houmous, taramasalata, tzatziki, washed down with Retsina. Waiters would dance on the tables, smashing plates on the floor.

She had drunk a large bottle of mineral water. Glass after glass, tangy with a slice of lemon, ice clinking, she had rinsed the dust of Salisbury Road from her throat. She would not go back for the camellia.

She scans Durham Road, looking for a parking place. The plane trees are coming into leaf. Spindly shoots rise from unnaturally thickened limbs, branches thrust upwards like a clutching hand against the blue sky. In winter the trees are pollarded so that in spring they produce a predictable canopy and their roots won't spread. Left to grow, they could undermine a building; inching through mortar, curling round the bricks, slowly tugging at her house. Each tree's growth, up and down, is checked. All that happens is the steady thickening of its girth. An orderly row of trees to shade the street. This weather can't last. Shifting fronts as the season turns. Highs and lows pushing and pulling. A maverick high has the upper hand today. Those new leaves will be battered and washed by rain before the full crop is out.

She can't park directly in front the house, blocked, as it is, with the builders' gear: a skip, ballast, the compressor. Desmond, stripped to the waist, shovels sand into the concrete mixer's greedy mouth. How will Roy manage to park the van? She pulls up alongside the skip as she sees Moss.

'Welcome,' his face is alive with enthusiasm. He's more excited than she is. 'I've put cones out there for the removal van.' He indicates a space in the other direction that he's saved for her. Moss is more familiar with her street and her home than she is. He chats to the neighbours she has yet to know. He's asked them to move their cars so he can commandeer a space for the removal van. Inside, he knows every crack, every joist, the dimensions of the windows, the irregularities in the walls and ceilings. Her home. His place of work. The Quinn's board stands proud over the garden wall: **Quinn Construction** – *specialists in quality renovation*. A building site. Her home.

Amy locks her car. Her eyes glance each side of the street, dancing from vehicle to vehicle, missing nothing. Moss's van with the Quinn logo, the beat-up yellow Bedford is the plumber's. It could be the white van with Keane Joinery on the side; or the dark blue estate. The family car. The car she has ridden in. *Will I give you a lift?* She had declined. *I'm going past the end of your road.* Hadn't he pressed her? *Will I give you a lift?* Kind words, quietly spoken. She could almost have ignored them. *I'm going past the end of your road.* There had been a determination beneath the kindness in that second bid. How can she read so much into two sentences. *Will I give you a lift? I'm going past the end of your road.* Innocent words that she's making too much of, yet in her head she hears the subtle shifts of tone. He had made something of giving her a lift. A quiet, eager determination was there in the tone. So much stored in the tone of those few words. She is not imagining it. She is not going mad; no need to see Dr Hampton.

She doesn't want this. She doesn't want to fall in love with the joiner. To fall in love. She allows the phrase to form. She puts a name to it; to the obsession, the preoccupation. *I am falling in love. I have fallen in love.* Standing in her new road, scanning the parked cars, the words come. She wants to laugh, shrug it off. A romance with the joiner; it sounds like a joke. Liz will laugh her socks off. Amy throws back her head, scoops her hair behind her ears, but the notion won't shake loose. It's real. A tug, a pull. A powerful current of energy that she can't switch off. He, also, has fallen. A current this strong needs two. She couldn't sustain a charge of this force on her own. They have fallen together through the joists. Down, down, together. Not wanting to fall, either of them; a one in a million chance that they stood on the same weak spot, the same tired joist, at the same moment. It gave way, they tumbled. Above them, pacing around on strong, safe timbers, are Innes and Fintan Quinn, Moss checking the programme, Maureen Keane, her hands full with four children and Alice and Imogen waiting to unpack their new lives.

Will I give you a lift? He was saying: let's get out of here, away from the Quinns, Moss, his men. Let's have a moment alone. A moment to notice the fall. What else could he do but ask her to go in the car. He feels the same. The utter need to dissolve into another human being. Beyond any rational act. No choice. This is the clear blue truth of it. He wanted her in his car to acknowledge the fall. Not in words. He had confirmed it with the look. They cannot speak about it. Not under the circumstances. No more lifts. From now on, they will discuss cupboards and shelves and window frames under the gaze of others. She will learn to avoid the weak spot, the hole in the floor. She scans the road again. Nothing.

'This is it then,' Moss points to the removal van arriving. Droopy moustache directs Roy into the space that Moss has saved.

'We're as ready as we will be,' says Moss. The route into the house is not as clear as it might be. Though the agreed rooms are ready, the hall and stairway are still being decorated. 'We're a few days out with that.' Liam's men are working hard to catch up. Wet paint on the walls gives Roy's men no margin. There's Desmond with his concrete mixer by the gate. In the cellar, men carry on a day's work. The plank, which makes a ramp down the stone steps and through the front cellar door, rattles as barrows of mud are brought up and loads of fresh, wet cement are wheeled down. Through this activity, Roy and his men must weave the thread of Amy's possessions.

'Mmm. Different,' says Roy surveying the scene, getting the measure of the task. Droopy moustache, helped by two of the others, opens the back of the van, puts the ramp in place. Amy's life in a strange configuration. The ironing board laid on top of the sofa. A bookcase on its side. A table with its legs pointing upwards.

She can't fault the Quinns and Moss, they are doing their best. They have installed the central heating, rewired, replastered. But, they missed the weak spot in the joists, found only by her and Conor. And they haven't finished the decorating.

'A few more days.' Moss is confident of his estimate. What is an estimate but an approximate calculation based on probabilities? What is the probability of falling through a hole in the floor at the same time as the joiner. Could Moss or Innes Quinn have predicted that?

Roy steps over the cable to the compressor and back up the van's ramp. Amy notices that he has a white smudge on his backside. Moss could have given the decorators an afternoon off. Should she tell Roy about the paint on his jeans.

'I'm not mucking about with that bed again,' says Roy. ''ere mate,' he calls to Moss. 'Need that window out of the front bedroom. Got a chippy, or shall we do it?' A chippy. Maybe their boss will be here later. Conor Keane has been out of her head for a few minutes, maybe as much as half and hour. One word: chippy. Down she goes again, through the floorboards. There he is, filling up her head. The space is getting bigger and bigger.

'The paint is barely dry,' Moss shakes his head.

'Can't be helped,' Roy is firm. 'Too many turns on them small runs.' He points towards the stairs. 'Besides, there's enough going on in there already.' The first sign of tension from Roy who has, so far, carried on as if nothing is out of the ordinary. As if every day he shifts furniture into houses that aren't yet built. Best not to point out the paint on his pants.

'What about unpacking, then?' says Roy. 'Strictly speaking, for your insurance, we've to unpack, see. Breakables in particular.

But with that kitchen in the bedroom I can't see how.' Amy follows Roy into her makeshift kitchen.

'Like I say,' both hands held up to indicate the size of the question, 'where do you want things putting?'

'It's OK,' says Amy. 'I'll do it.'

'Have you found the kettle yet, Amy. Have you?' Moss squeezes round the door and smiles down on Amy as she squats before a carton of mugs and bowls.

'No Moss, and even if I had . . .'

'Joking, Amy, only joking.' Amy was starting as she meant to go on. Making tea for this lot could become a full-time job. They have been here for weeks without her to make tea. That's the way it's going to stay.

Alice and Imogen will be home soon. With the three of them working together they would soon put a shape on this chaos. If she didn't have some semblance of a kitchen by bedtime, if they couldn't wake up tomorrow and have breakfast, she would be defeated before she had begun. The kitchen in some sort of order. She can't spend all her time beneath the floorboards with Conor Keane.

The kitchen. She still thinks of it as Mr Byrne's room.

'Just the three of you? A big family house you'll make it, for the three? I used to have a big family.' Mr Byrne had been the last tenant to go. Mr Byrne's room had had a cracked hand basin in one corner with a curtain draped beneath. On a shelf above it stood a shaving mirror, a mug and a toothbrush with flattened bristles in a glass thick with rings of limescale. Mr Byrne had a portrait of the Blessed Virgin which hung by a metal hook which curled over the picture rail. Plaster saints lined the mantel. The only sign of life had been a spindly cyclamen which had more yellow leaves than green. Mr Byrne told Amy that he had not been at Durham Road long.

'Temporary accommodation till I get back to my family.' The owner said Mr Byrne had been there for twenty-five years. Now his room is a temporary kitchen for Amy and the girls. She starts to pile crockery on top of the washing machine, then thinks better of it. Not a good idea when the machine is in full spin. Along the wall opposite the fireplace is the base unit which Moss has installed. She has filled its cupboards with packets and tins;

its surface is taken up with the microwave, kettle and toaster. The fridge and freezer are squeezed into an alcove between the window and the fireplace. The space is a fraction too small for them to fit snug, so the freezer juts out. The fireplace gives the room a homely touch, but she will have to butt the table right up to it.

'Where's this for then?' Roy calls from the landing. Amy hears the effort in his voice, he's handling something big; a large, solid-backed bookcase.

'Label says your workroom but it won't fit. Sloping ceiling.'

'Anywhere you can find where it will fit,' says Amy. 'Wait a minute.' She rummages in her bag for the steel tape measure she's never without these days, and measures the only available wall space left between the washing machine and the base unit.

'In here,' she says, feeling better than she has done all day. It fits. Somewhere to put things. Roy manoeuvres the shelves into place.

'Getting there?' Moss again.

'This isn't safe.' Amy touches the bookcase and the whole thing rocks. 'You'd better put it in my bedroom, Roy.'

'Let's see.' Moss checks the instability. 'These floors aren't true, you know.' A weak spot in the joists. A million-to-one chance that they stood on the same spot together. Enough hazards in this house; she doesn't want crockery tumbling around her ears like plates in a Greek taverna on a Friday night.

Moss straightens the back of the shelves against the wall, as he does so the base raises off the floor a good inch.

'Needs a wedge in there.' Things can be fixed. 'Keane's men are here, no problem. Dave, down here a minute, will you?' Keane's men. Is he coming too?

'It'll not budge now,' says Dave slotting the hammer back into his joiner's belt. He taps the base of the bookcase with the toe of his boot, it doesn't move. It has taken him no time to cut two wedges and ease them in place. A simple task to stop a bookcase full of crockery crashing to the floor. Could he mend the weak spot in the joists? Too late.

Where are the girls? It's nearly five. The sounds around her are changing. Roy and his men have finished. The site is packing up for the day. The throb of the compressor and the grind of the concrete mixer have ceased. She can hear the broom on the front path as Desmond clears up for the night. She can hear the voices of the men down below in what will be her real kitchen. There is no ceiling down there. The floor of her temporary kitchen is all that stands between her and them. Over the years the wood has shrunk leaving gaps. She can hear their voices as if they were in the room with her. Two men agree to meet in the pub later. Two others negotiate a lift with a third. A day's work coming to an end. Then another voice. She drops the plate that's in her hand. It doesn't break, but spins on the bare boards. When it stops, she crouches to pick it up. She peers through the cracks, but it's dark down there. She cannot see.

'Moss here, is he?' A soft voice.

She kneels, lays her ear to the floor.

11

House Rules

'Keane. I wasn't expecting you.' Moss, that's definitely Moss.

'I was passing, anyway.' There's a defensiveness in Keane's reply. 'Floor measurements. She wants a final quote for the beech.'

She. Me.

Amy presses her ear to the floorboards. Why, when she can hear perfectly well? She could hear even if she stood up or sat on one of the three chairs arranged around the table that she's placed across what she still thinks of as Mr Byrne's hearth. What's got into her? Ear to the floor. She wants to know what he's saying.

Is he coming up to see her?

She doesn't want to miss a word. She lifts her head slightly. She can hear better if her head is a few inches off the floor. If she presses down too tight, their voices are muffled by the draught that whistles through the space between the planks. A noise that's like hearing the sea in a shell. The hiss of the sea muffles Conor's voice. She raises her ear till the whooshing stops. The sharp, damp smell of raw clay slices through the crack. She feels the coldness of down there and shivers even though the day outside is still warm, even though the sun plays on her back as it cooks the air in her makeshift kitchen. She must buy a blind for the window before summer.

'Bay or a flat wall at the end there? You have both on the drawing.' Their voices move off as Moss leads Keane out from the kitchen space, into what will be the dining area. They are no longer directly underneath her. If she wants to hear any more she must move into the bathroom. There, with the window open, their voices will travel up. The bathroom sits above the first part of the dining area. When it is built, the rest of the room will jut out into the garden, ending in a bay with French doors onto a patio. Keane needs to know where the end will come now that she has decided on the bay. He must be at the far end. He could even be outside by the trench, freshly dug to take the foundations of the extension, increasing the space that was once a scullery. The old scullery floor had been hacked up to create a void. It's like an archeological site. Rising from the ruins, laid out in the sticky clay trench, are the first clean red bricks of the foundations waiting to take the load. The beech floor will be laid over the void and on into the kitchen. *A ballroom of a space.* New joists across the void, new planks of beech snug as each tongue fits the next one's groove and a breathing space around the edge. *Your floor will float.*

Amy floats.

She hardly knows where she is or what time of day it might be. Kneeling with her ear to the floor she gives in to the exquisite lightness that spreads through her belly and down her legs. Would they move, take her weight if she needed? She is weightless. A warm swirling in her stomach. Dissolving. Liquid with the anticipation of seeing this man she hardly knows.

What is she doing?

Spying through the floorboards. She watches herself in disbelief.

In the bathroom she doesn't want to push up the sash window. They are directly below. The noise would make them look up. She would have to acknowledge them. She's not ready.

She fills the brand new sink with water. As she leans over to swill her face she smells the fresh oiliness of the plumber's putty smeared around the taps. HOT and COLD, it says, in crisp black letters on the white porcelain buttons which are sunk in the top of each brass tap. The contents of her old bathroom are stacked by the window in unpacked cartons. There's nowhere to put anything. Sink, bath, toilet are plumbed in. Clean white tiles rise to the height of her shoulder, then comes the frieze of deep blues and greens. An underwater scene. A world of lacy-gilled fish beneath the lily pads. Fish tails swish the lily roots, their mouths reach up for air. The wall above is the flesh pink of smooth new plaster, still to be decorated. The electrician has wired up wall lights the shape of scallop shells either side of the brass-framed mirror, but apart from these things there is nothing. No cupboards or shelves. She rummages in the cartons until she finds soap, a flannel, toothpaste and brush. She washes her face, cleans her teeth, enjoys the mintiness on her breath. Her T-shirt is damp with sweat. She can't strip off. Not with Keane and Moss so close. She cannot hear much now, not words, what she hears is the rise and fall of their voices. She knows who is speaking. She sees herself, suspended above the two men. The bathroom is supported on steel girders that will eventually disappear into the dining room ceiling. For the moment, the house down below is like a dolls' house with the back wall missing. She sees it clearly in her mind. Conor and Moss, standing by the trench. Her raised above them in a room which sits on steel girders. She wriggles the flannel beneath the T-shirt, washes her armpits. As she bends to pick up the towel she sees right into her neighbour's kitchen. The hole would need at least three bricks to fill it.

'There's boxing-in to do behind the toilet but it all functions.' So that's what Moss meant. If she can see into their house what can they see?

Voices.

Clear through the hole she sees the wood-brown curls on the crown of Conor's head.

'You'll wedge the boards, secure the back here. I can leave you to it then?' says Moss. 'Good man, Keane.'

Conor, alone. Moss is leaving.

She could go down. Show an interest, discuss the floor. Too obvious, like being caught with your ear to the floor. It's not as if she can naturally walk down the stairs to the basement. Moss was as good as his word, he's blocked off the door. This stops the men tramping through, separating site from living space, but it stops her too. She will have to go out of the front door and down the front cellar steps.

Pretend she's looking for Moss. Say she heard noises, wondered if Moss had gone. Look surprised. Conor's not to know that she knows he's here. She dries her face. She's such a mess. Not at her best for playacting.

As she comes out of the bathroom she sees a figure outlined in the stained glass panel of the front door.

Heart thumping.

'Everything OK?' It's Moss. 'I'm off now, wanted to wish you well for your first night.' He says not to worry if she hears sounds below. It's only Keane. He'll lock up. Not to worry about down there. Any problems she's to call Moss and he gives her his home number.

'The lads'll be here from eight tomorrow. I'll be here meself at seven thirty.'

No feigning surprise now. Conor will know that Moss has called in.

He will hear their voices. He can hear her speaking at this moment.

Amy fills the kettle at her makeshift kitchen sink. The sound of the rushing water takes up what little space there is. He'll hear this too. The pipe makes a knocking sound as she turns off the tap. Conor will hear this. He will hear her feet on the bare boards. She takes down the teapot from her bookshelves of crockery. The first pot of tea in her new home. Home. So utterly strange. It's the silence.

And knowing he's down there.

She's alone, yet not alone, in a half-built house. Beneath her feet there's a man she hardly knows, yet he fills her head. She's making tea in a kitchen which is really a bedroom. She can't even retreat to the loo with that hole in the wall. And the silence. There's more silence than furniture.

He's taking his time.

The kettle rumbles up to a boil. A gathering cloud of noise scuds against the silence. Will Conor hear it as muffled, distant? Will he hear that? The sharp click as the kettle switches itself off. It makes her jump. Then another sound startles her. His mobile.

Ear to the floor again.

There's no mistaking the irritation in his voice.

'I can't say exactly . . .'

Heart thumping.

'I've to talk to the client yet.'

Talk to the client.

'Look Maureen, I'll call you when I'm on my way, OK?'

Maureen.

'Well it's the best I can do.'

She pulls out a chair, sits at her kitchen table, careful not to scrape the chair on the boards, careful not to draw attention to her presence while he talks to his wife.

His wife.

He's talking to Maureen, here, in her house. And after he's said goodbye to Maureen the silence is greater than ever, so she really jumps when she hears Conor talking again.

'Still at Durham,' he says. 'Not sure how long.'

Ear to the floor again.

'OK, Gerry.'

Who is Gerry?

He's telling Gerry that he won't be back at the workshop. Delayed at Durham Road.

He might be some time.

Gerry can lock up. And he's to mind now that those trainees clear up properly. Gerry's to remind them it's a matter of safety.

Safety.

Is she safe in this house? Amy can't quite grasp that she must sleep here tonight. She must clean her teeth in that bathroom with a hole in the wall. She must turn off her bedside light (if she can find it in the first place), lay down her head on a bed yet to be made.

Sleep.

How can she sleep knowing there is no wall on the back of the house. All that keeps the world out is a sheet of plywood to be wedged by Conor when he's finished down there. Doing what?

You'll secure the back. Good man, Keane.

Good for her?

It won't always be like this. There will be windows she can lock and strong new doors. Made by Conor. Curtains. Carpets. Furniture. Things to soften the place. The girls and their friends will fill it up.

The girls. They will be home soon. Coming here as home for the first time. Five fifteen, they won't be long. *I'll be here for some time.* How long? It can't take much longer to measure the floor. He must intend to come up and see her after all. *I've to talk to the client yet.* The girls will be here. They can't be much longer.

Conor, herself, the girls in one room.

No.

She must go down. *Make the right move.* She can't greet him with the girls as audience. There's not much that Imogen misses. Offer him a cup of tea. *Moss said you were down here, I've made some tea, would you like a cup?*

Breaking her own rule about tea-making on the first day.

She could call through the floorboards. *Conor, I know you're down there, would you like a cup of tea?*

She takes the bunch of keys from the mantel, in case the front door slams behind her. Moss has laid a plank down the cellar steps to make a ramp for the wheelbarrows. She walks the plank, wobbling, into the front cellar. On a makeshift desk there's the site phone, a temporary line which Moss had put in. There's a file full of delivery notes with a label in Moss's writing: DURHAM ROAD, SITE OFFICE. The programme of works is pinned to the wall by the gas meter. It's dark, even with the lighting on. Large neon strips stand vertical, held up on tripods. They look like stick men, bathed in the eerie purple glow of their own light. This is the light the men dig by. Not much digging to be done here in the front half, it's across the passageway to the back of the house, the room for the girls, but they must bring the clay up through here. Digging like miners. It feels like a mine. Hard to imagine this site office as the utility room it will become; humming with the purposeful sounds of the washing machine and tumble dryer, warmed by the boiler that will heat the whole house.

She makes her way through to the passage. Conor is up a level from where she is standing. The stairs aren't made yet. What will be the kitchen floor is level with her nose. It's like looking at a shelf. A shelf full of bricks and breeze blocks. Through the stacks she can see him, over by the archeological site. Making notes on the scale drawing, using a stack of bricks as a desktop. Engrossed. He hasn't heard her. He must be twenty feet away. He will hear the outdoor sounds, the children two gardens away squealing as they play in the late afternoon sun, glad to be out in the surprise warm weather. Can she reach him before he becomes aware of her? There will be stairs here, no more than five or six, so she won't even think about getting up and down from kitchen to lower basement. But she's still to agree dimensions and positioning. So there are no stairs, just a drop that is over a metre deep. There's usually a plank here too, but it's been pushed up onto the kitchen floor. She doesn't want to pull it back down. A plank that size would be heavy, he would hear it scraping. She presses her hands onto the shelf which is really the kitchen floor, eases up her weight. Push. A bit higher and she could swing herself round, sit on it, like climbing a wall. It's too high and even if she did succeed she would be covered in dust. She finds a plastic milk crate to use as a step. She puts it squarely in place, raises herself onto the crate, raises her head to see where she can get a footing.

'Will I give you a lift?'

Conor Keane smiling down on her. He offers his hand.

Adrenalin. He must hear the thud.

Thud. Thud. Thud.

Faster and faster. She will die of an overdose of her own adrenalin. She doesn't need his hand now or the milk crate. She could leap the metre-high drop. Heart pumping so much she starts to shake.

He takes her hand.

A kind, firm grip. Freckles. So many freckles on the back of his hand. She's up there beside him. Unsteady, she stumbles against a stack of breeze blocks. She catches her head on the underside of the staircase which is exposed above them. These are the stairs she walked down a few minutes ago. The stairs from her makeshift kitchen down to the main hallway. She's below them now. With no plaster to cover them it's like looking inside a garment without its lining. She can see the seams. Look how they are joined together, wedges reinforce each tread. She's never studied the underside of a staircase before. New electric cables sag beneath its treads: white spaghetti waiting to be joined to something else. More wire in a tangle at their feet.

'Steady,' he laughs, and grips her arm at her elbow. Gently, barely touching, but enough to stop her falling over and back down the drop.

'Dangerous down here . . . You OK?'

'I don't know.' She laughs, talks too quickly, at the speed of her thudding heart, about how the removal men and the decorators criss-crossed. And before she can stop herself she tells about the paint on Roy's backside and how all the crockery is packed tight on her bookshelves. And what is Moss thinking of leaving that hole in the bathroom wall? Can this really be the same day that she left her old home. Words tumbling this way and that, piling up like the rubble, no particular order, until she's out of breath. Laughing, she loses her footing again and grabs at the wiring.

'Take it easy.'

'It's OK.'

Gentle again, the squeeze on her elbow. Tender. And no question about it, remember this, no question, he searches out her eyes and holds them, gentle as the touch, but definite.

'Take it easy.' All the time looking into her eyes.

His mouth is open, lips parted.

So is hers. She feels her toothpasty breath slide in and out.

His mouth. His eyes on hers.

Make the right move.

The sound of her breath. The sun visible through the cracks in the floor upstairs. No ceiling just the underside of the same floor she had her ear to ten minutes ago. Up there, her and Keane in the virtual world inside her head. A fantasy world beneath the floorboards. Now she is in the real world beneath the real floorboards.

Slow motion. Lips close to the point of contact. Each leans on the cushion of air between them, a kiss-width away, following the natural pull. Going with what can't be helped.

And yet.

At their backs a tug that's as strong.

I'll not have men behaving badly on a Quinn site. Innes Quinn was clear. *No smoking. No loud radios. No bad language. No impropriety of any kind.*

Held. Caught between the pull forward, the tug at their backs.

The best I can do, Maureen.

A look now more vulnerable than she can bear. A squeeze at her elbow. She shifts her feet, raises herself onto the breeze blocks. It's like being on a step. She's slightly taller than him now. She's safe up here. But he can still look at her that way, even though she is taller than him. *Make the right move.*

It's done before she knows it. She leans forward. Her hand touches his shoulder. Lightly, ever so lightly. Not so much a kiss; she touches him with her lips. She touches his lips with her lips. His lips are as soft as his voice. The flesh of his shoulder feels solid beneath the cotton shirt.

A thud from above.

The bare-backed staircase is falling down on their heads.

Thud. Thud. Thud. More than one pair of feet striking the boards.

'Mum. Are you here. Where are you?'

Click. Like the automatic kettle. Their eyes switch off.

He's business-like. 'I need to make things secure down here.'

She thinks of the girls. 'It's OK. I'm here.' She calls up through the stairs, wondering what she is doing here anyway. How has she got here? Like a sleepwalker waking suddenly, she must find her bearings, make her way back to where she should be.

'I'm down below. Don't come down, I'm coming up.'

12

Champagne

'It's me.'

Liz. Relief.

Amy didn't really believe it would be Conor. But she sent Imogen to the door anyway. He must have gone by now.

She can feel him.

His presence around her, the touch of him filling her up. The lightest brush of lips. That was all. From this trace, she feels him as though he were still here. The slightest touch but it's left a strong mark. So strong, surely others will notice.

Liz will.

Amy puts a hand to her face, gently, to protect the touch of Conor. To keep it there. To stop Liz seeing. The tea she made before will be stewed. She could busy herself out of this. Make a fresh pot now Liz is here.

'Glasses?' Liz holds up a bottle of champagne, triumphant, like a racing driver. She has flowers too. Tulips. Red, orange and the deepest pink, a mass of heads on the verge of opening.

'You're early.' Amy spreads her arms for a hug. She grounds herself in the solid warmth of Liz. 'Tea?'

Champagne. Perfect. Amy's ready for a celebration. But if she drinks now, even one glass, she will be fit for nothing. She's struggling as it is to be here, present in this room. Her head is as light as the bubbles that will dissolve on the wine's surface. Her insides slip and roll like the plume of froth finding its way down the side of the bottle, released from the pressure. She flows, liquid, through the gaps in the boards, finding her way down there again. She holds on to the image: her and Conor standing on the edge of the kitchen floor, two figures on a shelf. Conor's lips, slightly apart. Not now. Keep it for later. Make the tea. The touch of him tingles on her face, spreading across her cheek which she knows is flushed.

Where is he?

In his van, or has he gone back to the workshop to check up on Gerry. Maybe he is talking to Maureen on his mobile, letting her know he is on his way home. His lips forming words for Maureen. When he arrives will he kiss Maureen, cover up Amy's kiss? Is he, too, feeling the brush of her lips on his face? Is he remembering the taste of her minty breath. Is it as sharp to him as his scent is to her?

She could drown in it.

The sweat of a day's work, the fragrance of new wood, and underneath that something else, something sweet. She would know it anywhere. The smell of a real life, a living man. A smell she could live off like a new element, replacing air. Raw. It brings her to full consciousness, sharp and sudden with a shock, like smelling salts.

'You've done it then. How did it go?' Liz sits down at the kitchen table, tilting back her chair, settling in for the details. As Amy fills the kettle once more and finds enough cups for them, she tells the story again but slower this time. The Kings turning up early. The chaos of men here. The paint on Roy's backside. The bed swinging though the window, hauled up on ropes. How, in this day of fierce activity she'd so little to do, and now there's so much to do that she doesn't know where to begin. She tells it slowly, concentrating on the order of events. This helps to keep the scent of Conor at bay. She can't keep the two thoughts in her head at once. But she can feel him on her.

'Well you've made a start in here,' says Liz looking round the makeshift kitchen. 'Cosy.'

'It's good,' says Alice. 'Better than I thought it would be.'

'These help,' says Amy putting Liz's tulips in a jug. 'There.' She places them on the mantel shelf where Mr Byrne's spindly cyclamen once sat, and remembers the Sacred Heart which hung above.

*   *   *

'Come on,' Liz is suddenly all energy. 'What's to be done?' Liz insists that they'll only do what's necessary to give them a comfortable night. The most important thing, she says, is to get to the champagne. They will make beds and hang the bedroom curtains. That's all. Liz can see an end to the possible tasks, whereas Amy can see neither beginning nor end. She simply emerges now and then from her dream state to do what is required so that she can pass for a reliable person. She washes the cups.

'Mum,' a sulky Imogen pokes her head around the door. 'I didn't want my bed over by the window.' Before Amy can summon up a reasonable impersonation of herself, a grown woman, this girl's mother, Liz comes to the rescue.

'Well, you and I will move it,' says Liz with a don't-come-the-young-madam-with-me tone. A tone that Amy would never get away with.

'Come on.' Liz gathers up Imogen. Alice has brought the suitcases full of clean sheets in from the car. 'We'll make your bed and move it wherever you choose.' They won't refuse Liz. 'You've time enough to get the room perfect. One day at a time.'

'Don't say that.' Alice bites her nails

'What did I say?' Liz softens.

'You know, I hate that, "One day at a time". It's what everyone used to say after Dad died.' Tears in her eyes now, she picks at the skin around her thumbnail. 'He'll never come here will he?'

A quietness gathers. They all stand still, huddled in the kitchen looking at Alice.

'No,' Liz says, quietly.

Amy puts an arm around Alice's shoulder.

'He won't know where to find us. When he comes back.' Alice struggles to get the words out. She's going to say it, she doesn't want them to stop her. 'It's not daft to say that. You know what I mean.' They all used to think it and say it, early on: *When Dad comes back. When Greg comes back.* Illogical, but it was real. They did it anyway, saving up scraps. *When Dad comes back I'll show him my new trainers.* Amy would clip things from the papers, a review, an article, a photograph by a colleague or rival. *I must save that for Greg.* They had all done it. Did it.

'Sorry, Mum.' Amy knows to let Alice pour this out, she can see the girl calming. Saying it is enough.

'It's all right,' Amy kisses her forehead.

'It keeps going through my head. Dad won't know where we are. He'll never come here.'

'No,' says Amy letting her own tears come. This isn't easy. She feels the impact of a collision. The hard stone coldness of a dead husband. The flesh warmth of Conor. 'No. You're right. He won't ever come here.'

In her own bedroom Amy faces the cartons stacked up in the square bay of the window. The giddy drunkenness brought on by Conor has receded. She's sobered by Alice's outburst. But the effect is not entirely gone and she could easily stir it up again. She's not letting go. She hangs on to a small, bright point she can't exactly describe, though she sees it in her mind. A speck of light, no, more like a sliver, like the strip of light seen under a door or between curtains not properly drawn. A thin strip of clarity not easily put into words except to say that at this point lies the knowledge that Conor is real. Conor is important. Conor is not wrong.

She doesn't feel guilty.

An insistent strip of light which she can't shut out. She will hold on to that. It needs time to grow. She raids the cartons, impatient to find the curtains. Roy's men have stacked them with her labels on the other side, round the back. She knows that the only way to find anything is to be systematic, to turn each of the twenty or so boxes around in turn until she finds the right one. Instead, she makes a haphazard grab here and there, chance might find them quicker than reason. She wants it to be dark when she lays her head on the pillow at the end of this strange day. The deepest dark, so she can see the brilliance of that light in her head. She looks forward to the peace and the dark, perfect conditions in which to see it and feel it again. Objectively, it is the briefest moment. Minutes only, if she measured it by the clock. Hardly anything happened, an observer would say. A few minutes, slight movements of their bodies, the briefest contact. Yet she could make a lifetime's study of it. So much couldn't be seen by the outside eye. So much in those brief minutes that days of reflection wouldn't exhaust her interest. Like some scholar in an important but narrow field of research, she could plough the furrow again and again, deeper and deeper.

'I've sent the girls for fish and chips.' Liz breezes in. 'It's time you stopped.'

'I can't find the curtains for in here.'

'Do you need them?' Liz has a point. The cartons, stacked six high all along, almost cover the window.

'They should be here. Maybe I sent them to storage by mistake.'

'They'll turn up. You need to relax.'

'Couldn't we just go through these?'

'A drink.' Liz takes Amy by the arm, leads her down to the makeshift kitchen. She takes down glasses and polishes them with a tea towel.

'Now,' Liz says, 'before the girls get back, tell me about this Conor Keane.'

'What do you mean?'

'It's the way you mention him, Amy. All the time. You'd think Keane alone was building this house with his bare hands.'

'I've told you, it's a relief to be working with people who really care about what they do. It's not what I expected, you know, a kind of bonus, that doing all this can be interesting too.'

'I've seen him.'

'Have you? How do you know?'

'Locking up the cellar as I was coming in. Curly hair and a smile that I could see you falling for. Got into a van marked Keane Joinery.'

'You spoke to him?'

'He said, "Tell her it's secure down there." Sexy voice. He looked at the flowers and the bottle, smiled, and said, "enjoy your evening."'

'Going as you arrived?' He stayed. Afterwards. What did he do? Compose himself. It would have taken a while to fix the boards up at the back. Longer, if he was feeling half the distraction that she felt.

'Not what I expected. Has the look of an academic about to do some DIY. So?'

'What do you mean?'

'Come on Amy, you've more than a professional interest in that man. And why are you the colour of those tulips?' She will have to tell Liz, but not now. It would be a relief, to speak about it, to get it outside of her head. But Liz would be practical, sensible, sceptical. She would tell her to stop it. Not to get hurt. Not to go any further with this madness. Amy doesn't want the spell broken yet.

'Two haddock, two cod, which do you want?' The smell of fish and chips arrives in the cramped kitchen just ahead of Imogen and Alice. Amy realises how hungry she is. There's not enough room for them all to sit at the tiny table. They take plates, knives and forks down to the front sitting room. It's a cool, north-facing room. Amy had Liam paint the walls in two warm shades of yellow divided by the soft grey on the woodwork. 'Puts a glow in there all right,' said Liam when the first coat was on. It's a haven in the chaos. A finished room. A deep sunshine yellow beneath the dado rail, the then paler, daffodil yellow up to the ceiling. Moss had someone in to sand the floorboards.

'You've good, old pine there, Amy. They'll come up grand.' And they have. The wood is slightly darker round the edge of the room. There's a lighter area in the centre where a square rug once sat. The boards are patterned with age and the maps of the lives which have passed through here: the dents of sofa legs, holes where knots have shrivelled and fallen out. The wood has shrunk over the years widening the spaces between the boards. The tongue only just reaching the next groove so it forms a ledge where dust has gathered, the sediment of this house's history, like geological evidence. And though Desmond cleaned the room after the decorators finished, it was a cursory wipe of the boards. He didn't get down into the cracks. Amy would like to scoop out the dust and put it under a microscope. A lot of new building dust for sure, and the sawdust from sanding the boards, but beneath that there would be the flakes and motes of everyone who ever sat in this room. Minute traces of skin, hair, fingernails. The dead amongst the living. She thinks of herself this morning vacuuming at her old house and it only just occurs to her that she probably sucked up the very last traces of Greg.

'Are you all right, Amy?' Liz is setting places at the low coffee table. There isn't much else in here. A sofa, an armchair, the TV and a bookshelf in the corner which she's yet to fill with books. The fireplace looks less imposing, more livable with now it's surrounded by the yellow walls. Like a piece of rancid lamb, Imogen had said when she first saw the brown marble streaked in greyish white. But it looks fine now. Liam's men have cleaned and polished the burgundy tiles which surround the black cast iron centre. A log fire in there in winter, this could be a cosy room. Right now Amy likes the blank yellowness. An orderly, empty place.

The four of them sit cross-legged on the bare floorboards around the coffee table.

'No chips for you then, Imogen.'

'Pure grease, thousands of calories,' says Imogen as if they should know better. She peels the batter off her haddock and picks at the white flesh.

'Toast,' says Liz bringing in the champagne and glasses on a tray. She struggles with the cork.

'Tight. Come on, come on,' shaking the bottle till the cork shoots upwards, hits the freshly painted ceiling leaving a mark.

'Ooops, sorry,' Liz lets a little champagne slide into each glass, then she goes round again until they are full.

'Here's to your new home.' They raise their glasses. 'And to your Mum for being daft enough to do this.'

'Yeah, to Mum,' says Alice. Even Imogen manages a smile.

'Never mind,' says Liz, as she watches Amy struggling to balance the washing-up on the draining board. 'You'll have a dishwasher in that state-of-the-art kitchen being built for you by James Joyce.' Liz finds a tea towel and starts to wipe plates to make more room.

'Stop it, Liz.'

'Well, he had more of the poet about him than a joiner. I'd say fairly intense wouldn't you?'

'You barely saw him. And I hardly know the man.' Amy tries to make light of it but she's not fooling Liz. Wouldn't there be something delicious about telling her? True confessions, like

being back at college. Amy and Liz over twenty years ago in
their bedsit above an ironmongers in the Kilburn High Road,
the day after she met Greg. Liz digging for details. Amy glad
enough to tell. A party at someone's basement flat in Ladbroke
Grove. Too many people in that low-ceilinged space. Amy in a
corner near the sound system. Stephen Stills plus backing chorus
billowing from the speakers with, 'Love The One You're With'.
She knew Greg by sight. He was on the periphery of friends, but
older, just starting out as a photographer, had something already
in a magazine. Everyone knew Greg would do well. Amy talked
easily to him, he was being polite because she was on her own. He
couldn't be interested in her. They laughed and had to shout to
hear each other over the speakers. Liz was dancing with someone
on the other side of the room, her hips pressing against whoever
it was, her velvet skirt swishing the floor. Amy knew she needn't
wait for Liz, so when Greg said he'd had enough and would
she like a lift, she said yes. They were heading the wrong way
down Ladbroke Grove, south towards Holland Park, and then on
through Shepherd's Bush. 'This isn't the way to Kilburn,' Amy
pointed out. No, but it's a lovely night and wouldn't she like to see
the river? They walked along the Strand at Chiswick. Pubs were
still open and they found the one that has a garden right down
to the water's edge. They talked until closing time. His work, her
studies, her application to the museum. Easy talk. And when he
finally dropped her back at her flat she hadn't seen it coming at
all. Him reaching over and kissing her gently at first and then
quite fiercely. 'You're such an innocent Amy,' said Liz back then
as they sat cross-legged on their patchwork floor cushions in a
fug of scented candles and joss sticks. 'You mean you really had
no idea?'

This time she could tell Liz how she had seen it coming for quite
a while. What a release to let Liz know. How crazy she's become.
Liz is going to get it out of her anyway. She won't give up now.

'Am I talking to myself again? Here, finish this.' Liz drains
the champagne into Amy's glass. They sit face to face at the
kitchen table.

'I kissed him today.'

'Who?'

'Keane. I kissed him.'

'You kissed him?'

'I did.'

'Where?'

'On his lips'

'No. I mean where were you.'

'Downstairs'

'In the dungeon, amongst all that rubble?'

'He was measuring up for the floor.'

'And what did he think of it? You kissing him.'

'He would have kissed me. He was holding back, you know, because of the situation, I suppose. It's been building up for some time. So, I kissed him.'

'Well, good for you. I assume he's available. Unattached?'

'He's very much attached to Maureen and their four children.'

'Amy are you all right?'

'Never felt better. The relief is wonderful.' She's not mad. She wasn't making it up. It's real. A small, real kiss. Not a story in her head. Not something she missed, didn't see coming. Who knows where it goes from here, but she's released the tension. She feels a surge throughout her, pent up energy discharging itself. Liz, for once, says nothing. She looks at Amy, Amy looks at her.

'Don't ask me what it all means. I don't know. I don't feel I have much choice in this. It's happening whether I want it or not. All I know is that in some odd sort of way it feels right.' Amy looks over her shoulder and lowers her voice. She can't say too much now with the girls still up and around.

'Look,' says Liz, whispering as Imogen clomps down the stairs on her way to the bathroom next to them, so Liz has to get up and push the door to. 'Meet me for lunch. You need to get away from here. Get a bit of perspective on this, Amy. I'm sure you've more to tell. I mean, would it help to talk it through? When will he be here again?'

Amy's seeing Conor again on Wednesday. Wednesday evening. It had been his suggestion to meet in the evening. To discuss the work. He had a lot on at the moment, the workshop was busy. He could come here in the day but he knows she has work to do. And she had not hesitated to suggest Wednesday, knowing that the girls would be out. It was the only weekday they were allowed out late in term time and they always went somewhere.

'Let's meet on Monday,' says Liz.
'Maybe. I'll phone you.'

This is the moment Amy has been waiting for. Her head on the pillow, the first night in her new home. Feels more like a temporary shelter. She thinks of the back of the house with nothing to keep the world out but the boards that Conor has wedged in place. *Tell her it's secure down there*. Down there. She'll revisit it now, play it again. Slowly. Approach it slowly. She relaxes into the touch of the sheets. Cool cotton with the smell of April air in them. Dried on the line in her old garden, the last washing she did there. She allows in the scent of Conor. How delicious it would be to have him here. Really here. To have the real scent of him coming in over the April air that is caught in the grain of the fabric. Air pockets trapped by the weave. She can smell him anyway, here or not. Everything is heightened, coming in clear and slow, to be savoured. Life the other side of that kiss.

The kiss. She is coming to that.

There is a wind gathering and the house creaks like a ship on the night sea. New timbers settling. A tarpaulin flaps somewhere, sounds like a giant bird landing or a sail filling. She will adjust to these noises. She looks up, opening her eyes for a moment. Over the top of the pile of boxes she can see the roofs of the houses opposite. Someone, if they cared to, could see in over those boxes. She must be careful in this house with holes in the bathroom and no back wall below. People will be watching her. But they can't see inside her head.

Conor's there.

He's looking at her. A look that says: I want to kiss you. And though she wants that kiss more than anything else, she shifts her feet. The pull towards him is tinged with fear. The exquisite terror of it makes her shift her feet. If she moves she will test the strength of the pull. If it's not real it won't survive the slightest movement. But if it's real it will still be there and she will have had a few more seconds to consider. Not to be done lightly, this kissing another woman's husband. No going back once it's done.

Consider?

Nothing like rational thought going on at the time. That's what she's making of it now. At the time it was all instinct. A thumping inside. Shifting the weight from right leg to left. Lifting her foot, steps in a dance, hands hugging her own waist. Shifting her feet until they hit breeze blocks. She stands on these blocks as if on a step. Slightly taller than him. No longer him looking down on her. She has made the kiss less possible, made it safer. It cannot happen. It must not, and yet it must. Kissing Conor is part of the dreamworld in her head. The place where she goes in these crazy days. A place she has invented. A story she has made up to escape the chaos, the disruption, the boredom of hanging around while her life is boxed and moved, hammered, sawed, extended and converted. Of course it cannot be acted on. Still, it makes the drama of the dreamworld more exciting if she knows he's thinking the same. If she knows he really wants the kiss.

Dream kiss. Real kiss.

Spinning and spinning as she wobbles on her breeze-block step, looking down on his curly head until the tension might kill her. She must release it.

A touch to discharge the static. So she lays her hand on his shoulder to stop her wobbling. She feels the softness of his cotton shirt and his flesh firm beneath. It's a surprise to discover how solid he is. He's looking at her in that way. Then it hits her. What his look says is: *go on Amy, it's up to you. I want to, but really it's up to you. Make the right move.* That's what his eyes say as clear as if he'd spoken the words. She leans down, brushes her lips on his, the lightest touch, just to the side of his mouth. Half cheek, half lips. He squeezes her arm. She moves her head back a fraction of an inch.

Waits.

He comes forward. Mouth slightly open, the softness of his mouth on hers. A few seconds. This small gesture utterly changes their lives. It adds layers of complexity whilst making it all so simple. No longer a story in her head that she makes up as she goes; a world of ambiguous gestures and looks out of which she spins a tale. Amy and Conor have a new existence outside of her head. Seconds, it can only have been seconds. The hinge on the door into this new place. She sees a fullness gathering, but destruction too, and looking for escape routes the word infatuation comes to her aid. An aberration brought on by the changes.

How does she know he's not some Romeo doing this all the time? Some womaniser and she's fallen for it. Making a fool of her.

This could be true.

But in her gut she knows, has known for some time, this is not infatuation. This has hit her in a deep place. Something has cracked open, a space inside which she barely knew existed.

13 ∫

Double Cappuccino

Amy walks on water. The river smells of mud and the sea. A warm breeze fills her skirt, strokes her thighs. The sun glints and flashes, broken by the metal railings. Vibrations in the soles of her feet gather force, flowing up and through her. Is it the train that makes this happen or is she powering the train? The train passes, headed for the coast, no doubt. He's here again. Anything can start it. Amy and Conor walking the length of a beach. Windswept or sunny? Deserted? Walking the shoreline, dodging the fizz of the sea as it swirls up to the firm sand, or, barefoot, walking through the waves?

No. This is supposed to be a day out, away from the house and her crazy thoughts.

She's walked across Hungerford Bridge hundreds of times but it's as if she's never seen London before. It's changed. The stone of Waterloo Bridge and the buildings that line the Embankment, look white, crisp, not the usual grey. The dome of St Paul's swells magnificently; she could reach out and touch its roundness. Big Ben will strike the hour before she reaches the South Bank.

'*Big Issue*.' She avoided the lean youth in the Strand. 'Buy the *Big Issue*.' This young man, with a weathered face behind a black beard, catches her eye.

She stuffs the magazine in her bag to read later. These days she can put most things off till later.

A few potent looks, some shared interests, his close attention to her needs as a client, and yes, all right, a kiss. A kiss that she offered. This is all it amounts to. *Perspective, Amy*. Liz is right. Amy is spending too much time in the house. In her head. She's too close for comfort. Out here everything is on the move. Traffic streams across Waterloo Bridge: bright red buses, mucky vans, a cyclist in orange Lycra. A constant flow of lives. Some of them will be in love. *I've fallen in love*. A riverboat swishes beneath her, thick with eager tourists. Its wake hits the bank, stirs up mud. The world is larger and more varied than she remembers. She has narrowed her world down to a half-built house and a fantasy. She stops for a moment to watch dredgers shifting silt, clearing the depths. When she brings Conor out into the bright Monday sun she begins to see it for the silly notion it might be. *Perspective, Amy*. She's glad that Liz persuaded her to spend the whole day in town, even though her meeting with Muriel is not until this afternoon.

'I can't,' Amy had protested.

'Yes you can.'

'I have to be here; there's always queries, people to see.'

'The joiner?'

It had taken some effort to leave. Amy didn't wait for her usual morning conference with Moss, she simply called down to him through the cellar door as she left.

'I'm out all day.' If she had hesitated, gone into the site office, she would have lingered. There was always a detail to take up with Moss. Today she could have made a fuss about the skip delivery at 5.30 a.m., waking the street with its clanking chains and the hollow, metallic rattle as the new, empty one dropped against the kerb. Once in the site office, she can't pretend otherwise, she would have been looking for signs. Deciphering Moss's end of each phone call. Was it him?

When was the last time she had a whole day out? BC, certainly. Before Conor. She's like a tourist arriving for the first time in a foreign city. It had started on the tube. For once she was not surrounded by builders. Instead, there were men and women in suits. Some of the women, on this warm spring day, had risked a summer dress and bare legs. There were large boys in school uniforms, blue blazers edged in red, and a party of Italian students talking when everyone else was silent, their English words slowing down the Italian flow: *British Museum, Totten-ham Court Road*. Forgotten places that Amy used to know well. The world beyond her house. There was no smell of paint or clay, only the mingling of everyone's soap, deodorant, dabs of perfume or after shave; the smell of a new week starting. In an attempt to blend in she had read the fax from Muriel.

Delighted you phoned. I liked your initial thoughts. This idea of re-imagining the domestic landscape sounds full of potential. Do keep in mind events and publications. CD Rom catalogue is a possibility. It might be the way to link new work to the collection here. So glad you're interested. I need your eye. The Monday afternoon slot suits me best. See you then.

She can't let Muriel down. Of course it would have been better if this project had come when the house was finished. This is too good an opportunity to miss. Muriel had more than hinted that there might be a permanent job if the new wing goes ahead. Muriel, passionate about the past but always with an eye to the future. Amy's done so little since Greg died. She needs this project to build up her work, but if she takes it on, she will have to deliver. It's an opportunity to divert herself from this madness, become absorbed in some real research. She has spent enough time on Conor Keane. Hours of attention considering the texture of his hair, the exact location of the large freckle on the back of his left hand and the way his nails are always trimmed. The known, observable data. She has speculated on the nature of his twin sister, once referred to, and his wife, Maureen. She has rerun each sentence in which he has made reference to Maureen and considered various interpretations of the tone: bored with, resentful of, respectful of. Never passion. Her research to date has been thoughtful, considered, painstaking. She might have enough to produce a catalogue on CD Rom with hot-links picked out in bright blue pixels. **Joiner** – of some distinction, designs own work. **Design** leads to **Art College** – began a degree in three-dimensional design, switched to sculpture, finished neither, used to make sculptural pieces in wood. Unclear why this stopped. Has it stopped? This could lead to **Wife** – Maureen – and that, in turn could lead backwards to **Cork** – home town, girl next door – or forwards to **children** – four, names yet unknown. **Siblings** must be considered too – several, exact number not yet known, but the twin sister seems to be important. Time to sort out the virtual from the reality. The kiss, of course, was not a fantasy, but maybe it grew out of a fantasy. Not enough evidence to prove the thesis. Yet.

Amy takes her coffee to a table by the window. The frothy head rises above the rim of the deep blue mug, sinking slightly at the centre under the weight of chocolate dust. She takes a sip, the lightness of air-bubbles in milk.

'Sorry,' says Liz. She wriggles out of her dévoré jacket and pushes her fringe from her eyes. 'You can blame the rust-proof corset.'

'Rust-proof?'

'Turn-of-the-century. American. The spiral corset. I've been on the phone forever trying to get through to the company archive. Anyway, enough of that. More coffee?'

'Yes, please.'

'Regular, or double to get your pulse racing?'

'Double.'

'I'll come straight to it,' says Liz, blending air, chocolate, milk and coffee to a muddy brown with a plastic spoon. 'I'm worried about you.'

'Me, why?'

'This Keane man.'

'Aren't you pleased? For the first time in three years, there's the house, work picking up – why not a man in my life?'

'It's not *a* man that bothers me, it's *this* man.'

'He's all I can think of. OK, I have fallen in love, I admit it. And there are indications that he is somewhat taken with me.'

'In Love? Please, not the "L" word. Do you know what you are saying?'

'Yes. I'm drawn to him, fascinated by him. He intrigues me.'

'So, off you go – have a shag.'

'Liz.'

'Don't go all prim and suburban. If you've got an itch, if the both of you've got an itch, by all means scratch it. But falling in love, well, think about it.' Amy's not prepared for the force of Liz's words. Liz has had so many men, she's coming at this from a different angle.

'In love is how I feel.'

'You'll get hurt. There's pain coming with this. You must know that.' Pain doesn't come into it, unless Liz means the exquisite torture of anticipation.

'Sometimes I think I'm going mad.'

'It is a kind of madness. Look, have an affair, by all means. There's nothing quite like an affair to revitalise you. But you must know that's all it will be. Affairs end, usually messily.'

'Aren't you rushing ahead? Maybe I'll enjoy his company. I like talking to him.'

'Amy, you fancy him. You've kissed him. Kissing is a prelude to shagging.'

'It's not possible. Living on a building site, I'm short of privacy.'

At Durham Road Amy hears everything. Moss on the site phone, men complaining about Moss or their pay, the odd remark about her: *left her a tidy sum*. They must hear her too; talking to the girls, on the phone to Liz and her footsteps on the bare boards. They will know when she's in the kitchen, the bathroom, the sitting room. She could barely imagine a private conversation with Conor, never mind anything else.

'You'll be surprised,' says Liz. 'You can shag anywhere, anytime. If you want to. But you're not talking about that are you?'

'You think I've forgotten how?'

'You're talking about attachment, involvement, romance.'

'He's interesting. A bit odd really, as if there's a part of him held back. We get on. An affinity. And yes, he has a great bum.'

'You've never had a fling have you. Never even had the hots for anyone?'

'No. I don't think he has either.'

'He's Irish. Romantic. It will be all in his head. Guilt. Amy do not underestimate the guilt. He won't be able to go through with this.'

'Go through with what?'

'When is he coming round to talk about your kitchen – the most well-planned kitchen I've ever heard of.'

'Wednesday evening. The day after tomorrow.'

'I bet you've counted it out in hours. What do you plan to do?'.

'Do?'

'Amy, don't tell me you haven't thought about it – a bottle of wine, offer him supper, that sort of thing.'

'I don't know. I'll take it as it comes.'

'I see you've had your hair cut.'

Amy's also worked out what she will wear, and tonight she will shave her legs.

'It needed cutting.'

'Ask him out, see what he does. Lunch. Ask him to have lunch. That's what you should do.' Amy laughs. How utterly unlikely.

'I've probably imagined it anyway.'

'It might be better if you had. Amy this man might as well be a priest, he's so unavailable. A priest would be easier, he'd only have to give up God.'

'Spare some change?' The girl sitting under the railway arch has an unblemished face, clean straight teeth and deep blue eyes. Her wavy blonde hair is pulled back in a pony tail. Clean hair that looks freshly washed; a wisp of it escapes. It floats on the breeze.

'Spare some change?' The girl speaks directly to Amy from her makeshift seat of a milk crate. She hugs a tartan travel rug around her shoulders. Amy fumbles in her pocket for change.

'Are you all right?' says Amy. The girl says nothing. She looks beyond Amy, her eyes fixed on the next passer-by. What could have happened to make sitting here the only option. A wrong choice, an accident, a sudden illness, an ill-timed word? It can only have been days since this girl was at home, washing her hair, doing her homework.

14

A Clean Shirt

The amber glow is like a dare. Conor could accelerate, drive through before the red light, but his foot is already on the brake. He stops. He's not entirely comfortable in his clean shirt. Its crispness has him tense. It's spotless, immaculately ironed; flattened under Maureen's hand. Stiff, it stands away from his body. The crease down either sleeve is sharp as a blade. The shirt only touches him where the safety belt presses against his chest.

A green light and Conor swings into the High Road again; it's not an hour since he made the journey in reverse.

'Important client, that must be,' Maureen had said, as Conor rushed upstairs to change. 'You driving back here for a clean shirt.'

Not something he always did, but he's done it before. Nothing she could take to be exceptional. New business, usually. He doesn't like to turn up to prospective clients with the workshop still on him.

Not a lie. He did not lie to Maureen about the shirt. Nothing deceitful about going home to change after a day in the workshop.

'Two,' Conor had shouted back at Maureen through the bathroom door. 'A new job, Highgate, all design work. And I need to finalise the kitchen on that big contract. Quinn is breathing down my neck.'

He's not going to Highgate.

He phoned the client on the mobile, as soon as he was out of the house in his clean shirt, to say could they make it first thing in the morning. So it had been a lie. The first of many? But Conor is not a liar. He's surprised himself. Look at him. He never was going to Highgate. He can see that now. He wouldn't have thought it was deliberate, but that's the way it's worked out. He only ever considered Highgate because of this damn shirt and going home to change and facing Maureen.

Normally he'd feel safe inside a clean shirt, ready to do new business, building the reputation of his workshop. A quality product. Designing, making, interpreting what the client wants. He's good at that. The best materials, a finish to the highest standards. Not the way he thought his life would go but, if he has to make a living, which he does, better like this where he can use what he knows. And normally he feels good dressed to meet a client.

Amy is not 'normally'.

He undoes the top button, loosens the tie. Interpreting what the client wants. Good at that, is he? What does this client want. She kissed him. He wanted her to. He can wrap it up any way he likes but that's the truth of it. He runs his finger between his neck and the stiff collar, rubbing the skin where it chafes. It's as if Maureen is with him, folded around him in an awkward embrace.

He had longed to kiss Amy. He had let her kiss him. Christ he's seen Quinn sack a man for *smoking* in front of the client. Kissing the client, well. Quinn could halve the turnover of Keane joinery if he got a whiff of this. God knows what he's supposed to do. Stop it before it starts. It can't develop. There can be no more of what he wants more than anything. More than anything he has wanted for years.

He passes The Crown. A drink. Not now, there will be too many of Quinns' men in there. Christ he'd like a drink. But he'll be late, and anyway she'll smell it on his breath. He does have to go over the kitchen plans. Though why, when they both know that they are picking over the details. Any excuse for a meeting. Legitimate contact. A way of being in the same room as her, noticing how sad she can look, and then how a smile can break out, the fine lines gathering around her eyes. Watching her listening to him. He hasn't forced it on her, he wouldn't do that. She's encouraged him to talk about other things. She asked him outright about

Luke's work. She was interested, very interested to find out that Conor had known him, briefly. She had wanted to hear about Luke's place by the lough. How Conor had visited him, watched him work sometimes. The sight of the lough can still take Conor's breath away even though he's made the journey scores of times. He can see it now, the climb up the pass, and at the top, as the road levels, there it is, deep below, hidden away in the hills. Amy wanted to know these things. She asked about Luke's carvings, his house full of bog oak. She drew it out of him. He's not forcing this on her.

This is not the usual occupational hazard. It can easily happen, if the woman is around all day. First it's tea, coffee, then a sandwich and wanting to talk, flirting. Sad. He's learned to deal with that over the years; a polite distance, don't get caught alone. Some of the lads toy with a woman like that, it's a game to them. The Quinns won't stand that for sort of thing. There's harmless flirting, of course, they all do that. Charming the client, Fintan Quinn calls it. Fintan Quinn charms the clients with his easy talk and his handmade shirts. Moss flirts with Amy. Moss is a big baby, he'd run a mile if Amy kissed him. Isn't that what Conor's planning to do. Run a mile. *Cowardy Custard*. He can hear his brother's taunts. *You're a cissy, Conor*. And Caitlin saying: *well show him you're not, Conor*.

Conor misses another light. He pulls up sharp. Amy's file slides off the passenger seat.

He can't mislead Amy. He mustn't do that. She's been through too much. They can't get involved this way. He must stop it now. However much he wants to go on.

Cowardy Custard.

Amy's strong. She must be, to have taken on that house alone. It's a difficult situation all round.

He'll maybe phone Caitlin. She'd tease him. *Have a fling, Conor. Go on, do you good. The cork is in too tight with you*. Amy is not someone you have a fling with. How can he do that to her. Maybe that's what she wants? She can look so vulnerable. He sees her, the first time they met, unsteady on the joists. He could feel the pressure that she was under. She's taken on a lot, a woman alone like that. Christ, if it's a fling she wants why pick him?

And what would he tell Caitlin? That a client had kissed him and he's scared stiff, that he wakes up at 5.00 a.m. in a sweat? Caitlin would probe to the heart of things.

'Doesn't feel right, eh Con, does it?' He can hear her now, all these years later as if she was in the car with him. He doesn't want to think of this now. Him and Caitlin, walking along the strand, a month before the wedding.

'If it's not right Con, wait, call it off.'

'She's good,' he'd fired right back at her. 'Maureen is a good woman.'

'Good for you right now, yes. After Judy.'

'Judy doesn't come into this, Caitlin.'

'Maureen is safe, Conor. Maureen is what you already know.'

An anger had risen in him that he didn't think possible. He didn't want to be this angry with Caitlin.

'Do you have to do that. Piss on everything? And what's wrong with safe?'

'Nothing. Just that I know you'll want more. What about your work? You've hardly started.'

'I'll get going again.'

'Not with Maureen.'

'That's crap, Caitlin.'

'Is it? You've not had a studio since you split with Judy. You've made nothing new since you moved to London.'

'It will come.'

'Not once you're married to Maureen.'

'That's not true.'

'Oh yes it is, because underneath the cheesecloth and beads she's mother bloody Ireland, that's what Maureen is. She'll want a child every two years, a nice home and . . .'

'Why do you have to piss on everything. Must we all be reinventing the world like you with your rallies and demonstrations?'

'Safe after Judy.'

The worst row they had ever had in their lives because Caitlin was right in a way. Judy had been volatile, difficult, not someone he would have spent the rest of his life with, but she had been a catalyst. He'd made his best work when he shared a studio with Judy. And Caitlin, who knew what he was thinking before he himself did sometimes, saw this clearly then and wouldn't budge an inch. He had left her by the shore, marched up to the headland alone. Above the wind, her voice at his back.

'It's your whole bloody life. Your work is part of your life. All I'm saying Con is, if it doesn't feel right, wait.'

Amy feels right.

How can he say that. He hardly knows the woman.

Amy feels right.

That's the hard part; he has to go in there and say, no. Push her away.

He turns into Amy's road. Dusk settles, lights go on in the houses although curtains are not yet drawn. Comfortable, ordered lives, of bookshelves, sofas, families watching TV. He pulls up outside Amy's. A yellow light flashes on the skip, bricks are stacked and tied down under canvas. Moss runs an efficient site. There are no lights in Amy's windows. She'll be at the back of the house, in her temporary kitchen that is really a bedroom. He takes off his tie.

The phone makes him jump. He clicks the button, takes the call.

'Hello.'

'Con, where are you? You sound as if you're in a tunnel. I'm so glad I got you. Maureen said you're on your way to a client.'

'Caitlin, how are you doing?'

'I'm in again, Con. It's happened again.'

Caitlin speaks fast. The line breaks up, he has to concentrate. She's in casualty. She can't pee, again.

'This damn thing growing inside me. I can't squeeze a drop out. It seems to happen now each time I have a period.' She's been waiting an hour already.

'Con, I swear I'm going to burst if they don't do something soon.' She sounds scared. Caitlin, who's afraid of nothing, sounds scared.

'I'm scared, Con.'

'Take it easy. You're in the right place. Do you want me to phone someone, find out what's going on.'

'No, I'll be OK. I just wanted to do something, talk to someone. I couldn't sit there any longer. I have to keep walking, pacing around like a madwoman. I thought if I phoned you it would take my mind off it.' He can't hear her properly. She's talking to someone else.

'I have to go, Con. The doctor's here now. Thank God. Don't worry. I'll be OK.'

'Will I phone later to find out how you are?'

'I have to go Con. He's here. I'll ring you when I know what's going on.'

He doesn't like the sound of it. She'd laughed the first time it happened. But this sounds worse. Christ. He pushes the hair back off his forehead with both hands. He's here now. He must go inside, they have an appointment, she's maybe seen him drive up. There's nothing he can do for Caitlin. She's in good hands.

He locks the car, takes his jacket from the back seat. As he walks up the path to Amy's door his hand reaches in the pocket. He runs his finger round the groove in the lid of Luke's box. A well-judged piece. Luke had known how far he could go, when to stop.

15

Platforms

Imogen squeezes the front door shut. Mum won't notice her anyway, she's on the telephone.

'It's me,' says Imogen as she passes the temporary kitchen. Mum is deep in conversation with Liz.

'Won't be long.'

It doesn't matter, Imogen wants to say. She's happy for Mum to talk for as long as she likes. Imogen wants to get ready without questions being asked.

In her room, she closes the door before she takes the shoes from the carrier bag. Shiny white patent leather. Two-inch platforms. She slides her feet into them, and walks across the room. They clomp too much on the bare boards. She hides them under her bed in case Mum or Alice comes up. If Mum sees her trying them on she'll know that Imogen has been into town today, bunked off. She won't mind so much if Mum notices them later, when she's on the way out. Imogen won't have time to talk then. Mum may not notice at all. Her mind is on other things.

'Imogen, I'm doing pasta for me and Alice, want some?'

'I'm going to have a bath.'

'You must eat something before you go out.'

'Not now, Mum.'

'Are you having something to eat when you go out?'

'I'm having a bath.'

'Do come and eat.'

Imogen hears Mum's footsteps on the stairs.

'All right. Leave some out for me. I'll zap it in the microwave later.' Mum's anxious to get supper out of the way early. She needs to clear up for her visitor. 'Oh dear,' Amy had said last night, puzzling over drawings of the kitchen. 'I need to have this ready for tomorrow. He wants a final decision.' She's overdoing the serious decisions routine. There's something strange happening to Mum. She's either running around like a wound-up doll, like now, or dreamy and vacant, like she's not here half the time. Mum thinks they're children. She thinks they can't see. Alice might not want to see, but she can say what she likes, Mum's looking forward to her 'difficult meeting' with Conor Keane. It's like she's going to a party. She looked so pleased when Alice asked if she could stay the night at Jane's. Normally, Mum makes more of a fuss about sleep-overs on a school day. Mum can't wait to get rid of them.

Imogen is glad she bunked off to buy shoes. She's tall anyway, but in these she will stand out. If Nick is there, he can't fail to see her. Also, she will be as tall as Desmond. She's not sure about meeting Desmond. It had seemed like a good idea when he asked. He's not her type. He's vain. He likes the way people watch him work. He likes to be looked at. Each morning he arrives early, sits on their front wall until Moss opens the site. He always has a cup of coffee, and when he's finished he crunches the empty polystyrene cup and throws it in the skip. He is beautiful. But he knows it. He works hard, labouring. He says he doesn't want to be there and, when he can, he does modelling and film work. That's the rumour. She's heard the teasing that goes on. Fintan Quinn joking with Moss about Desmond: 'When those film producers come around tell them Rudolf Valentino here's not available, so he's not.' Imogen hears a lot up in her new room. If she opens the window in the roof, the noise slides in. Moss thinks Fintan Quinn ought to pay Desmond more money.

'He's a good worker.'

'Will we put him on the higher day rate or give him a bonus?' Desmond will be here for months.

Desmond had smiled at Imogen for the first few days. A smile and a nod as she passed him on her way out in the morning, and on her way home. He packs up the site around five. He's nearly always at the front of the house clearing up when she comes home. It's hard to avoid Desmond. On Monday he was hosing the path. He turned the water off so that she could pass. Head in her Walkman, she didn't need to say anything. She nodded a thank you.

'Garage?' he said. She hadn't realised how loud the music was.

'Yeah.'

'Ever been to Charlie's Studios?' he said, pushing the water into the gutter with a stiff broom. Desmond grooms the site at the end of each day.

'You're Imogen.'

'Yeah.'

'Desmond.' He looked at her laden bag. 'Exams? "A" levels this year?'

'Next.'

'Gave up on them myself.' He turned the hose on again once she'd passed and was on the doorstep trying to find her keys.

'Not locked,' he said. 'The door's on the latch. Moss is in with your Mum.' She could feel him watching her as she put her key away.

Yesterday he stopped her again, asked her if she went out in the week, having so much studying. He mentioned a pub. She's heard talk of it in the common room. Nick Baxter goes there.

'Come for a drink tomorrow?'

'OK.' She said it without thinking. It was only one word. Saying no would have taken longer.

'Will I pick you up. I'll have the van.' No. She will see him there.

She collects what she needs: razor, foam bath, tweezers. In the bathroom she turns up the radio. A wall of sound to keep Mum and Alice out.

What will Desmond look like out of his work clothes? There's no mistaking him. His black hair ripples half way down his back.

Mostly, it's tied up in a ponytail. Some days he wears a head scarf knotted at the back like a gypsy. The ends of the scarf float down his back, riding on his ponytail. In his left ear he wears two golden hoop earrings, one, slightly smaller, sits inside the other one. He works stripped to the waist, his khaki trousers tucked into his boots. He's not hefty, and not much taller than Imogen. He looks like a dancer. He carries bricks through to the back of the house. Hod after hod of crumbly yellow bricks. He balances the hod perfectly on his shoulder as if it weighed nothing. Once, when a new skip was left awkwardly, jutting out into the road, Desmond had moved it on his own. He placed his hands, arms outstretched, along the outer edge, his face tight with concentration, his arms metal-hard. With one huge push he had flung the skip square against the kerb. At the end of the day his back is spattered with concrete. He will look the same, only cleaner.

Imogen wraps a towel round her hair, and another one round her body. She pads across the landing.

'Can I borrow your French dictionary.' Alice is on the stairs.

'I think it's at school.' Imogen doesn't want Alice in her room. Not now.

'You had it yesterday.'

'I'll have a look,' she says. Alice follows her in.

'Here. Don't lose it.' She hands it to Alice.

'I won't, but I'm staying over at Jane's. I can meet you at lunchtime tomorrow.'

'I know. Funny how Mum didn't make a fuss.'

'What about?'

'Well, she usually wants more of a reason than doing French homework for a sleep-over mid week.'

'It's only Jane's though.'

'She's pleased you're going.'

'Why?'

'She can't wait for us to go out. He's coming over tonight.'

'Conor Keane, you mean?'

'Yeah, and now she's got the house to herself.'

'Where are you going, then?'

'For a drink.'

'Who with?'
'A friend.'
'Who?'
'No one you know.'

16

Mining

In Love or Insane? The headline had caught Amy's eye earlier; a personal message meant for her. She longed to read the article, but Imogen had been watching. Now that the girls have gone, she's devouring every syllable before Conor arrives. She'll try anything.

She's still not decided where to take him. In here, the sparse sitting room, they would be forced to sit side by side on the sofa. Too intimate. In the kitchen they could sit at opposite sides of the table. Eye contact, unavoidable. That leaves her workroom at the top of the house. Business-like. This is silly. Lighten up. Be natural. If only.

In Love or Insane? Should people be allowed to make important life decisions while in the grip of the temporary insanity we call love? The journalist has interviewed an eminent psychologist, an agony aunt and some ordinary people who are smitten. The psychologist talks about the collapse of ego boundaries, the illusion of merging with another human being. He claims that passion in mid life may bring about transformation but only if the person recognises that being in love is about loss as well gain. He warns that extreme and obsessive behaviour must not be underestimated; the insatiable longing has the power of an extraordinary hallucination, a temporary psychosis. The agony aunt says that if you think any of the following you are in not fit state to marry: *1. You will change him/her. 2. You were meant to meet. 3. You are only complete in the presence of him/her.* The ordinary men and women are frank about their obsessions. All names changed, of course. With his beloved away on business, Anthony, a lawyer, had sat outside her flat simply to feel her presence. Linda, who could only see her lover once a fortnight, couldn't bear to change the sheets. Definitely not in here on the sofa into which they will awkwardly sink.

Amy climbs up to her workroom. There is a sense of order emerging from the corner of the room where she has arranged her desk. Her computer is wired up. On the shelves are the house files and things she might need for the museum project: exhibition catalogues, reference books. The other side of the room is still a stack of unpacked cartons. *MAKE THE RIGHT MOVE.*

She turns her swivel chair to face the room. There's another chair which she arranges a careful distance away, on the diagonal. She places two storage boxes in between as a table.

He could stay for two or three hours. This block of time has a physical presence for Amy, like finding an extra room in the house. No builders, no daughters. She will never have spent so long alone in his company. She planned what to wear this afternoon. She had to draw the bedroom curtains because one of the decorators chose that moment to appear at her window, preparing the outside woodwork for painting. It's as if they know. They do it on purpose. She's chosen a short, straight black skirt, a soft cotton sweater in a subtle mauve, silver earrings, warm red lipstick. She's put white wine in the fridge, opened a bottle of red, and drunk one glass. She's cleared the kitchen, arranged anemones in a jug on table.

Another drink. She drinks the red wine like water, then cleans her teeth. Last time she saw this man she had kissed him. She's acting like a teenager. They are mature adults. She will know what to say when the time comes.

Conor sits awkwardly in the chair opposite Amy.

'Elevations and plan.' He hands her the drawings. She's looked at these before. They both know that she's not going to change anything.

'You'll order the fridge?' She knows he will, they've discussed it already.

'That's right.'

He double checks her colour choice, the type of handles for the cupboards.

'And it was the etched glass, you said?'

'Yes.'

'The beech work top and the beech floor.'

'Yes.'

He writes the details in his file.

'You can keep the drawings. Your reference copy.' Formal, like an insurance salesman. Smart, in a crisp, clean shirt and trousers, not jeans. Did she really kiss him?

'Look, the other day, I was . . .'

'It's OK.' He puts papers in the folder with slow, deliberate care.

'But . . .'

He turns in the chair and faces her, kind, open. His voice is gentle, low.

'It's OK.' He says it again.

Is that it? What does he mean. It's OK that she kissed him? Or, although it is not OK that she kissed him, he understands, and therefore it is OK? Or, OK as in, forget it, it happens all the time.

'I want you to know that I'm not in the habit of . . .' The words rattle in her head: the brittle script of a soap opera. But she's started the sentence. A smile spreads on his lips; a kind smile, not mocking. He finishes the sentence for her.

'. . . kissing the joiner?'

'I don't do things like that. I don't kiss strange men.' He's silent, his face neutral.

'I'm an ordinary sort really, nothing strange about me.' Then, the glimmer of smile: a lifeline. They both laugh: mutual amusement and embarrassment.

'I don't mind that you did.' He seems to be about to say something else but he pauses as if he's forgotten what comes next. He shifts in the seat, clears his throat.

'I don't know what else I can say.' He's fumbling. 'I mean, please don't feel bad about it.'

There's a gathering certainty now about the way he holds his body. He sits up straight and looks directly at her.

'Don't feel bad about it.'

'I need a drink. Would you like one?' says Amy

Down in the makeshift kitchen they sit at the small, square table. She pours them both a glass of red wine.

'I'm sorry I, well, brought it up so abruptly. I can hardly pretend it didn't happen.'

'No.'

She can see that he doesn't want to go back over this. He may be in the same insane state but she can see that he's not ready for a head-on discussion. He shrinks into himself, tense. She must coax him out. She offers him the glass of wine.

'I'm thinking of taking on an exhibition.'

'A lot of work.'

'Yes, but things are going well here. Moss has it under control.'

'You'll be working at the museum then?'

'No, I'll work from here. There'll be some travelling. Visiting artists' studios.'

'Sounds interesting.'

It is warm in the kitchen. He leans against the fridge, his arms are stretched before him. His fingertips stroke the velvet petals of the anemones.

'These are lovely,' he says, and still concentrating on the flowers, not looking up at her he says: 'I don't think we can take this further. It's not you. It's me too I feel the same, Amy. But we can't. We can't do it.'

'Do what?'

'Become involved.'

'We are involved. I mean the house, you are part of my daily life.'

'You know what I mean; I mean, you know . . .'

She watches his lips rather than looks him in the eye. She could stop this awkward conversation, seal his mouth with hers.

'What I'm trying to say, is that we cannot become lovers. Leave aside the fact that I'm married, think of the situation.'

'What?'

'I don't want you to think, I don't want, well . . .'

'What?'

'Coming into your house, a client's house. And this. How will it look, as if I seduced you. God knows Amy, I . . . We must stop it, now.'

Stop what? If he carries on like this she may scream. Perhaps men handle it differently. Do they feel as mad? Anthony the banker said he did. No different from Linda.

'Another drink? Have you eaten?'

She finds cheese and crackers. As she fills his glass she slows up the flow of wine. As long as she is pouring the wine she need do nothing else, but when his glass is full, what then?

'No, of course you're right,' she says. 'These things happen.'

She could ask him to leave, go now. Instead she steers the conversation towards Luke Marsden. Safe territory. A common interest. He talks easily about Luke.

'I watched him work. Turning or carving he pushed everything to the limits. Nothing he did ever came out of taking the certain route. He would find a piece of wood, a difficult piece with knots and flaws, and work it till he found a form. Then the doubts would set in. The work was too finished, too refined, and he wanted to make something rougher, messier. He drank himself silly. Judy found him one night drifting in the boat, on the lough.'

'Judy?'

'Judy was someone I was with for a time. Back in Ireland, before I came to London.'

'What brought you to London?'

'A fresh start.'

'You set up the business then?'

'No, I took up mining.' Laughing at himself now. 'You don't want to hear all this.' There is nothing more in the world that Amy wants to hear.

'Mining?'

'Jubilee Line. Twelve-hour shifts.'

And he tells the fairy-tale of his mining days in Marylebone. Lowered in a cage down a shaft at 7.00 the morning and didn't come up till 7.00 p.m. Or, more often, it was the other way round; 7.00 p.m. and up 7.00 a.m. Drank all day to be numb for the next shift.

'I kept on going, thinking I'd either die or the light would come at the end.'

'Why?'

'Money. The money was good. I was broke.'

'There must have been other jobs.'

'Hiding, I suppose.'

'From what?'

'Long story.'

'I like your stories.'

'This one isn't very interesting.'

Conor Keane's shopping list would be interesting.

'Did the light come.'

'How do you mean?'

'Well, you didn't die. Did the light come, did you dig your way out. What happened to end your mining career?'

'I got married.'

Up to now both the telling and the listening have held them steady, but they've hit the barrier. There's a limited space and they're up against it. The cage clanking down the mine shaft.

He will go. She can't bring up the subject again. He doesn't want to talk about it. *Can't take it any further*. She will avoid him, deal with him through Moss.

'Coffee?'

He lays his hand gently on her forearm and squeezes it.

'Yes, please.' His hand is still on her arm.

'Amy, I didn't come into your house with intention of seducing you. I want you to know that.'

'I never imagined that you did.'

'You smell nice. What is it?'

'Perfume. Body heat.'

He takes the back of her hand to his lips, kisses it gently. As he lowers her hand, he leans towards her, brings his lips close to hers. Both mouths are slightly open, as if sighing. A soft lip touch. Mouths that match, feel comfortable together. It's a touch, no more. The softness of his lips is a surprise. He pulls back, looks at her as if that might have been it. He comes back again, slowly, slightly more pressure this time. Their lips close firmly on each other. His tongue fills her mouth. A perfect fit. Her mouth, his tongue. She is falling through the floor. The joists open. Down, down they go, deep as a mine shaft, way past the cellar. Or is it up beyond the roof, through the new rafters. She has no sense of direction, no body. She is entirely the kiss. *An extraordinary hallucination.*

17

A to Z

Thursday, Friday, he wouldn't ring. The end of the week. Conor would have wages to do on a Friday. He was busy. Hard to find the right moment to phone. *I'll call you later*. Understandable that he wouldn't ring over the weekend. Not even on the pretext of the job. Not with Maureen around.

It's the best I can do, Maureen.

That's what Conor had said to his wife, in Amy's house. Amy has considered the sentence, weighed and measured Conor's tone. Each word was etched with irritation. Out of these seven words she is building a picture of Maureen. She can't see her yet, not her features. She senses that Maureen is a woman who never smiles. A strong woman, maybe. A disappointed woman. She can't yet see her with Conor. What she sees is Maureen in perpetual motion around four lively children. Four loved children. Will they look like Conor, or like her? All of this from a snatch of one side of a telephone call. One piece of grit is all the oyster needs.

She has not imagined Conor's tongue filling her mouth. His hands stroking her back, feeling the length of her body, feeling the curve of her backside. Tentative at first, then squeezing her flesh as if trying to hold all of her at once, growing hard against her.

All blissful fact.

It happened.

He hasn't phoned since because he's busy.

She's planned this day of work in order to remove herself from the house, but she can't leave Conor behind. Conor accompanies her everywhere. He will be on site again soon. His work will bring him back, if nothing else. If she'd stayed at home she wouldn't have been able to concentrate for the growing weight of silence around the telephone. She would have been straining to hear, wondering if she'd missed it above the rasp of a saw, the sudden screech of a drill.

She's making a start on Muriel's project. 'Get out, do some studio visits.' Muriel had known how to coax Amy. 'I trust your eye.' Amy's agreed to develop the exhibition idea and to write a proposal to present to the committee. 'Some reason for putting together this group of objects. Something that makes people see things afresh and, ideally, takes them back to look at the museum's collection. That's what I want, Amy: the innovation in relation to the tradition.'

Lucy Henderson had sent slides of new work to Amy. Ambitious new pots: luscious, fat-bellied jugs with edible glazes which had the presence of sculpture. Work that couldn't be ignored, larger in scale. These were female jugs that went beyond daily use, filled with exuberance. Amy's not been to Lucy's studio since she moved from Hackney to Camberwell. It's in a yard behind an office block off the Peckham Road. Not marked in the *A to Z*, though Amy's brought one anyway.

She knows the route well enough as far as Elephant and Castle. She picks her way through Bloomsbury. In Brunswick Square a huge horse chestnut tree is heavy, its cream candles spreading out, thrusting upwards. Swinging round Russell Square she follows the curve of lilac bushes. So many shades from deep purple to pale mauve. Eager branches reach beyond the confines of the railings, their blooms erect.

Had she pushed him away too quickly. Had she put him off? She had wanted the confirmation of his hands on her body, but it was late. She was alert for the sound of Imogen's key in the lock. She hadn't meant to pull away so abruptly.

More than twenty years ago, she and Liz would skip lectures to sunbathe in Russell Square. That Amy, the one who had stretched out on the grass, bare-legged in hot-pants, would have ridden the crest of the wave. To be in love then was less complicated. If this were happening to Amy the undergraduate, she would be soaring. Passions were soon begun, soon over then. Until Greg. Had all of them felt like this? With Greg she can remember the sensation of herself opening up; her future gathering, expanding for her to walk into. She feels it again, now. A future, a possible future, expanding, opening. But she can't simply run towards it. She can't ignore the obstacles. There isn't a clear route. Where is all this going? She feels the absolute truth of Conor's body on hers. The bliss of mutual need. But she can't see a place for it to be. She can't stop the sensations either, the filling up, the expanding. She must become the Tardis: infinite possibilities inside, but outside the same regular telephone box.

She had to pull away. Any more and she would have been too far gone. She wouldn't have been able to stop even if she'd wanted to. She pictures the absurdity of her and Conor Keane up against the fridge in her temporary kitchen, fumbling under garments and Imogen bursting in.

'I'll call you . . . Can I?' he'd said.

'If you need any more information but, I think it's all there.' Why had she done that, pretend he was referring to the job?

'Not the work.' His eyes looking straight into hers.

'I know.'

They had walked down the stairs, saying nothing. In the hall, one more kiss, he squeezed her arm.

'I'll call you, then. I'll call you later.'

She had stood behind the front door, looking through the stained glass. She saw the glow of his headlights and waited, listening as the noise of his engine grew fainter, until she was sure she could hear it no more. Like a teenager behind the stained-glass door, listening so hard into the distance that Imogen was up the path, her key in the lock before Amy noticed.

'I'm not late, it's only half eleven.'

'I was putting out the milk bottles.'

'You were looking out for me, weren't you?'

'No, no. Did you have a good time?'

They had stood so close together in the hall with the distance between them growing. How easy it was to lie. Stupid thing to say, when there weren't any milk bottles. For once she was glad of Imogen's accusation. At least Imogen didn't suspect that her mother had been listening to the receding hum of Conor Keane's engine.

I'll call you later. How much later?

The traffic grinds to a halt at the Aldwych, thick with buses being diverted up Fleet Street. She's in the wrong lane. She needs to move over, swing into the Strand, take the turn for Waterloo Bridge. Only the motorbikes are moving, dispatch riders. When she first married Greg the bikes would come and go from the house, carrying his contact sheets and prints to meet deadlines, when there were still newspapers in Fleet Street.

She inches towards the lane that's moving, eases herself into the flow. If she stays too far over she'll miss the bridge and have to go along the Strand, past the Savoy. Ten years ago, more. Photographer of the Year. Greg's work was in demand. Huge round tables, an army of waiters. There were speeches. Greg said they should book in for a weekend. Amy's mother could have the girls. They often talked about it; a treat held before them, something to look forward to in the crazy rush of Greg's job. They never did go. She can't help herself, the thought has been there pushing its way in.

Booking into a hotel.

Her and Conor. What else could they do?

We can't take this any further, Amy. His words resisting a pull that is stronger than gravity. He said this only moments before his actions said otherwise. Perfectly intelligent people, both of them. Talking sense with words while their bodies speak another language entirely.

We can't take this any further, Amy. How much further could his tongue go? Could it wrap itself around a hotel booking? There could be no steamy afternoons for them while the girls were at school with her house full of Quinns' men. The appalling practicality of it. How would it be done? Who would book? Who would pay? Would they split the bill? Cash. Maureen would check the credit card statements. She adds this to her growing sense of who Maureen is. Coldly, after it was done, would they sit down with the bill, and work out how much they each owed? They could take it in turns.

Turns.

See how the thing grows. It's not something that can happen

once, is it? Wouldn't there be a tendency to want to do it again, and again, and again.

'Dream on.' That's what Liz would say. A regular room at the Savoy. Dream on. More likely be one of those anonymous tourist blocks in Bloomsbury.

His hand moving down her back, tender, tentative. Filling his hands with her flesh. Filling her mouth with his tongue. Spontaneous, deeply felt, nothing could have stopped this happening. There was nothing spontaneous about planning to book a room in a hotel. The web of lies. Finding a time when they could both get away.

On the approach to Elephant and Castle she's aware of the screech of sirens, a flashing light in her rearview mirror. The traffic parts. She mounts the pavement as the ambulance ploughs through. Emergency. Which service? An ambulance to take her to an isolation ward: she needs treatment for the virus that has taken hold. Fire brigade to dampen her down. Police to caution her. All three.

It is a virus. Seized suddenly, spread rapidly through mind and body. If only there was a pill she could take. How many times over the years has she watched Liz in this state. There was the art dealer in New York. Amy had stood by her through the highs and lows. Liz waiting for his calls. Liz buying new clothes each time he came over. Liz convincing herself that it was wonderful to have a lover at a distance, waiting for his faxes in the middle of the night. Amy, comfortable with Greg, had watched from afar. An alien world. She had felt sorry for Liz living a life of permanent adolescence. She remembers thinking: thank goodness I won't have to go through that again. Smug, she had been. And now Conor has walked through her front door. She cannot be accused of having sought him out. These things happen. She can see now how addictive it could become. Even the pain is exquisite. If there was a cure she's not sure she would take it.

She sees the office block, as described by Lucy Henderson, looming. She makes the right turn down an alleyway that is barely a car's width. At the end of the alley there's a gate falling from its hinges. An awkward turn but she squeezes through.

She must leave Conor here in the car if she and Lucy Henderson are to have an intelligent conversation.

'Conor Keane,' she says out loud, pausing before she opens the car door. 'Conor Keane.' It has a weight and shape in her mouth. 'Conor.' Her whole mouth rounds the O, curls on the R. Smooth. 'Keane,' makes a long, easy shape of her lips. A smile. The shape and weight of his name is a precious thing. She ignores the other name that's trying to form in her head. Maureen Keane. Doesn't have the same ring.

18

Tea-Break

Amy arranges the slides on the lightbox. She takes the eyeglass down onto the image of a huge pumpkin form. She wants to see the texture close up. No one would make tea in Lucy Henderson's teapot. The pot sits firmly on its generous rump, the cleavages of its belly inviting. The curve of its handle rests like a hand on a hip; the spout is raised in a flamboyant reach. It's all three things at once: pumpkin, teapot, female. Lucy Henderson's jugs are even more audacious. Amy plays the interview. 'I'm drawn to positive natural forms,' Lucy says. In her studio there had been heaps of fruit from the street market. 'Everyone can relate to a jug; they are like people,' says Lucy. A jug has a shoulder, foot, lip, and a handle for an arm. Lucy's work is surreal, sensuous. Studying each image in turn, listening to the tape, Amy, for once, is absorbed by what she's doing.

She's been at her desk since eight. She's avoided Moss. She's trying to get through the day, or even the morning, as if she were leading a normal life. She has shut the door on the noise below. Last night she spent time in here unpacking more books, putting things in the cupboard, arranging files in the filing cabinet. A sense of order. No message on her answer phone from Conor when she returned yesterday. She had been tempted to open a bottle of wine, drink herself to sleep, giving in to her worst fears. It's an illusion. It didn't happen. He's a womaniser. Instead, she came up here and thought about Muriel's project. She didn't get very far, but she cleared a space in which to work.

This morning she opened a file on her computer and marked it 'Muriel.' She made a space for the lightbox, cleared piles of unsorted books from the mantelpiece so she can stack up heaps of slides. The fireplace is a piece of fiction. Its surround has been painted a cool jade and the cast-iron insides freshly blackened. A grate waiting to be laid, yet she can never light a fire in here. The plumbing for Imogen's bathroom above runs in the cavity behind the chimney. The chimney from which Grimmet had plucked the bird. She sees the cool, clean skeleton. An image from another life. Is she the same person who watched the soot fall away.

'Will you put that kettle on, man.' A voice from below edges in.

Amy doesn't want to shut the window. Her small room will soon become stuffy. The conversation below thickens, becomes harder to ignore as the men stop work. Without looking at her watch she knows it is ten o'clock. Builders' breakfast time. They call it breakfast not tea break. They eat bacon sandwiches and cheese rolls washed down with steaming mugs of tea. They must leave home early to be on site by eight. Desmond makes the tea in a large aluminium pot; kettle, tea bags, cups are stored in the site office. Moss brings milk each day. They're sitting outside this morning. It's warm again. They sit below her window, on make-shift seats: piles of bricks, upturned milk crates, a bag of ballast.

'As true as I sit here, so it is.'

'Arrested?'

'Arrested, I'm telling you. She set the law on him. Her own husband.'

'He wouldn't hurt a fucking fly.'

'Fintan Quinn went to the police station, spoke up for him.'

'Has this story come from Fintan Quinn, has it? 'Cos he's full of blather.'

'I swear to God it happened. Danny told me himself.'

'The woman has the green eyes, won't let him out of her sight.'

'Danny? Danny's an innocent.'

'Wedded bliss, eh?'

'As my mother used to say, "what cannot be cured, must be endured."'

* * *

Builders' breakfast takes half an hour. She can't listen to this. Amy shuts the window. Below, her neighbour's garden is a contrast to her own. A neat lawn, newly cut and striped with the marks of the mower, curves around mature beds of shrubs and flowers. Her garden is a rectangle of uneven grass, uncut, the ground full of holes. The last time she went out there she nearly twisted her ankle. There's a yellow patch in the green where Moss had stacked window frames. There will be another yellow patch when they remove the portaloo, where the men will queue before getting back to work.

'The men need facilities,' Innes Quinn said. In the very first week of the work, when the house was being torn apart, Amy had walked in on one of the labourers sitting on a chemical toilet in what's now Alice's room. Towards the end of the garden a mature plum tree and a pear tree are coming into blossom. Beyond them the grass is longer. The grass will recover.

Back on the lightbox, Amy slides the magnifying glass over a Lucy Henderson jug, its surface encrusted with fish. The glaze on the bulging fish eye is a swirl of blue and green. *She has the green eyes, won't let him out of her sight.* Does Maureen have green eyes? Maybe Conor can't phone because she won't let him out of her sight. Would Maureen have Conor arrested if she found out. This Danny, the one that Fintan Quinn bailed out, he must be from another site. Amy doesn't recall a Danny. Quinn company gossip. See how it travels from site to site. Like a big family, each knows what the other is up to.

'What I like,' says Lucy Henderson, 'what keeps me interested, is that play between intuition, the gut reaction, and the science of it, you know, standing back to look at what you're doing.' Lucy explains the unpredictability of glazes. She mixes the chemicals intuitively, noting the amounts, so that if it works she can do it again. She has built a data base of two thousand recipes. She doesn't know if it's worked until the final firing. Each colour must go into the kiln to be fired. And each time, she risks ruining the pot. Amy stops the tape. She makes another file and calls it 'events'. In it, under the heading 'gallery talks' she notes: Lucy Henderson on alchemy.

The next bit of the tape is hard to hear. There was a pneumatic drill going somewhere near the studio, beyond the unmarked yard. Amy fast forwards. She wants to find the bit where Lucy talks about spontaneity.

'Doing something new,' says Lucy, 'it's a leap in the dark.' Mindset is important. Working through each step at a time. She has a vision of the finished piece but she has to work through the stages, instinctively with the clay. 'Each step you take, builds on the last.'

Amy taps at the keyboard, makes a note of Lucy's comments. The work is good. Muriel will like it. Once she's finished with the tape and looked again at each slide, Amy is stuck. She picks up the magnifying glass, places it on the back of her hand and studies the enlargement of her own skin. A criss-crossing of ridges. Etchings that are not so visible to the naked eye. Wisps of blonde down. A freckle. If this were Conor's hand she would see more freckles, more hair. His left hand, she can see it on the gear stick the time he gave her a lift. On the left hand there is one large freckle which stands out amongst the others. She sees Conor's firm back, taut against the olive-green cotton of his shirt. Is his back covered in freckles? The freckles on his hand, the fall of his hair, the shape of his mouth. Images that stay with Amy. The shape of his mouth. From their first meeting she had watched the way his mouth moved. The way it formed itself around the shape of his words, moulded to his accent. Is his mouth shaped by the shape of his words?

'Romantic Celt.' Liz's view. She has talked to Liz several times since Wednesday. Since she pressed her mouth against Conor's, unambiguously. 'You're beginning to sound like one of those high-pitched women in a forties movie. Admit it, aren't you enjoying this longing, this waiting for him to ring. It'll be an anti-climax when he does.'

It is a shrill metallic sound. Once, twice. Let the machine take it. She grabs the receiver before the fourth ring. The noise of her heart, fast in her head. Her stomach burning. Breathless as she tries to say, hello.

She says yes to Freya Hill in order not to prolong the conversation. A call from another life. The School Parents' Association, could Freya rely on Amy's help at the summer fair? June would soon be here. Yes. A session on the bric-a-brac stall. No. Too busy this year to be on the committee.

Amy turns back to her work. She makes a list of artists she needs to visit. People whose work make sense alongside Lucy Henderson's. There could be a garden element or some outdoor work. Muriel said to keep in mind the courtyard space. She makes another file and calls it 'gardens'.

'Sorry to disturb you, Amy.' Moss has brought up her morning post, but that's not the only reason he's here. Work in the basement is moving along. He needs to order things. Things that she's not given any thought to. He hands her a list:

– ironmongery to basement, does not include privvy set, please specify

– sanitaryware to basement lavatory, please specify

– decision on paving samples for rear patio and front path

'You've seen the paving samples, have you?'

'Sorry Moss, I'm a bit behind.'

'Later today if you could.' He leaves her the ironmongery catalogue and the sanitaryware supply list.

'Innes Quinn would like a word with you. At your convenience, but it's a matter of some urgency.'

'Is there a problem?'

'Nothing we can't fix, Amy.'

'You mean, nothing you can't fix if we revise the estimates.'

'He'll be on site later with the surveyor and engineer. Will I tell him you're here?'

'Engineer?'

'Basement. Party wall, something we didn't anticipate.'

He turns to leave. 'Oh, and by the way, almost forgot, Keane was here yesterday. He said to be sure and say that he'd called.'

She brings the cup of tea back to her desk. She could phone him, acknowledge the message from Moss. She could, but she will wait. He will phone.

She knows, the moment before it rings, that it is about to ring. The instant it does ring, she knows that it's him. This is not wishful thinking. She would swear the thing had a different sound.

'Amy, hello.' Warm, shy.

'Moss just told me you were here, I was about to ring you.'

'I'm sorry I didn't ring before. I got caught up in things here.' This sounds like evasion. Things. Here. Where is here. What things: work, Maureen, children?

'I've been busy myself; the project I was telling you about.' Amy talks quickly, creating a protective layer of activity.

'Only, I hope you don't think I was avoiding you?' he says.

'Oh.' So much that can't be said.

There's a pause that's too long for comfort and Amy almost rushes in. Conor turns business-like, says he needs to come round tomorrow with drawings of the French windows for her dining room. It will have to be around lunchtime. He'll have to be quick, another big contract. Hiding behind the work.

No mention of tongues in mouths and hands full of flesh.

'What I mean Amy, is I'd like to see you. Beyond the job . . . it's hard for me to talk now. I won't be able to talk tomorrow. Could we meet sometime away from the house?'

Somewhere we won't be seen. Coffee, lunch, dinner, a room at the Savoy? He doesn't say any of this. Tap dancing around the possibilities. Is lunch safer than dinner?

'I'm going to be out a lot over the next few weeks.' She hadn't meant to sound so distant.

'Your work?' He's taken it as a brush off.

'Studio visits, for the exhibition. I'll be all over the place.'

'Out of London, you mean?' Is she imagining this: *Out of London, you mean. Could I come too?* She will read that much into his tentative tone. What the hell.

'It's probably difficult, I know, but, if you could get away for half a day – why not come with me?'

The pause is endless, an ocean of silence.

'I'd like that Amy. I'd like that very much.'

Wet Blanket

One good thing about the rain, Imogen won't have to face Desmond in the morning when she leaves for school. After last night, she hopes she never sees him again.

For the last few days Desmond has not been out front with the concrete mixer. Moss has had him round the back, pumping the water that gathers in the sunken area that will become the patio off the 'den', as Mum calls it. Mum says it's not just the rain that causes the flooding, there's a problem with the drains and the foundations. It might make finishing down there take longer. Imogen hopes not, because when it's all done she will have a party. It can't take much longer, even with these set-backs. It must be finished before the end of term. She can wait that long if she has to. She will make sure Nick Baxter can come before she spreads the word. She won't go as far as the article in the magazine suggests: *How to turn your crush into a boyfriend. Ten ways make him to notice: 5. invite him to a party at your house, forget to invite the rest.* She wouldn't do that, but she would have a party, down in the basement room that will be their 'den', as Mum so quaintly calls it.

After last night she can't think what else to do. When Desmond had seen her talking to Nick Baxter he had claimed her, like some cave man. She could have died. Taking her arm in that way. She won't go out with him any more. She should have said something last night but he was really nice to her once they were in the van. He apologised. Said he didn't know what had come over him. It soon became obvious why. He pulled into the car park at the back of the cinema. After midnight, it was deserted. His hands on her knee, up her skirt. Couldn't she come back home with him? Sex with Desmond was not what Imogen had in mind. Desmond was meant to wake Nick Baxter up, now what could she do? Desmond has made it look like they are an item. She didn't want Nick to think that. She wanted to make him notice, then she was going to ask him out. She can hardly do that now. Not right away.

Even if she tells Desmond she doesn't want to see him anymore, she'll see him here every day. What had seemed so simple has become a muddle which she can't unravel. She's read the advice pages in all of her magazines. Nothing quite fits her situation.

> *I've been going out with my boyfriend for two months and he's never suggested having sex. I know he's had sex with other girls. Does this mean he doesn't like me? I am a virgin, he knows that. He's two years older than me. Should I make the first move?*
>
> *Lynn(17) Manchester.*

Imogen is pleased to know that there are other seventeen-year-old virgins. Desmond is not the way to lose it.

What would she write to Angie D's Advice Desk?

> *Dear Angie, I had a plan but it seems to be going wrong. I really like this boy in the year above me at school. He's doing 'A' Levels. We got on great once on a school trip to the theatre. I sat with him on the coach. I know he likes me. He doesn't go out with girls much. He hangs around a bit, goes to parties sometimes and the pub. He's working hard for his exams. I thought if I let him see me with someone else it might make him more interested. I've been going out with Desmond who is working on our house. I can have a laugh with him. He's very good looking. I like being seen with him, but he wants me to have sex.*

Angie would probably refer Imogen to *How to turn your crush into a boyfriend.*

Desmond is not what she wants. It's one thing being seen around with someone like that and snogging's OK, but she couldn't. She couldn't. Not with Desmond. Imagine doing it with him and then every morning seeing him out there. He wanted her to go the whole way last night. He would have done it in the back of the van. Imogen shudders. She sees how it might have been: the van with the Quinn logo, shaking from side-to-side in the empty cinema car park.

She could do it with Nick Baxter though. She really could. He has kind eyes. He's a virgin. He must be. Although he did go out with Wendy Burton last year. He has a few friends who are girls. That tall girl in his tutor group. Imogen saw them at the pictures once but not holding hands or anything. He's working for his 'A' levels. A party at the end of term. She must wait. It's not long. He's taking a year out; he might still be around next year when she's doing her exams.

Imogen bashes her fists into the pillows. She puts her head under them to shut out the drumming of the rain on the roof window.

Imogen's exchanged the beat of the rain for the hum of the washing machine and tumble dryer. Down in the temporary kitchen, she takes a can of diet Coke from the fridge. Alice is doing homework at the table.

'Funny smell,' says Imogen.

Alice shrugs and moves papers from one section of her folder to another, all concentration.

'Ali, is this your stuff in the machine?'

'Mmm?'

'You can stop the absent-minded professor impersonation.'

'What do you want?'

'What are you washing here?'

'My stuff. PE kit. Stuff.'

'It stinks.'

Alice keeps her head in her files. She picks the skin around her fingernails, pushes her hair behind her ear.

'How much longer?' Imogen leans over to check the dial on the tumble dryer. She clicks the door open to feel if the smelly load is dry.

'Christ, what's this?' She removes a tattered travel rug. Steam rising from the worn tartan. It's heavy with a smell that is more than damp wool.

'This is Esther's isn't it? You're doing washing for that bag lady? You're bonkers.'

'What's it to do with you?'

'You can't bring stuff like this in here. It's probably full of bugs and germs and they'll be all over the machines. I was going to wash my stuff later. It'll stink. We'll never get rid of that smell.'

'It's rained for nearly two weeks. Everything Esther owns is soaked. I offered to dry some things for her. A few things that I've washed and dried. OK?'

'You'd do anything she asked wouldn't you?'

'She didn't ask. I offered.'

'Esther will be dropping round for tea soon, I suppose.'

'Shows how much you understand. Esther wouldn't come here.'

'You wait. She's seen how soft you are.'

'I've already asked her and she refused.'

'You asked her to come here? When?'

'I asked her to come today, to have something warm to eat, to dry out. She wouldn't come so I offered to dry her blanket and stuff.'

'Mother Teresa.'

'Better than sitting around sulking about boys.'

'What would you know about that?'

'Everyone knows you want to pull Nick Baxter.'

'So?'

'So, nothing.'

'Does Mum know you're using the washing machine to wash some stranger's clothes?'

'Does Mum know that you are going out with one of the builders?'

Imogen squeezes the empty Coke can, chucks it into the swing bin.

'Had a drink with him. Hardly "going out". Anyway I don't see how Mum can object to me going out with one of the builders when you think what she's up to.'

'What do you mean?'

'You know, I told you before.'

'You're just saying that about her and Mr Keane.'

'Mr Keane. He's mister keen all right. He phoned her today.'

And it wasn't business. Phone calls from the joiner on a Sunday, Alice.' Imogen had answered the phone, afraid it might be Desmond. She recognised Conor's voice.

'Is Amy there?' he'd said.

'Who is it?' Imogen had asked. She wanted to make him say his name.

'Keane from Keane Joinery, Conor Keane.' He'd said, making it sound official. Mum was about to leave. She was meeting Liz for an exhibition and then the cinema.

'She went all red. Said she would take it in her workroom. Came to check that I'd put the receiver down in the kitchen. Very odd.' Imogen wasn't exactly listening in, but anyone could hear things in Amy's room from the top bathroom. The walls are only plaster board.

'There wasn't much talk of joinery.' Imogen hadn't heard everything but she could tell they were talking about going somewhere. Amy said, '. . . shame we couldn't go this week . . .' and 'wouldn't be worth it in this rain.' Amy had laughed a lot.

'She was giggling, Alice.'

Then Amy had said she was sorry, she had to go. She'd love to talk more, if only she'd known he was going to ring. But she's meeting a friend. She's late. It was lovely of him to ring. How she wished she was going with him to the exhibition.

'You're making that up.'

'Why would I bother? I've better things to do.'

'Mum's not like that. She still thinks about Dad. She wouldn't.'

'You must have noticed how dreamy she is lately.'

'She's worried about all that stuff in the basement and the drains.' Fintan Quinn has made a video of the pipe into the sewer to show the damage. Innes Quinn explained about the shifting foundations of the party wall. The house next door might fall down as well as theirs.

'It's all stuff she didn't expect,' says Alice. 'It'll cost a bomb.'

'You don't see what's under your nose.' Imogen rises from the chair, sweeps out of the room with a gesture of the head that demands Alice follow.

In Amy's bedroom Imogen opens the wardrobe door.

'If she's so worried about the extra costs, why is she buying all these new clothes?'

Imogen reaches for the linen jacket, a soft, dusky blue. The label still dangles from a pearl grey button. Imogen points to two pairs of summer shoes. Blue suede sling-backs with open toes and a modest platform sole, and black suede with heels higher than Amy ever wore.

'Mum's been slobbing around in the same leggings and loafers since Dad died. Why would she buy all this now if she didn't have a reason?'

Alice shrugs

'It's coming into summer. She's making a new start.' Alice doesn't sound convinced. She frowns. Thinks hard. Imogen picks up the black suede shoes and tries them on. Her feet are the same size as her mother's.

'It's her work.' Relief spreads across Alice's face. 'She's really into the exhibition project.' Alice reminds Imogen that Mum hasn't worked like this since before Dad died. Can't Imogen see that Mum's picking up her career again?

'She's out seeing artists, looking round galleries. She needs to be smart.'

'Why would she dress up to visit scruffy artists' studios? And, she's had her hair cut and hennaed. Mum never puts colour on her hair.'

'It is. It's because she is working again.'

Imogen opens one of Amy's drawers. She takes out several pairs of new, lacy knickers. Some are black, others are oyster grey.

'Come on, Alice.'

20

Foundations

'What else would you call it?' Liz pours more wine for both of them.

'I don't know, but it's hardly an *affair*.'

'So, Maureen is happy with this intimacy between you and her Conor, then?' Liz is not letting Amy off the hook. They've had versions of this conversation a dozen times over the last couple of weeks.

'I think it's great, Amy, don't get me wrong. Have a fling but don't kid yourself that this is innocent and containable. Don't give me "we're just friends."'

Liz is not buying Amy's current line on the subject: she and Conor both know it can't happen, they enjoy each other's company, have common interests. They have a tacit agreement that things will go no further.

'But you're making preparations just in case.'

'I need new clothes.'

'Look, I loved the shopping trip. I'm happy to come with you anytime. It was wonderful to see you paying attention to yourself again. I was glad to give you the benefit my expert knowledge on underwear, but don't tell me that deep inside you aren't working towards consummation.'

'It's not that simple.'

'Too true.'

'Of course I want to. That's the weird thing.'

'What, that you've discovered sex again?'

'No. I mean, to want it so much, both of us, and yet, not to act.

I never would have thought, you know, that, well, that it would be this difficult. That we wouldn't, you know, do it. I mean we used to, at college.'

'He'd die of guilt. Probably wouldn't be able to perform. A good Catholic boy. I've been there Amy. He won't deliver.'

'It feels right. Natural, inevitable. It's physical, of course it is, but it's more.'

'The urge to merge. You've got it bad.'

'Demented some days, Liz. That's how it feels, as if I'm crazy. When I think it through, where it might lead, well, part of me can't believe what I'm doing.'

'Thought you weren't doing anything?'

'I can't stop the feelings. On the days when I let myself go, just go with how it makes me feel, well, how it feels is bloody marvellous. So much energy. I could do anything. I could light the whole of London with this much energy. I feel like me again.'

'So, the big day out is going ahead, then. He's got a late pass has he?'

'He's coming with me down to Kent. I want to look at Derek Jarman's garden. It will be an afternoon.'

'And you'll be wearing the Wonderbra?'

'Maybe. But if I do it's because it makes me feel good.'

'You'll be wearing it and those lacy knickers because you know they might be seen. Underwear of that sort is worn to be seen.'

'Here, fill my glass.' Amy holds out her empty wine glass and turns her face up to the sun.

'Promise me one thing. When it finally happens, if he's a Y-front man, cut your losses. Boxer shorts or tell him it's off.'

'Liz, sometimes you . . .'

'Y-fronts tell a lot about a man. Too retentive, finds it hard to let go.'

'Is this all going in your book? How is the book?'

'The book is fine. I'm looking at the Second World War, rationing. No metal or elastic, silk gone to make parachutes. If this was a wartime romance you'd be knitting a woollen vest for Conor.'

'Listen to us,' Amy laughs. 'Too much wine, too much sun. Give me more!'

Amy and Liz have taken deck chairs to the end of the garden. They've disobeyed Moss's site rules. Amy's not allowed in her own back garden. 'It's a live site, Amy.' Moss keeps reminding her. 'All Quinn sites are run according to current health and safety regulations. No exceptions.' But it's so hot today, she wants to be out of the house. She wants to talk to Liz without the girls listening in. Amy had unlocked the front cellar door. She and Liz made their way through the site office, found the switch for the lights, neon strips on stands. There were steps now where, a few weeks ago, she had encountered Conor. Where she had stood on a breeze block and kissed him lightly, by the corner of his mouth. Six new wooden steps rising to what will be her kitchen. There was still the old floor in the kitchen, but beyond that, where the dining-room will be, there was nothing. A ditch, a void.

'Should we be doing this?' Liz dropped down awkwardly from the kitchen floor into the ditch.

'I'm not spending the first sunny Saturday in ages shut in up there.' Soon Conor will lay a new wooden floor in here. After that, the kitchen he is making will be installed. The last phase of the work will have Conor in her house daily.

Liz and Amy had to remove the boards that seal off the open end of the house.

'I hope we can put these back,' said Liz.

'It's my garden and I'm going out there.' Once they were out of the house, they had to clamber over a heap of hardcore, assorted planks and broken bricks. They picked their way through the garden, getting as far away from the house as possible. Past the heap of blue tarpaulins, past the portaloo, beyond the yellow patch of grass that is turning green again after the rain. They settled their deck chairs beyond the old pear tree, where the grass, untroubled by builders, was long, speckled with daisies and dandelions.

Amy puts her feet up on the makeshift table, a plank on two piles of bricks. She pulls back her skirt, feels the sun on her legs.

'Mind you don't burn,' says Liz.

'I want to get some colour in them.'

'Bare legs on Wednesday?'

'Stop it, Liz. Look,' Amy nods towards the house. 'I can't

believe I'm living in that.' The upper part looks reasonable enough but on the lower floors there is much still to do. A green hose snakes out from what will be the girls' den across the heap of hardcore, into the drain by the kitchen window. This is how they pumped out water during the wet spell, before they dug the trench. Moss hasn't bothered to block off the entrance to the girls' room. Looked at from the end of the garden, through the glare of the sun, it's a black hole. The newly dug trench reaches into it, stretching the full length of the garden. A pipe lies in the trench. Innes Quinn had come up with this solution to the drainage problems, 'Just enough of an incline, Amy, only just enough. A degree or too less and we'd have a serious problem there.' He'd also come up with a way of making good the foundations to the party wall. 'Differential movement. Clay dries unevenly. Too many trees, too many dry summers.' They would dig, two metres at least, to where the bearing capacity of the soil was more consistent. With the cracked earth below and all the disturbance above, the house was bound to shift. 'A house is a living thing,' Innes Quinn said. 'It expands, contracts, things change. And after the work is finished, the house will need time to settle.'

'Imogen was quiet at lunchtime.'
    'You know how she is.'
    'Ms moody moo, you mean.'
    'She's seventeen, needs to get on with her life.' Amy's trying not to think too much about Imogen. Since they moved, she's been pulling away from Amy. Secretive. She stays in her room. Alice, too, goes out more. Protecting themselves from the chaos. Making up for lost time. Amy is letting them go. They are nearly adults. They don't need her telling them what to do.
    'Boyfriend trouble?'
    'Imogen? I don't ask.' Six months ago, Amy would have worried about the ever-shut door, the coming in late. Now, Amy has her own distractions. Imogen missed out on a lot after Greg died. She needs to catch up.

'He's quite something, the one with the ponytail who poses around out front.'
    'Desmond?'

'Hardly recognised him today with clothes on.'

'Today?'

'He was sitting in the van up the road. I parked in front of him.'

'Today?'

'Do they always come in on a Saturday?'

'Sometimes. But no one worked today.'

'Well he was there in the Quinns' van.'

'I hope he's not been chatting up Freya Hill's au pair again.'

Amy rubs cream into her pink legs. She's had a shower to cool off, sober up. Imogen arrived home shortly after Liz left, but she went upstairs to her room, didn't even say hello.

Amy slides into her new black lacy knickers, hooks herself into the Wonderbra, amazed at the cleavage she's managed to achieve. In front of the long mirror she breathes in. *Underwear like that is worn to be seen.* She could send the girls away for a weekend, suggest they go up to her mother's. Conor could come here. A Saturday or Sunday afternoon. He has rung her at the weekend from the workshop more than once. He must be able to get away for an hour or two.

He'd die of guilt.

Does he feel guilty when he phones from the workshop, spends an hour on the telephone? Are some actions more guilty than others? Would Maureen be happy to hear the tenderness in his voice. What do they talk about, her and Conor? Everything and nothing. Amy would be happy talking to Conor about the weather. He'd phoned yesterday, late. Seven o'clock and he was still at the workshop.

'Wanted to catch you before I went off for the weekend.' He wanted to hear about her work, what had she done this week? She coaxed him to talk about the sculpture he used to make. Couldn't he find time again. Couldn't he use the equipment in the workshop. He laughed, 'If only, Amy. If only.' What he didn't say, what was left unsaid, was this: it's not simply the pressure from work that stops him, but the pressure from home. Here is a man who has to be home at night. A man who can't easily get a late pass. She realises, as she thinks about it now, how they avoid the subject. They pull away. An unspoken rule, an instinct. He never mentions home. Maureen or the children. He often says, 'I' as if he were a single man.

'I might go to the cinema tomorrow.' When really he means, 'We'. He sometimes mentions his sister, Caitlin. His twin. She's not been well. He doesn't go into details. It is a strange mixture of deep intimacy and guardedness. When Amy and Conor talk they are in a world that is theirs. It has no past, no future. It is only the present. Voices down a telephone caressing each other. It doesn't matter what they say. The softness of his voice strokes her ear. It's a sound that feels like the shape of his mouth. Talking to Conor, sound becomes touch. Her senses collide. Each conversation is a physical thing. Talking is sexy. And yet when he comes to site, like last week when she and Moss and Conor agreed the final details of the kitchen, Conor is formal. Amy noticed that with Moss around Conor avoided eye contact. She did too. What would Moss notice more: the fizz of electricity as their eyes met, or the careful way in which they avoided each other's gaze?

Amy checks her watch as she reaches to answer the phone. Seven thirty. Please let it be him. It won't be. At seven thirty on a Saturday night, I/We are probably on the way to the cinema.

'Liz. Are you all right?'

'I'm fine apart from a red nose. The sun was strong. Is Imogen in?'

'She's upstairs. Why?'

'Where was she this afternoon?'

'I don't know. Camden Lock, town. Who knows.'

'I saw her as I drove off from your place. She was getting out of the van, she was with the ponytail.'

'Desmond?'

21

Driftwood

'About tomorrow. Will I wait, or will I lock up?' Gerry's making sure he's clear what's being asked of him. Conor knows he won't be back by 5.30.

'Assume you'll lock up.' He's being deliberately vague, which is not like Conor. That's why Gerry looks confused. Nothing more. There's no reason to suppose that Gerry suspects where Conor is going.

'See you Thursday, then,' says Gerry.

'Good man, Gerry,' says Conor, as if disappearing for a day with only a vague explanation of his whereabouts was something he frequently did; when, the fact is, the business runs on maintaining a link between workshop and sites. He's the boss, and if he chooses to do things differently for once, so be it. Conor turns to the drawing board. He waits until he hears Gerry's motorbike splutter away, beyond the workshop yard. Maureen knows that Conor's working late, as he will be. He will finish the drawings for the new job in Essex Road. It won't take long. There is time to call Amy.

'Hello there,' Conor is relieved when Amy answers. Relieved that it's not the older girl. Prickly. Always asks for his name. 'Who shall I say is calling?' Then she shouts up the stairs, announcing him, deliberately, so the whole world knows Conor is calling Amy. There's an edge to the way that girl talks. He had hung up the last time she'd answered.

'That's grand,' Conor says when Amy tells him there's a pub

by the lighthouse that does the best fish and chips in England. It's easy to talk about being there. They spin it out.

'Hot and dry again,' says Amy. 'I heard the forecast. We could swim.' Laughing. As if they would. Circling around the awkward bit. How to get there. How and where will they meet? Is it possible to bring any dignity to this kind of arrangement.

'I'll have my car, not the van.' It has to be done. They won't both arrive by chance at the pub with the best fish and chips by the lighthouse. A simple enough matter. Two people meet, get into the same vehicle, to go to the same place. Two people who have every right to meet in some situations. They agree the details briskly, awkwardly. Even though they agree to meet in a public place, it feels like a furtive act.

'Ten to ten thirty.' He can't be precise. He will go to Essex Road first thing. He doubts he will get away before ten. Why don't they meet at Angel. They agree a café near the Underground. That way if he's held up she's somewhere to sit, have a coffee. No hanging around the street corner, no pacing or skulking in shop doorways. They agree that picking her up from the house is impossible. Neither of them could be that blatant. That's what they mean. Blatant. But it's not what they say. What they say is: 'not a good idea . . .', 'might get caught up with Moss, the Quinns . . .', 'never get away . . .' As if not doing so was simply a matter of convenience. When he suggests picking her up from the end of the road, she says, 'I don't think so.' Voice lowered, her tone letting him know that she's not prepared for this level of indignity. Neither is he. Wishing he hadn't suggested it. He's trying to make it easy for her, doesn't want to put her out. The café is far enough away from Amy's house, but easy enough to get to. Perfectly ordinary people meet for coffee every hour of the day.

Neither wants to cut short the call even though they will see each other tomorrow for more time than they've ever spent together before. He asks about her day. She spent the morning in an old button factory in Bow, artists' studios now. She watched a woman blowing glass. He loves the way Amy describes things.

'Like toffee,' she says. The woman lifts the molten glass, swings and blows, filling it, shaping it with her breath and the rhythm of her body, judging when it's right to stop. As the day went on, she watched the woman join the elements together. A study in light, colour, form. This is what she's looking for, it's perfect for the exhibition. She's looking for artists who are finding new ways to work with old skills; transforming the materials of everyday things to make something that hasn't quite been seen before. He could listen all night when she talks like this. Amy had been hot standing by the glory-hole; too hot for a day by a furnace. She was looking forward to being by the sea. She had been so absorbed watching the glass artist that she was late for her meeting at the museum, but never mind. The museum is pleased with her work. A busy day. A busy day, in a world he once thought he would be a part of.

He shifts the drawing of the bedroom cupboards to one side, reaches for the sketch. Will he tell her now, or wait till there is something to show?

'A start. A doodle,' there's not much to tell.

'When can I see?'

'When it's further on. When I see where I'm going with it.'

'I'll book you in for a studio visit, shall I?' Amy teases. And he almost says: that'll get the lads talking. But he stops himself in time. An easy joke to make, a quip, a throwaway remark.

An admission.

The limits are soon reached. They both seem to have it, a sixth sense, a tacit agreement that, for the most time, avoids the danger zone. It's not a conscious weighing of what he says, but an instinct that keeps their talk in their allotted space; bands of snatched time in the no-man's land between their other lives. It doesn't need to go further. This is enough. This is better than nothing. Why can't he have a friendship with another human being. Why can't he talk to this woman about the things that matter to him, something other than the VAT return, cash flow, estimates. This is, and is not, an illicit relationship. Of course he won't tell Maureen that he's spending the day down on the coast. If she found out would it matter? Nothing need happen. Nothing too damning has happened. All right, some wine and a kiss. The kiss that he couldn't stop once it started. The feel of her shape in his hands, her warmth, the curve of her back. Wanting to go on, while another part of him was ready to run down the stairs, out into the night. She drew the limit, pulled away. The situation avoided, averted. He could still say with some honesty to Maureen that nothing has happened. And since then, easy talk. It hasn't gone further. They avoid the kiss, they talk around the kiss.

They talk rather than kiss.

He's only seen Amy in the company of Moss and the other men since the kiss. But he's talked to her many times on the telephone, the safety of the disembodied voice. What's the harm in talking to her on the phone about the things that interest them. They both know it can't, won't, go any further.

'Let's just say the germ of an idea.' Of course he wants to tell her, to let her know that he's started to think about making things again.

'Too soon to tell.' He wants to share it with her but he won't claim too much in case he can't go through with it.

'I'll maybe tell you more tomorrow.'

'Sleep well,' she says, taking that as the cut-off, time to go.

'You too.' He starts to put the phone down.

'Are you still there,' he says, pulling the receiver back to him.

'I'm still here,' she laughs. Neither wants to break the link. They don't need to talk. He could listen to her breathing.

If it worked, it would be for her. A gift. He considers what he's drawn. A spiral. The elevation of what might become a large bowl or maybe an abstract form. He didn't use to work this way, drawing first. The years of cabinet-making have formed new habits. He's started as he would for a job, with pencil and paper. But if he makes this, it won't be to fit a space, to meet the specifications of others. He will make this piece as large or small as he wished.

He would please himself.

It's been a long time since he has worked so freely, going where the ideas take him, an open-ended brief. That's how he always worked before, directly with the wood. Driftwood, or the section through a tree. Things he found, collected. Not the stacked, processed planks and boards of the timber yard. He used to work with green timber that would crack and change after a piece was finished, went on having a life. Sometimes he could anticipate where the weakness would come, and so he worked with it, allowing for it. But still there was the chance element; knowing how to work with the unexpected, letting it happen.

'You can't plan it all out in advance, Conor,' Judy would say. Working alongside Judy in their shared studio, he would push things further, take risks. 'Go with it.' Judy pulling him to her. The press of her body and in no time they'd be making love on the cold stone floor. Judy never felt the cold. 'Here, let me warm you.' A catalyst. Unpredictable as her final departure.

It's here somewhere, Conor's sure of that. He makes his way through the stacks of new timber. Planks of yellowish pine that his workshop will transform into doors or window frames. Dark reddish hardwood for newel posts and outdoor use. Fibreboard out of which almost anything can be conjured and painted so that it looks as if it's always been part of a house. Somewhere in the back of the lock-up store there's other wood. He tries a couple of keys in the padlock before he finds the right one. He hasn't looked in here since he can't remember when. It's dark in this neglected cupboard. He shines the flashlight. A thick stack of driftwood, some wedges of ash, elm. It's mostly the driftwood. There are pieces nearly the height of him. On the floor, smaller pieces. He picks one up, turns it in his hand. Light, smooth, dry. Traces of salt, the bleaching of the sun give it a whiteness. Its dry smoothness against his palm makes a swishing sound. He fingers a split that runs the length of it. A dark crevice that might stay like that forever, or, it might ease further open, fall apart. Small powdery flakes of wood scatter from the surface, attach to his jeans. The driftwood is beautiful in its own right, marked by time and the elements. He's not sure there's anything he could add.

It's not duplicity.

The Conor who talks to Amy, the Conor who will spend tomorrow with Amy, is not the same as the Conor who goes home to Maureen. They are different people. Separate parts of him. As different as the driftwood is from the manufactured sheets of ply that are at his back, stacked floor to ceiling. A different part of him that he's not had dealings with in a long while. Like the cupboard at the back of the lock-up store that he hasn't opened in years. A part of him that Maureen had wanted out of the house.

'That stuff, it's in the past,' Maureen had said, after Michael, the second child, was born. He'd brought what remained of his materials to the workshop. The space in the shed at home was needed for tricycles, somewhere to put the garden toys in winter.

'It doesn't seem to make you happy,' Maureen said. He hadn't protested. There hadn't been a row. It was necessary.

'I'd say you give more satisfaction with the work you do now, than you ever did with that other stuff.' It's always been Maureen's line. Trying to carry on with the sculpture and the carving didn't seem to get him anywhere in Maureen's view. They had a life to live. A real life of children, a home, family back in Ireland. His talent was not going to waste, she would argue. He designed and produced useful things that made a difference to people's lives. Wouldn't that give anyone satisfaction? Wouldn't that make anyone happy?

Happy.

Has he ever aspired to the condition of happiness. Caitlin said he could be happy by making a wish. If he did it right, it would come true.

'It works Con, believe me.' He and Caitlin, six or seven, nuzzling through the hazy red blush of the fuchsia blossom. Bushes of it, higher than a man, formed a grove, off the road on the way to the store from Gran's house. They lay on their backs and watched the bees going from bell to bell. Each red flower drooping from its thread-fine stem. Red petals splayed, purple inside, rich as church robes. Bees, hundreds of them, suckling at the dangling stamens, like a calf at the teat.

'Listen Con, close your eyes'

The hum of the bees amplified in the canopy of blossom.

'Lie still, you won't get stung.' A magic place. They would make a wish, gather the fallen flowers and carry them up to the standing stones. An offering. Later, sitting on the flat, grey slab, legs dangling in Wellington boots he asked Caitlin what she wished for, but she wouldn't say exactly.

'I want to know where that wire goes.' Even on a calm day the air would catch in the telegraph wire. A whistling from pole to pole across scanty fields and bare rock. When the wind got up it rose to a moan. He can't remember what he wished for.

Only that Caitlin said: was that all? Hadn't he asked for more than that?

He won't ask for anything more than a day out with Amy. It will make him happy to spend a day with her by the sea. He won't ask for anything beyond the next day. What harm could there be in that? The one part of him wanting time off from the other. Separate parts that would both be present at the same time tomorrow morning. Breakfast. Maureen hurrying the children to be ready for school, checking lunch boxes, PE kit. What time would Michael be home? 'I need to know, Michael. If you're walking home with friends: half past. You must be here by half past four. And Kevin will you mind Maura while I take Clare to her dancing class?' Into this he would have to speak. Late again, out of London. A prospective client. Say it at a time when she is most distracted, when she won't register that a client out of London is something he avoids. Plenty of business close to home. She will quiz him on that, want to know more. But he'll time it so he can't stop. No time. He'll be off with the Essex Road drawings in his folder.

Beyond a day out with Amy what would make him happy would be to work through this idea on paper, bring it into being; achieve the shift from two to three dimensions. The driftwood's no use. The drawing in front of him couldn't be made from unseasoned wood. Trial and error with the proportions. The drawing would only take him so far. He must spend time in here at the weekend, try to make the thing. Not the driftwood. Something new, not going back to what he's done before. He needs time to play around with different materials. Take a few risks. Where's he going to find the time to do that. Maybe that's asking too much. Maybe wishing only makes you want more?

'You have it in you, Conor,' Caitlin would say. 'Take the risk. Don't give it all up.'
   'I have to make the business work.' Caitlin always prodding at the bit of him he'd hidden away.
   'You have it in you, but you'd as soon hide it as use it.'

How he would love to talk to Caitlin now. To tell her. But she's enough on her mind.

'Nothing sinister,' the doctor had told her.

'By which you mean I don't have cancer.' Caitlin bold even in the face of her illness. Nothing sinister, but an operation is likely. It can't be ruled out.

22

Flower Arrangements

Amy regards the pearl-grey satin knickers as they slide to her ankles; they seem to belong to someone else. The thighs are undeniably hers. If only they were longer, thinner, firmer. How has she become this person obsessed with clothes, her appearance, the condition of her body?

'Please be there,' she says out loud. The words are lost in the swash of the toilet's flush. And if, when she climbs back up the stairs to choose a table and order coffee, Conor hasn't arrived, she might have to come back down and stay in the ladies' lavatory for the rest of her life. She checks herself in the long mirror.

Her new haircut has settled. It had seemed too short when she first had it cut. Her wavy hair needs a certain length to sit easily. Now it's grown, the effect is altogether softer. The waves give the bob a lift, creating a pleasing shape that rises from just below her jaw line. The colour too has eased, leaving a reddish sheen on her own warm brown. She feels and looks comfortable in the new blue linen jacket and white skirt. She might regret the suede, slingback, platforms on the shingle beach. She redoes her lipstick. A waxy smudge of Rocket Red on her lower lip spreads to her upper lip as she draws her mouth in tight. Both lips disappear then re-emerge, scarlet. She traces their outer edge with a brush making a fine red line, then adds more colour, filling in the blanks till her lips are solid red. With a tissue she blots the surplus.

It's not as if she's been careless about her appearance all these years. Things may have slipped since Greg died, but she's always cared about how she looks. Cared, yes, but not this much. It's a huge preoccupation to accommodate in her life; everything down to the last blocked pore. She hasn't given such scrutiny to each detail since she was at college. She and Liz on a Saturday afternoon plucking eyebrows, soaking in the bath with mud on their faces and afterwards, trying every permutation of their combined wardrobes.

Is this what it feels like to be Imogen?

It's as if Amy's returned to something which she thought was long since done with; like being forced to re-sit 'O' levels even though she passed them the first time. She eyes the machine on the wall: ribbed, coloured, flavoured. Since she last studied the subject there have been changes to the syllabus. If she hadn't called in the chemist for mouth fresheners it wouldn't have occurred to her to *buy* condoms. Ribbed, coloured and flavoured she might come to later, right now she's getting used to the presence of a packet of 'ultra safe' lurking at the bottom of her bag. Suddenly she's not so sure: superstition creeps in. Having them there might make it *not* happen. Wasn't it more likely to happen if she didn't have them. There was always the morning-after pill.

Liz would carry condoms as surely as a comb or purse. The thought had passed through Amy's mind last night but she dismissed it: nothing to do with her. It returned, unbidden in the chemist, half an hour ago, as she waited to pay for the mouth fresheners. A major symptom of the virus is the sudden, urgent need for incidentals. As she emerged from the Underground at Angel all she could think of was the rankness of her own mouth. In the chemist she was dismayed to find that mouthwash came as livid blue liquid in bottles larger than her bag, until an assistant pointed out the discreet, pocket-sized dispensers of deodorising pills. As Amy queued at the till, she wasn't aware of having made a conscious choice; the packet appeared in her hand. How had she selected from the baffling variety? Beyond the novelty packs – out of the question – how had she chosen between ultra fine, ultra safe and super strong? It must have been the word safe that prevailed. She had handed it over as if it was part of her weekly shop, with no more significance than soap or toothpaste. And it was her own paranoia, not a real knowing look on the face of the assistant, that noted the connection between sweet breath and safe sex before 10.00 in the morning on a weekday.

Amy brushes her cheeks with blusher. Too much. She dusts it off with her fingertips. The amount of time Imogen spends on her appearance has, until now, been a source of exasperation for Amy.

See how things change.

Amy's efforts are entirely motivated by Conor. It wouldn't be possible to be like this as a matter of course, to make this much effort for the world in general. Amy exfoliates for a purpose. Is it different for Imogen? Amy tries to remember, to recall her own seventeen-year-old motives. A different time, a different world. Perhaps some things remain the same.

For whom is Imogen making all that effort?

Maybe she and Liz have read too much into seeing Desmond last Saturday. There is no doubt that Amy and Imogen are avoiding each other. Amy begins to enter Imogen's world; in her current, deranged state she can't be far off the mark. Desmond is a stunning creature. A lean body. Muscle that is finely tuned rather than overdeveloped meat. Desmond does not labour at his labour. Each movement enhances his beauty. Amy had watched him this morning. Desmond is careful with his body as if his movements have been worked out in advance, rehearsed. His day is an extended ballet. He paces himself, cannot be hurried. For today's heat he was stripped to the waist, wearing khaki battle fatigues that gather in at the ankle. His skin is smooth, brown as the newly creosoted fence he's been working on in the back garden. With his red peasant headscarf and near black ponytail, he looked like some exotic desert bloom; a stray from the set of *Scheherazade*. Amy watched him take a fat, square mallet to the inside of the concrete mixer. A slow, strong cracking of mallet inside the metal drum. Desmond loosened the stuff that had hardened overnight. He turned the wheel that tips the drum, captain at the helm, till the porthole faced the ground, then he started the motor. The drum whirled. Pebble-sized lumps of concrete tumbled out. Next, he cracked the mallet hard on the outside of the revolving drum methodically till only a few brittle flakes fell. He turned the wheel again so the drum faced upwards, open-mouthed. Sand, ballast, water, he fed in the ingredients for a fresh mix. The black gape of the concrete mixer reminded Amy of Masaccio's Eve, expelled from the garden of Eden, high on the wall of the Brancacci chapel, eyes clenched, hand clasping her breasts and her mouth upturned, a black hole of despair. And when Amy had left the house, avoiding Desmond's eyes, the concrete mixer seemed to have a life of its own; a turmoil of sand, stone and water thrashing against the blades.

If Imogen is seeing Desmond, his looks, his perfect body, must come into it. Amy and Imogen have talked about contraception. Her daughter knows what the options are and where to get them: GP, clinic. Amy knows, or thinks she knows, that Imogen isn't on the pill. She knows, or thinks she knows, that Imogen hasn't yet had sex. Amy also knows that most of Imogen's friends have. But then, for the last three years they've all been held back. She must find a way to talk to Imogen.

Amy shakes her head to make her hair look less combed. The attention to detail must result in her looking perfect without apparently having taken any trouble at all. She plucks stray strands from her shoulder and aims them at the bin where the shape of her own red mouth gapes back at her.

If he's not here by eleven she will leave. She's ordered coffee. She will drink it and then leave. Now that she's moved to a different table she feels less anxious. From here, through the gilt-framed mirror, she will be able to see Conor arrive. She can turn her back to the door and see him at the same time.

A large, clean-faced clock hangs from the centre of the ceiling. An old clock that, years ago, might have hung on a railway platform, steam clouding its glass. She tries not to look up too often. Thin fingers point to worn, Roman numerals. The smaller finger is at the X, the long bony one has just reached the centre of the VI. Any further forward movement of that finger confirms Conor's lateness.

Ten to ten thirty. Ten thirty at the outside.

What if he doesn't come?

What if she's in the wrong café?

Is this the right day?

What if he's been stringing her along; enjoying the spectacle of her falling for him?

*   *   *

The café's interior is dark wood and brass; bentwood chairs at marble-topped tables. Today's newspapers hang on poles. Fans, like propellers, suspended from the ceiling stir the already thick air. A sign above the doorway down to the lavatories shows a running white figure on a green background. Emergency exit. If she were to see him now through the mirror, she could still get away. There will be a door onto the street down there. The coffee is a bitter continental roast that sends her pulse shooting up; a knocking under her collar bone.

A man behind the bar in a white apron over black trousers and waistcoat, polishes the wooden surface. Amy is one of a handful of customers. By lunchtime each table will be full. In the mirror Amy sees a couple arrive. The man kisses the woman's forehead. They perch at the bar on high stools and each orders a cappuccino. The man in the white apron stops his polishing, packs coffee into the machine. There's the screech of steam through milk. As he hands the man his change the telephone on the bar rings. When he's finished the call he goes through the door marked *Staff Only*.

She could ask to use the phone, call Conor's mobile. Something may have happened. People do get held up. Are they two adults who have agreed to spend a day out and one of them is now late, or is this strictly boy/girl stuff subject to the rules of adolescence? Checking out on the mobile would be a reasonable, adult thing to do. Reason doesn't seem to apply.

Play hard to get. Leave now. He's late.

The man in the apron brings out a large clear glass cylinder filled with tall white lilies. He places them carefully at the end of the bar, putting the finishing touches to the arrangement, easing out the long, leafy stalks so that the blooms have space to show themselves. Though the bar is a good few feet away, Amy catches their heavy, sweet scent. Only three or four of the waxy trumpets are fully open. There are many more to come, long pale-green pods, that will split and whiten in the heat. Proud lilies. These are summery, less solemn than the one Arum lily she laid on Greg's coffin, before the first shovel of earth rained in on him.

A single lily.

Greg, the coffin, the lily.

Thoughts that she doesn't want to have. Not today. Not now. Often after he died, she would think of Greg, alone, so cold in the earth with the single lily lying on his chest. The flower and the man both cut off from air and sunlight. An unbearable thought that would make her shudder. Irrational thoughts that would come in the depth of her sleepless nights, thoughts that made her want to act, to drive to the graveyard, there and then, at 3.00 a.m. with a blanket and a warm drink. She was always at her worst thinking of Greg in his cold grave, next to his grandparents in a Suffolk churchyard, blasted by winds off the North Sea. By now Greg and the lily have dissolved into the earth. Has it become less unbearable or is it that the thought is now so familiar?

She thinks: Greg wouldn't mind.

The coffee has left a bitter taste. She finds the mouth fresheners in her bag. Pale green pills, cool on her tongue tasting like the rinse-out at the dentist. Will she smell too clinical? Better that than the treacly aftertaste of too much coffee.

'Excuse me,' the young man from the bar, leans to take her empty cup. 'Finished?'

'Yes, thanks.'

'Amy Beardsley?' He's saying her name. How does he know her name?

23

The Lighthouse

'I can't decide.' Amy leans against the bar, reads the blackboard once more: *dressed crab, shrimp salad, deep fried cod or plaice.*

'Whatever's fresh today,' she says, not sure she'll be able to eat a thing.

'Fresh?' says the man behind the bar, smoothing the carbon in his order pad. 'All our fish was in the sea until dawn, madam.' Can she eat anything so recently dead?

'Plaice for me,' says Conor.

'Me too,' says Amy, surprising herself, following his lead as if she's not capable of making her own selection.

She's in no doubt about what she wants to drink. Her need for alcohol is urgent.

'A bottle of white wine.' Pleased to hear that she sounds like a grown-up again.

Outside there is only one wooden picnic table left. The pub is filling up, others might join them. Hardly a romantic, intimate lunch. What had possessed her to suggest that they come to this place?

'Unconventional as a garden,' she'd said to Conor in the car, as if she had to justify wanting to see Derek Jarman's place. 'But it's the way he's used the found materials that interests me.' Keeping the tacit agreement they were on a recce, a work trip. No suggestion that they've both seized this opportunity to come to the remotest place possible, less than two hours out of London, while keeping within her working brief. Conor pours the cold white wine, filling a glass for each of them. They're having lunch in this pub because there's nowhere else to eat at the end of the earth. It is pleasant enough in the sun trap formed by the angle of the building. It would be too hot here but for the breeze coming off the sea. In London it would be stifling.

'Cheers.' They clink glasses, both smiling, regarding each other with a mixture of eagerness and shyness.

'Quite a contrast, isn't it?' says Amy.

Look one way and the old lighthouse stands bold, purposeful despite its redundancy, against the grey slab of the power station. Somewhere in the heart of that impenetrable concrete mass neutrons collide with nuclei in a chain reaction, a contained explosion. In the other direction there's the stark beauty of a wilderness of sea kale, orange and red poppies, deep pink valerian, triumphantly pushing through the shingle. A line of fishing boats perches on the shore. Perfect backdrop for the photo shoot that's in progress. Wispy young girls in transparent garments, all leg and eye-liner, throw back their heads, manes flying in the sea breeze.

'Something about the light here,' says Amy, a piece of knowledge surfaces, 'makes it a good location.' Something Greg must have told her. She knows it, but doesn't quite know how she knows.

'I wouldn't piss on her,' a voice booms from the next table.

Conor and Amy exchange a surprised glance. They both look, without seeming to, towards the voice which emerges from behind a bosom the size of a pillow. The woman in black shorts, hefty thighs splayed against the bench, has feet thrust forward beneath the table into terrifying boots.

'Did you see the way the blonde one pushed her food around her plate?' Hefty legs and her friend ogle the stick-insect models.

'A woman needs love handles,' says hefty legs, laughing and squeezing the flesh of the woman beside her.

'Another world,' says Conor.

The Lewisham ladies or Dungeness?

An elderly man flanked by two middle-aged women leaves the pub. As the women ease the man into the front passenger seat one of them kisses him on the cheek.

'Wasn't that nice?' he says. 'Let's have some more of that.'

They all laugh.

Some more.

Amy wants to reach across and kiss Conor, an affectionate kiss. A soft brush on his cheek. She watches the way his lips form around his words, following the contours of his accent. *Romantic Celt, Amy.* She can't take her eyes off his mouth. An immense energy gathers between them, clusters of particles headed for a collision. A rush of wine to her head, warmth swimming through her body. The beach is deserted. Along the beach, away from the pub this could be another planet. Alone with Conor. Not here with hefty legs and her friends. Alone with no one to see the way Conor listens so attentively when Amy speaks. Where only she and Conor will notice the awkwardness, the trace of hesitancy between them. Alone, held in each other's attention, as if some bubble existed around them.

Being in the car was easier, the bubble was intact on the motorway, anonymous in that no-man's land; a corridor from their other lives to here. The client had been a talker, a pain, hard to get away. Conor had arrived shortly after his telephone message. When Amy saw him in the gilt-edged mirror he was obviously relieved to be there, so pleased that she had waited, full of apologies. Her doubts had evaporated. In his car she relaxed back into the passenger seat banishing, the minute it formed, the thought that this was Maureen's seat. Deleting the image of the four children who would, at another time, in another life, be ranged along the back seat.

Conor tossed coins into the auto toll booth on the Dartford Bridge, the barrier went up, a pulse of relief passed between them. Who would see them now? They were like any other vehicle, unexceptional doing a steady 70 mph through the polite, green orderliness of the Kent countryside. Driving into the clear blue of a June day.

They had talked easily. She studied his profile, noticed a tiny shaving cut on his neck and the way a crease formed in his cheek when he smiled. Watching his hands on the steering wheel she learned by heart the constellations of freckles on the back of his hand. This alone could be a life-time's work. Had he done any more with the sketch?

'The sketch will only take me so far,' he'd said. 'The thing will only come right in the making. I need to play around with materials.' Amy said she hadn't realised what tough beauty there was in ordinary building materials: breeze block, bricks, roof timbers, slate, lead, copper piping, sheets of hardboard, ply, plasterboard. The house eats it. There's a potency about the stacks of new materials that arrive daily.

'You know, when I see a fresh batch of plywood it looks like great blank sheets of card, as if you could do anything with it.'

'Plywood is dead, processed wood. Inert.' But he knows what she means. He's had a thought in that direction himself; it needs testing in the making.

Amy had asked about his sister. The twin. What was it like to be a twin.

'The worst thing,' said Conor with a smile, 'about being a twin amongst seven was that we were treated as one person.' A single entity: the twins. Caitlin was the reckless one, he had all the common sense.

'The family joke was that together we made one reasonable human being.' Caitlin had made a career of her outspokenness. She has a good academic post now: Women's Literary Studies. She speaks at conferences around the world, has another book on the way. Out of all of them she'd railed most against what she calls the patriarchal structures of home, state and church, yet she was the one who had stayed in Ireland.

Treasure.

A glimpse into Conor's life. His past. Who he is. The way he tells it, it might be a fairy tale.

They had passed signs for the Channel ports. A hoarding at a service station said: *Get your tickets to France here*. They could drive through the tunnel and be gone. People do. They go out for a packet of cigarettes and never come back. Conor and Amy would have the whole of Europe in which to disappear. The girls would have the house. Greg's family would step in. They would survive. Too much to ask of Conor's common sense. An afternoon together offers acres of space. More than they've ever had so far. A continent is asking too much.

Amy cracks the fragile shell of batter on the fresh-caught plaice.

The white flesh tastes of the sea and is almost blue in its white-ness. She must eat or she will keel over. She has drunk too much, too fast. It's only an illusion that the sound of her swallowing can be heard by everyone.

'More wine?'

'Mmm,' and a nod of the head. Words aren't possible.

Their eyes meet with a look that says: *what are we doing?*

Eyes welled up with longing. No room for common sense.

'Such a strange place,' Conor says.

'Other worldly.' A parallel universe. Here, they can do any-thing.

Amy can't eat any more. She pushes her plate to one side. Conor toys with the flaky white plaice. They share the last of the wine.

'Not the fish's fault,' Conor laughs. 'Will we go now?'

As they leave the pub behind, walk back towards Jarman's cottage, there is nothing to come between them. No words, just the taking of each other's hand simultaneously, fingers interlacing.

Isn't this enough? Simply holding his hand, the bliss of mutual touch. An acknowledgement.

So little. So much.

'Here,' says Conor, once they are out of sight of the pub. He turns to Amy, lifts her face gently to his. A soft, tender kiss.

Why want any more? They turn their backs on the sci-fi cityscape of the power station and head towards the shore across flat shingle that is dotted with fisherman's huts. They walk into the wide open space between sea and sky. A high, perfect sky rinsed by the recent rain, clear as a fresh start. Beneath them the steady crunch of their feet. Arms around each other, their joint shadow spreads before them on the grey and ochre pebbles; their other selves, inseparable. On they go past the huts that are blackened with pitch, protection against the salt-scouring winds. They are lucky to be here on such a hospitable day. On past the fishing fleet until the boats thin out and there are just a few smaller craft dotted here and there, ropes coiling beside them.

They sit with their backs against the clinker-built hull of boat called Mermaid. Saying nothing, arms linked, her head on his shoulder. The tide is out. They might be studying a vast, abstract painting, a work of colour, texture, light. Cutting the scene in two is the deep blue line of the horizon where sea and sky merge. In the foreground the shallows are the buff colour of the sand beneath, the surface is feathered with white wisps. Next comes the glisten of firm sand, and finally, the richness of pebbles rising to where they sit. The bands of colour and light shift and alter with the rhythm of the sea. Into the frame comes a lone man, a dot, way down the beach, head bent digging for lugworms.

How well their mouths fit, the one onto the other. Sweet, hesitant kisses, taking time in between to look closely at each other's face. Conor strokes her hair. A light touch that sends a charge down to her toes; then urgent tongues. Conor filling her mouth. His hand finds her breast.

'I feel as if I've known you all my life,' he says.

For Amy words aren't possible. She sinks her hands into his hair, her tongue tracing the tip of his ear.

Instinctively, with no discussion, they stand, climb into the boat. Conor first, his hand reaching to ease her in. They lie against a pile of orange netting. The bleached bare boards are warm against Amy's leg. Conor's hand strokes her thigh. Her leg across his, feels his hardness.

For a moment it shocks her, as if it's her first time. She's forgotten. The softness, velvet smooth yet full and hard. A strange, beautiful thing that she holds, stokes, tracing its length. She pushes the zip further down, eases him out. His breath, quick and shallow, his stomach taut. A noise from deep in his throat. A pulsing in her palm that can't be stopped.

'I'm sorry,' he says.

She feels the force of him, holds the sticky warmth.

'Sh,' says Amy. 'Sh.'

They lie still, side by side, on the netting. Amy hardly dare open her eyes. When she does, she sees the beam from the new lighthouse. It doesn't miss a beat. The regular pulse of light turns and turns. A beam so strong that it's visible even against the brightness of the sun.

24

No Parking

'She's so obvious,' says Imogen. 'She was phoning on a mobile. *His* phone.'

'How can you tell?' says Alice, facing her sister across the kitchen table.

'Because it cuts in and out.'

'A bad connection.'

'That's what she said. Honestly, she must think I'm stupid.'

'At least she phoned.'

'It sounded so made up. I mean, Mum never listens to the traffic news.' Serious delays, she said, both the M25 and the Blackwall Tunnel. She's going to stop for something to eat while the traffic eases. They were not to wait for her, go ahead and eat. If they were going out, leave a note, let her know where they were.

'*We* have to account for *our* movements,' says Imogen.

'Doesn't bother me,' says Alice. 'I've nothing to hide.'

'And stopping to eat. Mum hardly eats anything these days. I can't see her bothering to go in a pub or restaurant on her own.'

'She's lost weight.'

'I know. Have you seen her new jeans? White ones.'

'Snooping again?'

Imogen won't rise to this. She makes for the fridge.

'Everything in here is going off. We'll get e-coli.' Imogen sniffs and inspects. 'Mum doesn't buy proper food anymore.'

'It's not much fun cooking in here. Why don't you do the shopping if you're so bothered? Anyway, I thought you could survive on salads?'

'Not this stuff, it's turning to compost.' Imogen holds up a pack of salad leaves that have liquefied in the cellophane packet.

'I'm going out,' says Alice. 'I'll get a pizza.'

'To share with Esther?'

'Piss off.'

'Strong words from a saint. So where shall I tell her you've gone?'

'I'll tell her myself,' says Alice, taking files from her school bag.

'Spend the evening with the bag lady if you want.'

Alice tears a sheet from her jotter pad, writes a note for Amy. She folds the paper over, writes 'Mum' and props it on the mantel.

'Since you'll read it anyway,' says Alice, 'what it says is, I'm going to Jane's to work on the environment project and I'll be back around ten. And I hope she's had a nice day. Which I do.'

Imogen hadn't planned to go out, but now that she's been deserted she might as well. Why shouldn't she have a good time? That's what Mum's doing. She's definitely with that joiner. She said she was going to look at some garden in Kent for her exhibition. An excuse to go off with him.

It's early. Fiveish. She'll wait until the men down below have packed up for the day, have a bath and think about it. Maybe phone Maxine. She managed to avoid Desmond on her way in from school. He had been talking to Moss, but he had seen her. He would have asked her out if she'd hung around. Desmond is all right as long as she doesn't see too much of him. He can be a laugh. It was fine spending a Saturday afternoon with him like she did that time at Camden Lock; a drink by the canal, checking out the record stalls. They bumped into Nick's best friend Mike Archer. She'd made a point of saying hello, stopping to talk to Mike. He would definitely have noticed that she was with Desmond. 'Better go,' Mike had said. 'I'm off to Nick's. See you around.' He was bound to say something to Nick. Or was he? Difficult to tell how much boys talked to each other. He might have said nothing at all. Anyway, being seen around with Desmond is all right. A laugh, a drink, being seen, that's all.

*   *   *

She ignores the doorbell. It's probably someone selling dusters. But after the third ring she takes a look. Desmond's ponytail is unmistakable through the stained glass.

'Your mum in?'

'She won't be back till late.'

'Only, Moss had to go early. He says to tell her not to park directly outside. I've left a couple of crates to mark the space, only she might move them.'

'I'll tell her.'

'Extra skip.'

'Well if you've marked the space.'

'Could come as early as six. She wouldn't want to be woken up would she?'

'That's fine. Thanks. I'll tell her.'

'Only she might park there even with the crates.' Desmond doesn't move. 'You busy?' His blue eyes lighten up. He'd looked quite serious talking work.

'I might be.' Imogen blunders on about coursework and assignments until he must think she's some goody-goody school kid like Alice.

'Do you want a drink?' she says.

Amongst the rotting food in the fridge there is lager and wine.

'Yeah. Thanks.'

Maybe she should make him a cup of tea.

He's pleased that she's invited him in. He makes a thing of wiping his work boots on the mat; their tough, round toes are coated with a layer of concrete, veined with cracks, like parched earth. In the kitchen he sits down at the table without waiting to be asked.

'Milk? Sugar?' asks Imogen, reaching for the kettle.

'I thought you meant a drink drink.'

His T-shirt is clean because he hasn't worn it all day. He has only just put it on, ready to go home. He was stripped to the waist when she'd seen him earlier. The red of his scarf is muted with a layer of dust, but his white T-shirt is spotless. Imogen fills the kettle anyway but doesn't switch it on. She opens the fridge.

'Lager?'

He drinks Becks straight from the bottle, rinsing his throat. His skin is a deep, even brown, like a conker.

'Haven't seen much of you lately,' he says.

Imogen times her exits and entrances well.

'Yeah . . .'

'Your mum out for the evening then?'

'She'll be back soon. She's working late.' Imogen doesn't want to give Desmond the impression that there's an evening stretching ahead in an empty house.

'Thanks for the beer.' Desmond stands, ready to go. He tightens the knot on his scarf. 'I'll leave you to your studies then.'

Imogen walks ahead of him along the hall.

'Don't forget to tell her about the parking,' he says, as she opens the front door.

'I won't.'

Halfway down the front path he turns.

'Have you ever been to Twisted Funk?'

'No.' Mum has a thing about her going into town on week-days.

'It's Techno night.'

'Yeah, I've heard it's . . .'

'Why don't you come?'

'Tonight?' He could pick her up around eight; he would need to wash up, change. 'Perhaps not eh, if you've work to do.'

Prissy little swot. That's what he thinks. He'd be a great dancer. She doesn't want him coming back to the house. She doesn't want to look too keen either.

'I'll see,' she says. 'I've sort of half arranged something.'

He shrugs.

'I'm going anyway.' And he tells her the name of the pub where he's meeting the others. If she wants to come she should be there before nine.

'Yeah, I might,' she says, 'need to phone someone.'

She'll see if Maxine wants to come. That way, she needn't end up alone with him. She and Maxine could share a cab back.

'Might see you later then,' she says, closing the door.

25

Washing

Amy props the note at the foot of the stairs: *Long, hot day. Need sleep. If I'm not up by seven please wake me. If you go to bed before Imogen leave a note to say she must lock up. Thanks. Love Mum.* Alice will see it as soon as she comes in. It's a relief to find them both out.

Amy glances at her post. There's a letter from Fintan Quinn with the final costings for the underpinning and drainage. Figures that don't bear thinking about. There's an invoice from the Quinns: her fortnightly payment, due tomorrow. On the fax is a message from Muriel; she wants to bring forward Amy's presentation to the committee. And there's an answerphone message from Freya Hill, reminding Amy about the school fair. School fair? What's that? An ancient custom from another culture. They will all have to wait. Impossible to make the transition without time alone. A decompression chamber. She will be all right in the morning.

Amy can't bring herself to wash, or even to clean her teeth. She wants to preserve the taste, the smell of him. She looks in the bathroom mirror. Her face is reddened by the sun and the wind, the unmistakable glow of a face that has spent the day by the sea. She takes her hand to her face, closes her eyes. Conor, on her skin.

In the bedroom she takes off her clothes, throws them to the floor. She feels her breasts; how had she felt to him? His touch was light, tentative. Kisses on her neck. A line of kisses. Her breast in his mouth. She can smell him on her skin.

It's hot. She turns off the light, opens the window. She can hear talking, a sudden laugh: her neighbours sitting outside to keep cool. The sky is the colour of lavender, it's not yet dark. She lies under a single, cool sheet. Beneath the sheet Amy traps the scent of Conor, holds on to him until morning.

Delicious. A whole day. Their landscape has expanded. Two real people in a real place.

So smooth. The velvety smoothness of him. Smooth, hard. And afterwards lying back on the fishing nets, cradling each other, Conor saying: 'I'm sorry, Amy. I'm sorry.' He couldn't hold back. Was she all right?

'I can wait,' she had said, quietly, surprising herself.

She wants him here in her bed, not furtive in a boat, wondering if a fisherman, or a man walking his dog, or a child flying a kite, will peep over the side and laugh at them or scowl with contempt. To be caught like that would diminish the beauty, the exquisite exploration rendered nothing more than a desperate hole-in-the-corner grope.

Sheets. Fresh, cool sheets and plenty of time. Time to explore. Time to make mistakes, to go too quickly and then try again. It will take time to learn what he needs, what she needs. He hadn't been able to hold back once she'd touched him. Was it a mistake, to touch him so soon? She hardly knew anymore and her head had been swimming with the wine. They will try again, learn the rhythm of each other's bodies.

Afterwards, as they'd walked back across the shingle to look at Jarman's garden there was a closeness that made perfect sense.

How can this be wrong?

Images and sounds, so vivid. The sudden cry of a gull, the unexpected strangeness of the steam train's whistle. A mournful note from a tiny engine pulling coaches, taking day trippers there and back again, there and back again. A glimpse of the past, a scene from a children's picture book. Amy had noticed the tension in Conor's cheek; a tightness which, for a moment, had frozen his face. It was probably not even a fully formed thought, more like something felt: in his other life he might be here with his children, taking them on the train ride to the lighthouse. He had squeezed her hand, releasing the tightness in his jaw, pulling them back into the moment.

'Got your notebook?' Laughing again as they stood before the blaze of colour at the front of the cottage. Orange, red and deep pink poppies.

'How do you put this in your exhibition?'

The arrangement of plants and objects couldn't be separated from the place. The sculptures were in the spirit of Amy's show, the transformation of the ordinary into the extraordinary, but they needed to be here. There was no fence around the cottage, nothing to say where the wildness ended and the garden began. That was the magic of it: objects, props from another story, carefully selected, placed, rearranged to tell another. Sculptures made from found objects: a plastic buoy, a coil of rusted chain, a wooden crate filled with worn cork floats, a fishhook and the great square timbers of old winding gear. All recovered from the beach where they'd been left for dead. Putting life back where there was once decay, making dead things live again, and Jarman only having the time to do this because he was dying.

To one side of the cottage there were blue overalls hung on the washing line to dry. Filled by the breeze it looked as if it were a person. The ghostly presence of the gardener watching over his garden. Had someone intended to animate the dead man's clothes? After Greg died, Amy had washed all of his jeans. She couldn't decide whether to keep them or give them away. The sight of them inflated by the wind on the washing line had shaken her. She had stood at the kitchen window, watched them lift and dance. Greg striding back to her.

Amy and Conor had been quiet together, not knowing what to say. Not naming what had happened; the tacit agreement not to put too much into words. Instead they had talked about what was there in front of them.

'An ancient form,' Conor had said, running his hand along the sun-bleached wood. 'The clinker-built boat.' The shape grows around the ribcage, one plank eased to overlap the next in an outward curve, then clinched together with copper nails which turn green, exposed over the years to the elements. 'Beautiful, isn't it?' Inside the boat there were traces of bright blue paint, but it was mainly bare wood, stripped and scoured by sea and sun. It was an older version of the boat which they had just lain in together. Amy looked over the side of Jarman's boat, noting the pattern of the wood and the nails. She could see herself and Conor coiled, wound around each other.

Hang on to the moments.

This is what she must learn. It might never be a whole thing, only a collection of moments. Saved, put together these would amount to something that was better than nothing. What will Maureen make of the heightened colour in her husband's face, a forehead burnished by the sun and the salt breeze? If Maureen were to smell Amy's perfume on Conor's shirt, Amy might never spend another day with him.

This is what she must learn: to take the moments as they come. Think of today compared with the snatched phone calls and awkward site visits. Think how much more there had been. The pleasure of touch, soft kisses, fierce kisses, all making perfect sense: past, present and future.

Not caring to rush back to London they had returned to the pub for a drink. What had they talked about? Her exhibition, the work he used to do, his family in Ireland. His parents, aunts, uncles, cousins, in Cork. The concern for his twin sister. He was clearly worried. Caitlin, the one who had stayed in Ireland. She lives in Dublin most of the time but she has a house on the west coast. She bought it because it was like their grandmother's house where they had spent their summers. His stories that she hopes won't end, always wanting one more chapter. He listens too, when she talks. Something in the quality of his attention; the utter certainty that she is not alone. The absence of solitude makes each of these moments infinite. Each one a pool that Amy can dive into yet never reach the bottom; an ocean's depth. How can this be put into words? How can she say what is not quite thought, but certainly known? A knowledge that doesn't come through words. There is more knowledge, more potency, in their finger-tip touch than anything that can be put into words. When he listens and she talks, or he talks and she listens, they are indivisible. She, Amy, extends into Conor. A clarity so limitless, it must have existed before either of them. A prehistoric condition to which they have been waiting to return.

I feel as if I've known you all my life.

The thud of the front door shutting brings Amy up too quickly, surfacing from the pool of thoughts. Alice. The nervous cough, clearing her throat. Footsteps which go into the room next door, a thoughtful tiptoeing. If it was Imogen there would be heavy feet above. Amy does not get up or call out. She resents the intrusion, being snatched from her thoughts. She wants to dive back into her day with Conor. Where was she? In the pub talking, afterwards. Start there. Or go back again to the beginning. Start the day again: waiting in the café, speeding down the motorway, the sweet awkwardness of lunch, walking into a perfect sky. Her concentration is broken.

Where's Imogen?

Imogen is seventeen. She can live her own life. Imogen doesn't need Amy, doesn't want Amy prying into her life. Amy can't face Imogen's adolescent longings, she has enough of her own. Amy will give no more thought as to who Imogen has been drinking beer with; bottles left blatantly on the kitchen table. Let her stay out late. Amy wants to be back in the garden.

'See this.' Conor leading her to the totem of old timber, part of some winding gear that would have launched boats. It had a square hole in its centre where another timber might have fitted. It was split from head to toe but still in one piece, its foot bound with the frayed and rusted cable once strong enough to haul in a boat full of fish. A fragment of the whole that now stands as a beacon marking the edge of the garden, encircled by sea kale. They had walked around it, noticing the disjunction of the views. Look past it one way and see a line of boats, fishing huts, the wide sky. Turn around and there were the steaming blocks of the power station. Depending on the light, the weather, the time of day, either might appear dangerous, beautiful. There was ugliness, bleakness, potential danger in both. At the same time, both have an awful, stunning beauty.

They had taken the slow route back, cross country. Conor had stopped just past the power station. He couldn't get reception down on the beach. He had calls to make. He'd stepped out of the car, the wind ruffling his hair, his forehead reddened by the sun. She looked away. She didn't want to see him lying. What had he told her? Not a lie, a necessary protection. Turning her gaze from him, she noticed the teams of pylons striding into the distance across the marshes; energy from thousands of contained explosions, enough to heat and light a city. Unchecked, the same energy could devastate, contaminate.

One day, Maureen. That was all. One day.

Holidays

'The last two weeks of August,' says Innes Quinn, 'we shut down. Annual holiday.' He's here to discuss the revised programme of work; the final push that will finish her house. Amy's temporary kitchen is not an ideal conference space. It's hot. The sun is fierce on the window. No point now in fitting a blind. Moss, Fintan and Innes Quinn have compressed themselves around her table. Innes, with his blue-blazered broad shoulders, looks bigger still against the white enamel of Amy's freezer. The scale drawing of the lower house is spread out between them.

To Amy, the lowest level of the basement is not real; it will never be finished or lived in. It's a ground plan, drawn to scale on paper, squares and rectangles on a grainy blue page. She's looked at the plan many times, considered the problems, the solutions, the costs: how to remove a metre of clay, compensate for poor drainage, stabilise the differential movement beneath the party wall. The kitchen which is on the next level up, is a secret place where she kissed Conor. She wishes it to remain exactly as it had been that day: no ceiling, electric cable trailing between the joists, the underside of the stairs visible. Amy wants to retain these forgotten, indefinable spaces; they will disappear if the house is finished.

'The back of the house is stable,' says Innes Quinn. 'We can proceed to finish your basement, rejoin it to the rest of the house. Six to eight weeks and your house will be finished, Amy.'

'Timing is critical,' says Fintan Quinn. Though Innes is the one who seems to do the work, Fintan comes along when there is pressure to be put on the client or the need to discuss the financial implications. 'I have the final costings here,' says Fintan indicating a folder he'd like Amy to look through. 'Overtime will be necessary. We'll be in Saturdays from now on, and the occasional Sunday.'

'Now that we've got the moisture level down in the extension area,' says Innes, 'we can install your new beech floor. You must be looking forward to having your house back, getting rid of us.'

'You'll miss us, won't you Amy?' says Moss.

'I will, Moss,' says Amy, pandering to the tease.

'We need to be ready for Keane by the last week of July.' The mention of his name and Amy is hot liquid. *Ready for Keane.* His mouth around her breast. She can't speak. His tongue fills her mouth.

'It's the middle two weeks that Keane's away?' asks Fintan.

Away?

'That's right,' says Moss, talking above her head. She's a midget in a land of giants. She can't trust herself to speak, can't ask the direct question: what do you mean, away? Think of another way to get the same answer.

'Is there any chance of fitting the kitchen earlier?' She pretends not to have taken in what they are saying. Innes Quinn strokes his chin, consults the programme of works. He can't see how. The beech floor, the kitchen, have to come last. There is an order to these things that can't be changed. With overtime they might make up the odd day but it can't make much difference.

'Not with Keane taking his holiday there in mid-July.'

Holiday.

She wants to say, almost says: Conor is not going on holiday. He would have told me. We talk everyday. Some days, two or three times. I see him once, twice a week. We've thought up ways to meet in the day; a precious half hour, always a different café or pub or a walk on the Heath. I talk to Conor Keane more than any of you do. We had an hour at lunchtime yesterday. We walked and talked for an hour around Kenwood. He said nothing about a holiday. It's not true.

'We're tight on everything,' says Moss. 'We couldn't bring Keane's work forward even if we wanted to.'

Sitting on a bench, trying to pick out the dome of St Paul's through the heat haze. He had taken her hand, tried to say something.

'Amy, you know it can't . . .' She had stopped him with a kiss.

'It's all right. This is lovely,' she had said, not wanting his words to contradict the absolute truth of his touch.

Innes Quinn talks her through the order of work: second fix plumbing and electrics, screed floor on the lowest level, plastering throughout, lavatory and utility room fixtures, glazing, installation of beech floor and kitchen, decorating. Innes is confident he'll have her house joined up in six to eight weeks.

'The plan is to hand back the whole house before we shut for the holidays. There will be more work to do, of course, but your house will be yours, not a building site.' The sign will be gone, the skip, the concrete mixer and compressor, the portaloo. In September Moss will send a couple of men to do what is outstanding. It will take pressure off this last phase if they can leave the removal of the temporary kitchen until after the holidays, incorporate this into snagging and decorating. Some of the outside work can maybe wait, though the patio will have to be laid, if she can confirm the paving.

How can it have happened? The imminence of a completed house unnerves her. Differential movement had sounded like a problem that would go on and on. As long as the house is unfinished she has legitimate contact with Conor. Once the hardwood floor and the kitchen are installed there will be no reason for her to phone his workshop as she does now, openly, if a little awkwardly. Couldn't they find another dodgy foundation? Halfway through June and the Quinns have their sights on leaving. Time isn't what it used to be. It doesn't have a regular movement which can be measured on a clock. She inhabits a different time scale, a new dimension known only to her and Conor, variable in its pace. With him, an hour goes faster than seems fair, two hours on the telephone might have been minutes, yet a single moment recalled in his absence could fill a morning. She was surprised to find that it was June. Last time she registered the month it was March. In six weeks it will be August. Legitimate time with Conor will end. For two of those weeks Innes Quinn is daring to suggest that Conor might not be here.

'Finished,' says Amy. 'August.'

If she is to see Conor after the house is finished they will have to talk openly, directly of the things they avoid. When she is with him she has the certainty of his presence, the knowledge that comes through the tips of his fingers. She has the truth of those moments, but she doesn't have the wider picture. Caught in the potency of the moment it is easy to keep the tacit agreement not to mention their other lives. It's a tight space that Amy and Conor inhabit; a forgotten space.

'Will you have a holiday yourself, Amy?' asks Innes.

'I don't know. I don't know.'

Imogen's asked Amy for money to buy a Eurorail pass. She and Maxine will make their way through France, Spain, Portugal ending up at Maxine's parent's place near Seville. Imogen wants to go away for the whole of the school holiday. She's never done anything like that before. Can Amy let her go? It will avoid the confrontation that's brewing around the matter of Imogen and Desmond. There's no doubt now that she's seeing him. Imogen won't be challenged.

'I'm getting a life,' she had said after she'd stayed out clubbing till four in the morning.

Amy will have to fix something for Alice because she, Amy, cannot entertain the idea of going on holiday when all that matters is the next phone call, the next lunch with Conor.

Amy stands, thanks them, makes it clear they must leave.

'I'll look at these later,' she says to Fintan, knowing he wants her comments on the final figures. If he stays he'll engage her in conversation. He's a walking definition of Blarney. She's heard it all before: how he couldn't complete his architecture studies, who he knows at the museum, who's getting the big Lottery refurbishment contracts for the Opera House, the new Tate at Bankside.

She wants to say: Go. Go now.

She will leave for Liz's soon, she needs to ask Liz a favour. But first, she will call Conor.

'What else did he say?' Liz pours more wine.

'Not much.' Amy kicks off her shoes, tucks her feet beneath her. 'Gerry was still there, he couldn't really talk.'

'So, he's going on holiday with his wife and children. Seems reasonable.'

'I know but . . .'

'What did you expect Amy? That he ask you to help him fill in the booking form? This is what it's like.'

'I just wish he'd told me.'

'Amy don't make a big deal of it. He's told you now. He would have told you nearer the time. Loosen up.'

'Two weeks. No contact. Not even a phone call.'

'Where did you say he was going?'

'Lanzarote.'

'Poor man, no wonder he didn't tell you.'

To be fair to Conor he had been trying to tell her yesterday. She had stopped him. When she phoned he said: 'I don't feel good about this. I didn't say anything because I can't bear to think about it myself.' Maureen's sister has a time-share, they have to go in the middle two weeks of July even though it means taking the children out of school. Maureen is prepared to do that until the eldest takes exams. And he didn't use her name once. What he said was: my sister-in-law has a place.

'Guilt. He keeps you both in separate compartments. He can't say her name, he can't speak her into your compartment. Guilt, Amy. And besides, why would he spend his time with you chatting about his wife and kids?'

'What he said was: it's a proper rest for her.'

'So the man's not a complete shit. He's concerned about his wife.' It's easy for Liz. She's done this a dozen times. She's an expert. Amy wishes she was Liz in her self-contained life. Her house is a sensible size. Her books are in order on the shelves: design history, textiles, history of clothing. Her walls are hung with objects and interesting pieces of cloth that she's collected on her travels.

'Come on, let me show you something, take your mind off him.'

She follows Liz up to her loft work space. More well-ordered shelves. Rows of box files of projects completed. A table laid out with images for the new book.

'I've had a good week on the picture research.' Amy tries to look enthusiastically at images of farthingales, corsets, bustles, chemises.

'Look at this,' Liz holds up her triumph.

'The inflatable crinoline.' A woman sits like a fly caught at the centre of a web, three maids hold the crinoline cage around her while they inflate each hoop.

Amy sees Conor standing in the skeleton of the new roof timbers, measuring the window frame.

'Short lived,' Liz reassures. 'It didn't catch on.'

Liz has a life, a job, men (plural) a house that is ordered, comfortable.

'What?'

'The inflatable corset. It didn't last.'

'You're so lucky, Liz.'

'Come on, help me clear these, don't sit there dreaming,' says Liz. Amy has managed to eat supper. She didn't think she would.

'You can stay if you like.'

'No thanks, not tonight.'

'Liz?'

'Yes.'

'Are you planning to go away in August?'

'I'm not sure. If the book is going well, I'll leave it to the last minute. If I go anywhere it will be Italy. Why don't you come?' Liz is enthusiastic, picking up that Amy wants something, but she's caught the wrong thread. 'If Alice goes to your mother's, why don't you come?'

'I have to be here,' says Amy

'Can't bear to be away from him?'

'It's not that. They're going to finish the house.'

'So, go away. Come back to it finished.'

'I couldn't.'

'He'll still be here and married when you come back.'

'It's not that, I've got to be here as they finish the house. There's always some decision to be made. It might hold things up if I go away. But I did wonder, if you're not here, could I house-sit for you?'

Liz looks Amy directly in the eye.

'It will be hectic at Durham Road. They plan to work weekends. It would be a break for me to live somewhere normal, and if the girls aren't here . . .'

'Will he be able to get an overnight pass?'

'That's not why I'm asking.'

'It's absolutely why you're asking. Get real. It's enough that he has all the Catholic-guilt-denial.'

'I'm doing what I can Liz. I don't have your years of experience.'

'If I go, you can have the keys. Do what you like as long as my house is in one piece when I come back. I don't want to find Maureen's been round here with a meat cleaver.'

Liz wipes the table, scoops coffee into the cafétière.

'Amy, if you're going to carry on with this thing, don't you think it might be a good idea if you, well, enjoyed it a bit more?'

'I do. I enjoy the moments.'

'You're getting off on the pain too.' Liz faces Amy across the table. 'This is the best bit, Amy, the bit you're in now.'

'What do you mean?'

'The madness, the magic,' says Liz. 'The highs, the lows, the exquisite torture, the surges of energy. Let me give you the benefit of my accumulated observations on the state we call being in love. One: it is the best thing that can happen to you. Enjoy it while it lasts. Two: it is most certainly temporary.'

'I know what you're saying,' says Amy, 'but it feels, well, more permanent. And yet it's impossible too, look at this holiday business. I don't know. It's the best thing and the worst.'

'It will be the making of you Amy. Use the energy, it can transform you. You'll grow. It's like something expanding inside you and I mean more than his dick.'

'Liz.'

'I know. You're still only holding hands and groping.'

'If it were only about sex . . .'

'You can't separate the two things. Don't even try. It is about sex, all that energy. If you're not going to shag . . .'

'Hardly likely with him off to Lanzarote. I mean after he's had two weeks of close proximity to his loved ones, he'll probably call the whole thing off.'

'Amy, whatever complaints you have, take a look at yourself. You're thriving on it. You've never looked better. You might be pissed off because he's going on holiday, but think of all the longing that will induce. A great big fix of longing.' Liz is in full flight. 'Look at you. You're three-dimensional again. You've been flattened by grief, a two-dimensional version of yourself, for three years. Now your eyes sparkle, your skin is glowing, you've lost weight, you care about what you wear, you're working again, you've built a house. You're having normal rows with your bolshie teenage daughter who, at last, is doing what she should be doing – going off with an unsuitable man. Amy, you're back.'

27

The Spiral

Conor selects a disc of plywood the size of a bicycle wheel. He's cut several from a large sheet; he can cut more if he needs to, there's stacks of the stuff in the yard. He selects a fine blade for the band saw. It may take a few attempts to achieve what he wants; a larger disc maybe, a finer blade. He'll find out by making it. There's no blueprint for this.

If only he could keep this thing with Amy as it is now. To be with her, talk, keep the contact. To be in each other's lives. To be in touch. A half hour on the phone to her can take him through a day or more. She stirs him. There's a new shape to his life, formed around each encounter with Amy. Why can't he have this?

Who does he think he's kidding?

He wants her, wants to make love to her. Will make love to her. He wants the visions that appear in his head each night to become real. Later and later he goes up to bed, waits till Maureen is asleep, her breathing slack beside him. He leads himself towards sleep down the trail of Amy's words. Things she's said run through his mind until he takes her mouth to his and the flow of words between them becomes the fluency of their bodies. Back in the boat. This time, in slow motion, he waits for her. They move gracefully together, smooth until he's held inside her succulence. It can only be a matter of time. It's bound to happen. And then what? At home will he be able to face Maureen, look her in the eye and make the kinds of excuses he did after their day at Dungeness? Excuses that hadn't altogether held. 'What's eating you, then, Conor?' Maureen had asked through the dark when

Conor thought he'd convinced her that he was asleep. 'Pressure of work,' he'd said, feigning sleepiness in his voice, when in his head he was wide awake, charged with the vitality of Amy. Maureen hadn't stopped there: why chase clients out of London and then work late at the workshop? And was there something wrong with the mobile or had he switched it off by mistake? It wasn't suspicion, not yet. Maureen was puzzled more than anything. Concerned. She's tuned into his movements. This is what happens to people who've been together a long time. It's a kind of mind reading, a knowledge that they almost don't know they have. It wasn't suspicion, simply Maureen noticing disruptions to the normal pattern. So, he had stroked her back, kissed her neck and prayed to God that she wouldn't turn round, wouldn't take hold of him and want more, when the touch of Amy was still on him even though he'd washed away all actual trace of her. He'd no choice; straight to the bathroom as soon as he'd entered the house. Nothing unusual about that, going straight for a bath, especially after a long day. He had soaped himself, rinsed, run fresh water, and soaped himself again. He had lathered shampoo into his hair. Then, submerged, he rinsed away the foam and her perfume, running clean water, but he couldn't wash off the memory of her touch.

He switches on the band saw; a fast-moving, lethal thing. A fine, continuous blade fixed at a right-angle to the bench. It can have a finger off before you know it. There is no margin for error. He must keep his hands clear of the blade. He holds the disc of ply, feeds it into the teeth of the moving steel belt. It's all intuition, going with the movement in his body. Following what he knows in his fingertips. He will try different dimensions. Will the line of the spiral remain equidistant, or will it need to become tighter as he reaches the centre? Make a start. He can do several versions; he has the time. He's told Maureen he needs to be here for much of the weekend to catch up on the paperwork. She was happy enough. 'If it makes things easier,' she'd said. She wanted to see her sister anyway. It was one thing lying to create time to work on this, he could justify it if he was ever called to account. But one day, soon, when words flow into bodies, how will he manage then? Something will give him away. Some small thing which, however hard he tries, he will not be able to hide.

However careful he is, once he has made love to Amy something will give him away. A sliver of evidence, a chance remark, an attitude. Whatever it is, it will switch Maureen's concern into suspicion. He's not made for the kind of creeping around that will be necessary. He sees again the sordid spectacle of himself the day after Dungeness, stuffing his boxer shorts into a carrier bag, chucking the bag into a litter bin on the High Road.

No margin for error. He must keep the movement steady. Not too fast, not too slow, a strong, steady movement of wood through the speeding saw.

He wished he'd told Amy earlier about the holiday, but he's trying not to think about it himself. He should have realised that she would hear about it from the Quinns or Moss. A sliver of information heard in the wrong place. It doesn't come naturally to him, there's no blueprint for any of this. Now that she knows, he has to look at himself. He has to admit how much he dreads the two weeks away. What kind of monster has he become that the thought of being alone with Maureen and the children, of being away from Amy, fills him with dread? And even as he thinks this he can't quite call it betrayal. There is a part of him which has a right to be with Amy. He's trying to keep that part of him away from Maureen. He's protecting Maureen. He wouldn't willingly inflict pain on Maureen if he had any choice.

Too far. He's taken the blade too far into the centre. It needs more surface area at the centre to form the base. If the thing is to stand firm it will need a base that is in proportion to the diameter of the outer rim. It doesn't matter if it's not perfect the first time. What matters is that he makes a few versions. He needs to go through the process, see what works and what doesn't. It's a challenge if he cares to accept it, stick with it, not give up at the first hitch. He's made a maquette in card, fixing the raised spiral in place with staples; he knows that the form works in principle. Easy enough to manipulate the card but now he needs to discover how the wood will behave.

Amy understands that making things is a kind of thinking; she can see exactly how one way of working can lead to another. Amy is curious about things and the way they are made. He sees her walking through the strange garden. She'd slipped her arm from his, walked over to the boat that is fetched up there in front of the cottage. He had stayed by the wire sculpture; a bunch of rusted steel cables, each of which ends in a tiny loop. They look like elongated versions of the thing Maura uses to blow bubbles. A half dozen of them enter the ground at the same point but splay outwards as the they reach eight, ten feet high. They swayed like giant stamens, the breeze catching them made a moaning sound. Through this spindly form he had watched Amy walk towards the boat, noticed the way her body moved beneath her skirt. The ripple of her flesh beneath cloth was like a call to him. How could he not answer? How could he not want to touch her again?

He had followed her and they stood by the disused craft that was a worn-out version of the one they had not long since lain in together. She wanted to know about the boat, how it was built. He showed her how one plank was eased over the next around the ribcage. It was made like the boat on the beach, the boat he returns to most nights in his head, so he can come to her again, slowly, in tune with her. They had stood a while talking about the clinker-built boat and that's what had started him off with this. It was the link he was looking for to get the drawing off the page and into something he could work at; hand, head and heart working together.

Once he has his spiral of wood he can ease it into the new form. He will lift up the disc that is left at the centre and coil the wood back on itself, working out from the centre, the band of wood overlapping itself with each turn. He knows the thing will work in the end. When it does, it will be for Amy. He would like very much to have something to give her before he goes on holiday. He will make another one for Caitlin. A late birthday present for last year when she wouldn't hear of marking it, or making it special. Now, with these things growing inside her, she's seeing things differently. When she called last week she was just out of hospital again. Down at the cottage for the weekend. It was lucky she had a friend to drive her.

'Every bump in the road, Con, I thought I would die.' And it had rained, a solid rain. 'A sky like Gran's mashed potatoes.' Driving rain. 'All that water and me not able to squeeze out a drop.' She's happier now she's back in Dublin. She's seen the specialist who said that injections might help to shrink the fibroids. But he would put her down as a priority for surgery. There would be a cancellation, no doubt, before the summer was out. Her choice, mind, but that would be his recommendation. 'Some choice. He says the one big fibroid is the size of a four-month foetus.'

'Give it a month or two more.' Conor had said realising what the operation meant.

'That's it,' she'd said. 'No kids for me.' Conor had one up on her there. He'd done something that she hadn't.

'I'll have to take being an aunt more seriously.' And when she had asked him how they all were he didn't know what to say. He thought of them, his four children: Kevin, Michael, Clare, Maura. Distant faces, people he once knew, still knows. They seemed at once close and yet standing far off. He'd almost told her about Amy. Almost said: I have a choice to make too. But the moment had passed.

'We could make it a wake,' Caitlin laughing to keep away her fears.

'You're not going to die, for Christ's sake.'

'No. I mean the party we were talking about. We could make it a wake. For my womb, and the passing of our youth.'

It's not right yet. A thinner blade, maybe. He knows he can do this. Glue maybe, though if he could find the right nail, a small enough copper nail, he could work the line of the nailhead with the curve of the spiral. He'd like to get that in, the reference to the boat. That will come later, when the form is right.

This is the saddest bit. This is what he can't get right in his head. It's not that he could say there is anything wrong with Maureen. If he were asked, he would have to say Maureen is a companionable partner.

'She confirms you Conor,' is what Caitlin said when she had tried to make him think again about getting married so soon after Judy.

'She confirms what is safe in you, what you accept in yourself and there is so much more. So much more.'

When he thinks back to the day they agreed to marry, it wasn't because he was nearly half-mad with the need for her. It wasn't because when she was with him he was alive, alert, ready to soar, like he had been with Judy. Like he is with Amy. It was because, with Maureen, he felt safe. They were emigrés in a foreign city.

- Pamela Johnson

A decent, safe life. This is what he has with Maureen. A life that postpones a good part of him.

Can he square the circle?

There's something here that could come right. He will make the disc of dead, processed wood hold volume, define a new space. This one is too tight, too cone-like. He wants it to be more open. A generous, relaxed form with a wide outer rim.

If he were to tell her, if he were to say: 'Amy, you're the love of my life,' that would be a commitment, one that he's not free to make. He doesn't want to offer her less.

28

Night Out

'It's me that's in a muddle,' says Imogen. 'She must have gone with Mum. It doesn't matter. Thanks. See you.' She doesn't want to give Jane the idea that anything is wrong. Imogen knows that Alice can't be out with Mum. So where is she? Imogen is not going to worry. Alice wouldn't do anything really stupid. If she's not at Jane's, and hasn't been there at all this evening, then there is only one other place to look. Why has Alice done this, what is she trying to prove? It wasn't as if she had been part of the row. She wasn't even in the room.

It had been Imogen and Amy. Head on.

Who is Alice trying to impress? Imogen's not going to feel bad about any of this. She doesn't regret what she said to Mum, and if Alice has taken it into her head to run off because of it, well, that's her problem. It's been a long time coming. She and Mum have been avoiding each other for weeks. So, Mum knows about Desmond. So what, what is there to *know?*

Amy is hiding more than Imogen.

Well, now she knows that Imogen has not been fooled.

'House rules?' Imogen had spat the words back at Amy, glared at her, eye to eye, standing firm. 'I'm happy to keep to any rules you care to name, if you'll stick to them too.' The look on Mum's face. She didn't say anything. She didn't say a word. An admission in itself. Maybe if Imogen had stayed there Amy would have said something. Why can't Mum admit it? Why can't she come clean and say she's seeing someone else's husband. Isn't that what all married people over thirty do? Why is she being so uptight, trying to hide it? Inappropriate. Amy had said that seeing Desmond was inappropriate. If it's appropriate to see Conor Keane why is she pretending she isn't. Imogen had wanted the last word. She didn't give Mum time to speak. She had walked out and locked herself in the bathroom. She had heard the front door slam twice, so Alice hadn't gone with Mum.

It's late now, almost midnight. Alice wouldn't stay out past ten on a weekday. She just wouldn't, and she can't have gone with Mum. No doubt about it, in that outfit, with that much perfume, lipstick and blusher, Mum was off to see her, her what? Boyfriend, lover, married man.

Alice is definitely not at Jane's. She will be with Esther. How far will she go; will she stay out all night, sleep in the doorway? It's a hot night. She might try it on, especially now she's finally twigged that Imogen has been right about Keane. That's what's getting to her, that Imogen has been right all along. Imogen hadn't meant to push it so far, it just happened.

'Have you put the cheque in the bank?' Amy had asked. Imogen had been reading a magazine, she genuinely didn't hear.

'Some acknowledgement,' Amy's tone was tense. 'That's all. I mean, I'm happy to make up the amount, but some acknowledgement would not go amiss. I haven't got a bottomless pit of money. Most of it is now in this house.'

'Oh yeah,' Imogen had tuned in too late. 'Yeah, thanks, I put it in the bank this morning.'

'Please don't spend it on anything else will you?'

'Mum.'

'When will you pay for the ticket?'

'Mum.'

'But you bought more clothes today. You must leave enough for the ticket, Imogen.'

'Mum. I know what I'm doing. OK?' If she'd stopped there things might not have escalated, but Imogen couldn't resist. Mum coming all high-handed like that about buying clothes. Imogen has enough for the clothes and the rail ticket. She doesn't need Amy doing the figures for her.

'Anyway, you seem to be spending rather a lot on clothes at the moment.' Imogen had flashed her eyes the length of Amy's body, taking in the new white jeans, the tight black top that showed Amy still had a waist and was wearing the Wonderbra. How obvious. Did she think they were blind? Amy let it pass, tried to diffuse things.

'All I'm saying is, please don't come back to me for any more money towards the holiday. I'm happy for you to go and I'm happy to buy the ticket but that's what the cheque was for. The ticket.'

'Look, I know what I'm doing. It's you Mum, you're the one who doesn't seem to know what you're doing at the moment.' And then the lid flew. Imogen let Mum have it. She told her how Freya Hill had stopped her in the street. Deep embarrassment. She told Amy exactly what Freya had said: 'Odd that your mother would forget. Such a stalwart of the summer fair in the past. Is she all right? I expect it's the building work.' Too right. There had been something in Freya Hill's insistent questioning that made Imogen realise that people knew, or at least suspected. Others can see what's happening: the new clothes, the hair, the dippy, distracted way she is, high as a kite one minute, miserable the next. Does Mum think she's invisible?

'It was so embarrassing. She said she would call in to see if you were all right because she said, "it's just not like Amy to be unreliable."'

'Unreliable? I missed my slot on the bric-a-brac stall. I forgot.'

'But Mum, you used to like doing those things.' Amy was sorry if Imogen had been embarrassed. She would ring Freya to explain, but really, she has other priorities at the moment. The house is nearing completion and the museum project means a lot to her.

'It would be nice to feel I could rely on you for support. Instead of which you seem hell bent on creating more pressure.'

'Pressure? Me? How?'

Amy had said nothing for a while. She had been weighing something up. She looked almost as if she couldn't be bothered. Then she said quietly: 'I don't want you to bring Desmond in here while I'm out. See him if you must – I know you are – but don't bring him in here.'

'I've had a drink with him. We've been to a party, a group of us went to a club. You know, normal things people do.'

'As I said, see him if you must, but don't bring him in here when I'm out. I hope you're not sleeping with him.'

'And what about you?'

'Imogen. It's one thing you seeing him, socialising. It's another entirely bringing him here. All I'm saying is that it's inappropriate for you to bring him here.'

'Why?'

'The man's working here.'

'So is Conor Keane.'

'We're talking about you, Imogen.'

'Well why can't we talk about you at the same time? What is the difference between me seeing Desmond and you seeing that joiner.'

'I'm not getting into this.'

'Why not?'

'I'm late.'

'Late for Conor Keane?'

'It's not what you think Imogen.'

'Where are you going tonight, then?'

Amy had turned away, rummaged in her bag as if looking for her keys or something. She had looked away from Imogen and mumbled something about going to a private view, she wasn't sure who would be there. A number of people she hoped to see, people whose work she might include in her exhibition. She might have dinner with some of them afterwards.

'You're seeing him aren't you?'

'He may be there. I believe he has an invitation too.' Amy looked weary. 'We'll talk about this another time. I don't want Desmond in here.'

'Fine. I'll keep to that if you do the same. No Desmond. No Mr Keane.' Out of the room, up to the bath. It felt as good as squeezing a pimple.

Imogen knows where Alice is. She's up the road, in the doorway with Esther. Mum need never know. Imogen could go up there now, persuade Alice to come home before Mum gets back. She could. But why should she?

29

Treading Water

The water is cold. Amy takes a deep breath, plunges her head below the surface, pushes forward. She scoops away the water, arms wide apart, then pushes forward again. Her muscles stretch, easing out the tension. Strong deliberate strokes, as hard as she can, up and down the length of the pool. She will swim for half an hour without stopping. She checks her watch on the turn as her feet push against the tiles, propelling her into another length. Her body stretches, extends. Each sure movement draws the energy away from her head, slowing down the tumble of her thoughts.

What has she done to drive Alice onto the streets?

Vulnerably accommodated, that's the phrase used to describe those in danger of becoming homeless. A phrase which now describes her own daughter. Amy remembers the young girl she had seen on the South Bank, hugging herself into a tartan rug, looking as if she had not long since been someone's daughter, doing homework at the kitchen table. A row, a build-up of tension. Is that all it takes?

'You're never here, Mum.' Imogen had been angry, accusing.

'And if I breathe down your necks, follow your every move, I'm an anxious mother. It's not easy.' She and Imogen had sat up talking till two once they'd brought Alice home.

'I mean, it's like you're somewhere else, even though you're here. You know what Alice is like. She needs someone to tell her that what she's doing is OK. You know, look at her homework now and then, or something.'

*   *   *

Amy stares through the clear blue water, takes an honest look over the last few months. She's been only too happy to let Alice go off at every opportunity to work at Jane's house. She'd convinced herself that this was a positive thing. This was Alice becoming independent. It was good that she had found a way to escape the building work.

'Alice says that Jane's mum shows more interest in her than you do.'

The shock of it. After a near-perfect evening with Conor, there was Imogen waiting on the stairs. No warning. The stark shock of it.

'Alice has gone.'

'What?' The warmth of Conor's acknowledgment pushed aside by words that had hit Amy in the face as sure as any punch. Imogen handed her the piece of paper.

'I found this on your bed.'

Don't worry, I'm safe. Alice.

Amy had little in reserve. She simply didn't know what to do.

Imogen had looked so grown up, so powerful. She was in charge. Amy had wanted to cry, to say: help me, tell me what to do.

'She'll have gone to Jane's,' Amy suddenly recovered, realised what must have happened, rushed to the phone to call Jane's mother.

'I've tried. She's not there.' Thumped again.

She could have coped with that. Alice going off to a friend's house, a house where she often stayed the night.

'What?'

'She's not at Jane's.'

'Where the hell is she? We must call the police.'

'No.' Icy determination in Imogen's voice, and the fix of her eyes.

'What do you mean, "No"?' More and more helpless, waiting to see how many blows Imogen had to inflict.

'I know where she is.'

'What? Where? Why didn't you say? Imogen what kind of game are you playing?'

No grip on the situation. She had gone upstairs to the temporary kitchen, opened the window. A hot night. No air. In the garden she could see looming shapes: the portaloo, a pile of ladders, stacks of paving, and up at the window, scaffolding. None of this will make sense if Alice has been driven out on the street. *Vulnerably accommodated*. The whole lot can fall down as far as Amy cares. The whole lot might collapse at any moment. She had turned to face Imogen.

'Here, sit down. Have a drink of water or something.'

'What's going on. Where is she?' The growing sense that Imogen was the adult and she, Amy, was the wayward girl who was being made to face her actions before being offered any relief.

'She's with Esther.'

'Who?'

'You know, the woman who sleeps in the church doorway.'

'How do you know?'

Imogen explained that she'd been up there to check. She had made sure that Alice hadn't seen her, but Imogen wanted to be sure that's where Alice was. If she hadn't been there Imogen would have called the police ages ago. Not knowing how long Amy would be staying out. Not knowing if Amy herself was staying out for the night.

'She's all right. She's with Esther.'

'Why didn't you talk to her, bring her home?'

'Because it's you she wants to take notice of her. Because it's you who should go up there and find her, not me.'

'But why this woman, why go there?' Amy had to listen to Alice's secret life. How she takes this woman food, washes her clothes, talks to her on the way home from school. Some homeless woman is more capable of paying attention to her daughter than she is. What has she done?

The chlorine stings her eyes but she can't stop now. She swims faster, changing from breaststroke to crawl. She pounds the water. She will have to end this thing with Conor. End what? It's hardly started. And what is 'it'? Her secret life. It's grown, taken all her attention. How could she kid herself that the girls wouldn't notice? She had meant to protect them, didn't want to involve them in her madness. Keep it watertight. The bubble. Her and Conor in the bubble: a ride in his car, a day out, talking on the phone, lunch. A contained, secret life. Liz is right. It's not easy to hide.

'There's a look adulterers have when they're amongst people who aren't meant to know. The harder you try to hide it, Amy, the more you reveal yourself.'

'Hardly adulterers, Liz.'

'Tell that to Maureen Keane. Tell her you went all the way to Dungeness to check out the weathered wood. Some fancy new effect for the kitchen?'

The madness has leaked out, contaminated Alice and Imogen. All of them. Things speak themselves even if nothing is said.

Amy recalls the look on Conor's face during that last site meeting with Moss before Conor went on holiday. Conor wanting to know when his workshop could check the final measurements.

'Gerry will come by to check the plaster levels.'

'Screed floors and plastering begin next week. Relax, Keane. Off you go, sunning yourself. We'll be ready for him when he gets back, won't we Amy?' Moss had looked to Amy for a confirmatory laugh, she had done her best to manufacture one. But she'd caught the look on Conor's face. She wanted to say: don't look at me like that. If Moss were to turn quickly and catch that same look, if Moss were to see all that was being said by Conor's eyes, they would be done for. A momentary thing, but dangerous. A searching look, almost as if he were trying to stand back, see Amy from afar. A deep, longing look.

The look on Alice's face when Amy had appeared shortly after midnight on the church steps. Neither mother nor daughter could speak. They had looked at each other for quite some time. Alice's face shot with pain, fear, what else? Worry lines on her brow. Trying to look tough at the same time. Alice doesn't have the defiance of her elder sister and it was painful to watch her try to emulate it. Behind that sad, trying-to-be-tough face, Amy had seen the years dissolve. Inside the awkward fifteen-year-old was the anxious baby who would wake at two-hourly intervals through the night, the clingy toddler who always needed another cuddle before she would join in the playgroup circle. Baby, toddler, emergent woman, sitting on the steps of the disused church, amongst pigeon shit and a heap of rags. The steps were streaked with Esther's urine and her VP wine. Alice giving up on life before it's begun.

'She's a good girl, is Alice,' Esther's hair matted, her teeth broken. 'No harm, she would of been safe with me. I said she oughta go home. She wanted to stay.'

Vulnerably accommodated, in a half-built house, with a demented mother, struggling to accept the loss of her father. It's more complicated than Amy had imagined. Alice's actions can't simply be explained by the effects of Amy's distractedness. It's more complicated. Alice still has this thing about Greg never coming to the new house. It's not all down to Amy. Alice is having to accept that Greg is never coming back. They all are. Amy too. But they are doing it differently. Each finding a different way out. Alice has been the most upset by the disruption of the house and she's worried about exams next year. It's all of these things; it's not simply because of Amy and Conor. The move has broken the tight way in which they lived through the loss. They are no longer cocooned together in grief. They have pulled apart, taking different directions. If not Conor, then Alice will have to accept that there could be a man in Amy's life. Amy is not going to live the life of a nun. Conor's away for thirteen more days. Even in the midst of this, coming slap up against her neglect of her own children, she can't extinguish the thrill of it. She will talk to the girls again tonight. She will tell them exactly what remains to be done on the house, reassure them that it won't be like this forever. She will try to explain about Conor. These things happen. Amy hadn't planned it. A deep attraction. An affinity with someone. She hadn't thought it possible after Greg. Yes, he is married, has four children. An impossible situation. She will explain that she's trying to be discreet not deceitful, trying to understand it herself, before any damage is done. She hadn't wanted to involve them. She doesn't know where it will go. Probably nowhere. Could they allow her to have someone in her life? Would it be all right now that she'd owned up? Amy hadn't realised that keeping a secret can etch away; things unsaid can have a powerful presence. They all need a holiday. Imogen has made her plans with Maxine. Alice could go up to Gran's with Jane if she cared to. Amy will have to stay here, see the house finished. Things will be back to normal in September. Amy could travel to see Alice at the weekends if Alice wanted her to. They each need to think more about what the others feel. Amy's not thrilled about Desmond, she's baffled by Esther but, she'll make an effort. So, would they please do the same for her? Tonight, after supper, they will sit down together and she will say all of this.

Amy's head breaks through the surface. She sees the handrail and grips it. Breathless. She treads water, lies back. Floats.

30 ∫

Carpets

Amy selects 'desktop patterns' from the control panels menu. Anything to put off the first draft of her proposal. A new delaying tactic; the digital equivalent to pencil-sharpening. Most of them don't stand a chance. She clicks past the tartan, the teddy bears, the pussy cats and all those that look like carpets. She settles on a deep, bright blue. The colour of the sky as she lay in the boat at Dungeness. The colour of the sky over the beach where Conor now lies with his wife and four children.

Three more days. He will be back. Amy will be forgotten.

He will have come to his senses, alone with his family for two weeks. No pressure of work, no contact with Amy. He will have seen what he has and won't want to jeopardise the equilibrium of his family life. However dull things are between Conor and Maureen it won't be easy to keep Amy in his life.

I want you in my life, Amy.

There will be nothing casual for Conor. No double life. He's an all or nothing sort of person. She is prepared.

Against this, she weighs the evidence of the last time they met. The one time they had allowed themselves an evening out. They met at an Italian restaurant in town, a place that she had suggested. They ordered asparagus, grilled sea bass and a crisp, cold wine. After mangoes and strawberries the waiter had brought glasses of *vin santo*; they dipped *cantuccini*, the heavy, sweet wine softening the almond biscuits. A long, leisurely evening, drinking, eating, talking.

I think of you all the time, Amy.

You are a beautiful woman.
I want to be with you, Amy.
It's as though a beam of light has been turned on in a dark place.

Words she has saved. Now, away with Maureen, Conor might have changed his mind, but these things he said were meant then, in the moment. He had been more open that evening than he'd ever been. Amy had dared to break the unspoken rule. She had asked him about Maureen and the children. Was he very unhappy at home?

Not unhappy. Not happy. Existing.

'Maureen's good.'

Good. Good is a word that attaches easily to Maureen Keane.

Amy can't think of her as a rival, she doesn't resent her but she is curious about Maureen. In one of her crazier moments she had driven to Queens Park, found the street where he lives. She had parked opposite the house. There had been lights on in the front bedroom and a dim glow through the glass of the front door, indicating a light on somewhere at the back of the house. The kitchen, perhaps. Was the upstairs light Conor and Maureen in bed? It wasn't late. Maybe it was the eldest child, Kevin. Conor and Maureen would be in the kitchen, eating, talking about their day. Conor would have to leave things out. A glimpse of Maureen was all Amy had wanted. To know what the woman looked like would make a difference.

When Amy and Conor had left the restaurant, walked arm in arm through Soho, leaning close to him she had caught the clean, laundered scent of Conor's shirt, the trace of washing powder. This is the smell of Maureen.

Maureen's good.

It is Maureen's goodness that Amy fears most. And the inertia. A safe, dull place, the well-tried comfort of compromise. Conor will wonder if the reward, the renewal, will be worth the risk. He wouldn't want to end up like Mr Byrne. *Temporary accommodation till I get back to my family.* Twenty-five years Mr Byrne had lived in the bedsit that is now Amy's makeshift kitchen. Two whole weeks surrounded by the protective layer of Maureen's goodness. Maureen is home. *Emigrés in a foreign city.* Amy is a foreigner; too much of an unknown. Unsettled, eccentric, perhaps, when seen against Maureen. How can she make comparisons with someone she does not know, and yet there is something to this, she's sure. This is not her imagination reading too much into too little. She pieces together the snippets Conor let fall that evening. Peepholes into his past. Maureen and Conor had been teenage friends in Cork, growing up in the same neighbourhood. Lost touch when Conor went to college. Afterwards, he set up his studio in Ireland. Exhibited in Dublin. There was a woman, a relationship. An artist. Judy. Passing references. *It was difficult. It didn't work out.* A grand passion? Does he still hanker after her? This is Amy's fantasy. It was a long time ago, he was young. Stick to what is known. Losing his way with his work must have come after Judy. Leaves Ireland, comes to London. No money. Long shifts digging the Underground. Takes a room in a shared house which is where he meets Maureen again. This is what he said when Amy asked why he married Maureen: *we were emigrés alone in a foreign city.* Not a grand passion. Maureen was a nursery teacher working in a rough school. *Maureen's good.* She coaxed him above ground. There were miscarriages. More than one. He holds back here, too. Amy has pieced the story together from a number of fragments, things he's hinted at before. There is enough to tell her how extra precious the four children must be to Maureen. To Conor. There are things that bind Maureen and Conor; the hard work of living.

Amy types quickly. The clack of the keyboard chases out thoughts of Maureen and Conor. She has put together a strong group of work which will form the core of the exhibition; young artists who transform materials and familiar objects into vivid, sensuous work. Conor's bowl sits on her desk, the curve of its spiral catches her eye. She would like to include his work in her show. Why not, it's an everyday material used in an unexpected way. Conor has put life back into the dead wood; produced something dynamic out of something inert. Two weeks with Maureen may mean the end, but neither of them will forget what has happened. She can trace the spiral downwards as it narrows to the base; or, she can start at the base and trace the curve upwards as it widens to the brim.

'Have you a minute, Amy?' Moss taps at the door. Amy clicks on 'save.'

'Carpets.' An announcement. Moss introducing his topic for the day. He pitches in about a firm that Fintan Quinn does business with. They'll colour-match to Amy's specification, weave to the widest room, no waste. Fintan Quinn could arrange a deal; a better price than the stores. If she orders now her carpets will be ready in September.

'You'd do well to lay carpets before you bring your furniture back from storage. Will I make an appointment?'

Carpets. Furniture.

That means she's staying. She's going to live here after all. Often, these days, she has the feeling that this isn't her home, that she's simply passing through. This is a stopping-off place on the way to somewhere else. A place where there is Amy, Conor and no one else. A perfect, blue-sky place.

Carpets, then. She confirms a time and a day with Moss.

'I need you below for a moment, if you don't mind. A surprise,' he says.

She walks down through the house with Moss, their feet echoing on the boards. She reads the movements of everyone in the house by sound. With carpets down she won't know where anyone is. By the time the carpets go down there will only be the three of them here.

Amy makes for the front door, Moss stops her.

'No need to go that way.' He points to the stairs that have been blocked off; daylight beams through the open doorway. There is the smell of fresh wet plaster and a roar like a jet engine. Moss takes her below. Huge heaters, fans behind wire mesh, blast hot air around the room. For months this has been a gaping wound at the back of the house. Now it's a room. It still needs a floor. Conor's floor.

'I want to be sure the plaster is dry by Monday. Keane's due first thing. Your kitchen's on its way.'

Amy feels a huge wave wash over her. Nostalgia for the temporariness in the face of encroaching permanence. The bare bones of the house are disappearing beneath new flesh. The spaces beneath floors, under stairs, behind walls, secret, potent places, will soon be out of reach, still there but locked away. Evidence of the months of work will settle in those spaces, untouched for years: fresh sawdust, a shiny nail, flakes of paint.

'And if you can bear with me another ten minutes, Amy, let's agree the snagging in the top of the house.'

He has a list. They go from room to room, checking: a faulty electric socket, escutcheon on the sash window, remove paint from marble fire surround. Each room requires at least one small adjustment.

'Innes Quinn wants no come-back from the client. It's more than my job's worth not to catch all of these, Amy.'

At the top of the house, in the new loft bathroom there's a man on all fours. He writes P I P E S, stretching the letters to make them reach the length of the bare board.

'Water can do more damage than fire,' says the plumber, as he rises, moves on to the next room. In Imogen's bedroom he does the same. He knows where all the pipes are, even though they are hidden. She stares at the word written in felt-tip pen on her bathroom floor, remembers the day she stood on that same spot, unsteady on the joists, feeling the updraft. That day, she could see through the whole house, right down to the deepest part of the basement.

The signal has faded. That's what's happened.

She's wary about Conor because she's lost contact. No word for nearly two weeks. In touch on a daily basis she knows what he thinks, what he feels. She can read the tone of his voice, the way he holds his shoulders. These signs confirm the mutuality.

'Don't look so worried, Amy,' says Moss, telling her a story about a woman who had cowboys in to lay a bedroom carpet.

'She sits below,' says Moss, 'feels water on her, warm water coming from above. She looks up: jets of steaming water at regular intervals where the pipes have been punctured.' Moss laughs. Blarney. True or a tease, it doesn't matter: it's the telling that counts.

New copper pipes run in the space between the floor and ceiling, holding in hot water to warm them. *Water can do more damage than fire.*

'Your phone, Amy. I think that's your phone.'

'Liz.'

'How are you today? You sounded, well, down, last night.'

'I'll survive.'

'You'll do more than that. Look, I'm sorry if I went on a bit, but that film – it's not real life you know.' Amy had met Liz from work yesterday for the early evening programme. The woman had a brief, passionate affair, then held on to the memory for forty years. A secret that her children discovered after her death.

'At least the girls know,' Liz had said over a drink afterwards.

The tension has eased since Amy's talked to Alice and Imogen. She's keeping a close eye on Alice; with Conor away, she's had time to catch up with her. Alice is a good person; is Maureen a vulnerable creature like Alice? Alice has kept up with assignments and course work, finding refuge with Jane. Amy read the environmental project which the two girls had done together. There was a section on nuclear energy, arguments for and against, with a picture, cut from a magazine, of a power station that might have been Dungeness. Amy read the notes that Alice had written next to it: *a series of controlled explosions* . . . If she and Conor could have a few controlled explosions this thing might work itself out.

'When is he back?' asks Liz.

'They fly on Saturday. I'll see him on Monday.'

'Counting the hours?'

'I don't know what to expect.'

'Two weeks with the loved ones. It could go either way. Whatever, it will have stacked up his guilt.'

'Liz, in the face of all evidence to the contrary, I can only think that something must come from this. It can't have happened for nothing. The strength of it.'

'Any number of things could come from it, but I doubt it will be the fairy tale you're hoping for.'

'I do try to be realistic.'

'You could be more, well, economical.'

'Economical?'

'Love in mid life, a married man? Messy, if you take the logical route. You're not twenty, looking to procreate. Have less of it. Eke it out.'

'I wish I knew what you meant,' says Amy.

'What worries me is that you're pure Hollywood. That woman in the film lived a fantasy for forty years. No relationship, not even a friendship keeps going with no contact, no context. It might go on in your head, but it's not real. Look, if you want Hollywood try this: "Why reach for the moon, Jerry, we have the stars." Bette Davies. Start thinking more stars than moon.'

'I know, I know. It's impossible.'

'It's easier for you to think there's a future. He has younger children, a wife. I don't doubt that his feelings for you are strong. If anything, he sounds deeper in than you. But he's rooted: family, a Catholic, being Irish. Roots that go deep, he'll have a hard time pulling them up, and if he does, then what?'

'You're racing ahead, Liz.'

'Maybe, but that's where your thoughts are. Don't deny it. You're crazy in love at the moment. When the magic wears off – as it will – you will have the full weight of his guilt. You know that in your head, your heart will catch up.'

'You make it sound so easy, as if I can work it all out in logical steps. Logic doesn't come into it.'

'You have more chance of keeping this man in your life if you let him stay with his family. Don't expect too much. You've got so much going for you. Anyway, enough of him. How are the girls?'

'Imogen goes at the weekend. Alice is still not sure if she wants to go away, I won't push her.'

'And are you ready for Muriel's committee?'

'Getting there.'

'I reckon you're in with a good chance.'

'I'm not so sure, they won't just hand over a contract.'

'I must go. Look, you make this exhibition a success and you could have a job in the new building.'

'That's what Muriel says. It's tempting.'

'You know, Amy, this falling in love is as much about *you* as it is about him. It's about you caring for yourself. Forget running off into the sunset. Don't blow the presentation. Not because of him.'

31

Heave

The floor is rising.

Amy tries to ignore it. She walks over to the corner of her new kitchen and it happens again; her foot catches, comes up against something. There is a bulge in the new wooden floor, in front of what Moss calls 'your larder'. It's not the word Amy would use to describe the proud cupboard that Conor has built. Larder, to Amy, recalls a dark room in her grandmother's house: cold, chalky walls, meat under nets, and a beaded muslin sagging over the milk jug. Conor has made a huge cupboard, floor to ceiling, with double doors that might be mistaken for the entrance to a room, but it's not possible to walk into this larder. He has cut a design in the door panels, long grooves each ending in a circle. The cast iron handles sit well on the warm green. She remembers the strip of brown paper laddered with Conor's colour samples. A memory from the other side of the divide.

Behind the green doors, on one side, there is a large fridge, on the other, a cupboard. Every time Amy goes to take something from the larder her foot catches. Moss had noticed it, too, this morning.

'Heave,' he had said. He wasn't happy. Innes Quinn will be here soon to assess the problem.

Heave is a word that comes with subsidence; a tell-tale sign of structural movement. There are no cracks in the newly plastered walls, but what else can make a brand new beech floor rise up into a mound? Surely the house can't move an inch. Innes Quinn had explained the underpinning process. Her house now stands on rigid pillars of concrete, poured into eight-foot shafts, deep into the ground. She walks down the steps to the lower basement in order to view the whole floor at eye level.

A ballroom of a space.

She sees her and Conor dancing on breeze blocks. Now, shiny new wood stretches, smooth as a pond, up to the French window. She had once watched Conor measuring the angle of the bay. No glass, no walls. A moment later he had surprised her, lifted her up because there were no stairs either. She turns her eye in the other direction, into the kitchen space. The mound is clearly visible. It's as if something is pushing its way through. A growth. An undesirable presence. Will she come down tomorrow and find the floor cracked open.

A live floor. Wood is unstable.

Conor will be called back to the house. Keane joinery finished working here a week ago. Now Moss will bring Conor back. Amy will have to meet him again, surrounded by the men, when she thought that was done with. Amy doesn't want to go through that again; the strain of the week when Conor was on site every day as first the floor was laid, and then the kitchen fitted. This is how she was forced to meet him for the first time after his holiday. She had spoken to him briefly on the phone the night before; without that call, meeting him with an audience would have been impossible. He'd called late on the Sunday morning. She had been in bed reading the papers.

'How are you?' His voice hesitant.

'Conor. You're back.' Silence. She wanted to ask how it had been. She wanted to know: what was it like being with Maureen for two weeks?

'How was your holiday?'

'The children enjoyed themselves.' He sounded flat, low. He was trying to say something. She was ready for it; ready for him to tell her that he had thought better of it, that once the house was done, well, that would be a natural break wouldn't it. She wished he would say it. Get it over with.

'Look, Conor . . .'

'I don't know what to say.'

Drowning. This was what it would feel like if she were drowning.

'You'll be finished here soon.' She would make it easy for him. 'If it would make things easier . . . I mean, after that . . .'

'I can't square the circle.'

'Don't try.' Yet how could it end, the potency was unexplored. End. They have hardly begun.

'I missed you so much,' he said.

'Me too.' Back to the surface. Air. Enough to carry on.

'I have to see you,' he said.

'I'll be here in the morning when you arrive with my floor.'

'Not like that.' He said he wanted to spend more time with her. He wanted to pay attention to what was happening between them. He couldn't exactly say when or how. Was there a way they could find more time to be together, relax, like the evening before he went away?

'I want to be with you, Amy.' She didn't tell him what she had come home to that night. One daughter on the streets, the other railing against her. She didn't tell him the price she paid for those few blissful hours.

'The job, the house confuses things,' he said. After his work on the house was done, they would talk. He couldn't take things further while he was working on the house.

Imogen would be away by the time Conor had finished but Alice might still be here. Amy will not put pressure on Alice to go away; she can't push Alice out of the house simply so that she can be with Conor. There was Liz's house. *Eke it out.* Not a fairy tale, not the moon. One more evening would be enough to be going on with. They would make love. Skin on skin. Conor deep inside her. Yes, this. But curling up on the sofa with a bottle of wine, talking, watching a movie. Lighting a fire. This would do, too. Not a fairy tale. A night in with a bottle of wine.

The next day Conor's men had arrived at eight with the wood for the floor. The site was busy. Both Quinn brothers were there. Conor was expected before ten. Amongst this activity, this was how she had seen him for the first time in two weeks. She had tried to work, sat at her desk, but she had left her door open.

'Good man, Keane.' She heard Moss greet him down in the hall.

She waited as long as she could.

He was talking to his men, checking the preparatory work.

They had marked the outer limits of the floor, laid a batten that marked the margins. Between that and the new plaster of the wall there was a gap, kept evenly spaced by small blocks of wood at regular intervals.

Your floor will float. A live floor needs to breathe.

'Double check, that expansion gap,' he was saying. 'Is it enough? Is it even the whole way round?' He had pulled the steel tape from its coil, crouched down to check, the fabric of his shirt tight against his back.

'Hello.' She had to see him, audience or not.

It had only been a moment, the look on his face: the slight smile, the depth of his eyes. A flood of warmth passed between them.

It wouldn't ever be possible to stop seeing each other.

He had stood up, and without uttering a word, he had said all that she needed to hear. Nothing had changed. The feeling, if anything, was stronger. It was the way he looked, the warmth and depth of his eyes, the slight movement of his shoulder: a hug stifled.

There had been no time to be alone with Conor while he and his men finished the kitchen. She had to get through this period of him working in the house. She had worked hard to distract herself, putting all her energy for Conor into her work. In the midst of everything, somehow, she managed to do the presentation at the museum. She performed well. Approving nods from Muriel throughout. Some tough questions from an intense young man in a collarless shirt, his hair tightly cropped. Who did she see as the audience? Would the gallery talks have the widest possible appeal? She had answered him, allayed his doubts. Any day now she will hear whether the exhibition has been confirmed into the programme for next year. If it has, she will begin work in earnest by September. There will be travel, studio visits.

Overnight stays.

'I want to spend some time with you, real time,' he had said, the day after the kitchen was finished. They had met briefly for coffee.

'I'll have the keys for a week.'

'Someone else's house?'

'She wouldn't mind.'

'You've told her?'

'She's my oldest, closest friend. I didn't need to tell her.' He clearly wasn't comfortable with the idea.

'Look, it's a suggestion. We can spend some time there and not be looking over our shoulders every five minutes. Only if you want to. No pressure.'

Liz had phoned last night, confirmed the dates. The week after next she could be with Conor in Liz's house. An evening, a night, whatever. A bottle of wine, curled up on the sofa. It could happen, which is why she doesn't want this set-back, this bulge in the floor tripping her up when she's come this far.

Conor back here. Working in her house again. It might take a week. Two. Unfit the kitchen, take up the floor. Put it all back together. Not to be contemplated. Conor would never come to Liz's if he was working on her house.

'It's not just that I'm a married man, Amy. Think of the way we met. Think how it will look if it comes out. Seducing the client, that's how the Quinns will see it. They'd finish me.'

Moss and Innes Quinn regard the bulge from all angles. They bounce on it, the balls of their feet pressing hard as if they might tread it back down.

'Weight distribution,' says Innes Quinn, confident that he's solved the problem. 'The fridge is taking all the weight of that larder cupboard to the one side. We need to distribute the weight evenly. It's a live floor. That fridge is not allowing for any movement.'

Amy watches. She knows what's coming next. Innes Quinn and Moss discuss what it is they will ask Keane to do.

'He'll remove the larder cupboard, let the floor relax, settle down.' Innes Quinn says he wants a solution to this right away.

'Upsetting for you Amy,' he says. 'Never had this happen before. Keane must find a way of distributing the weight of that cupboard. I'm surprised he hadn't taken account of it. The fridge was always going to make it heavier on the one side.'

'That'll be Keane now,' says Moss as door bell sounds. He'd called him early, caught him on the way back to the workshop.

Why hadn't Conor warned her he was on his way?

She tries not to look directly at him. They don't need her.

'Wait now, will you, Amy,' says Innes Quinn as she turns to go. 'We'll need you here if we've to decide how to dismantle your kitchen. Good job we left the temporary one in place.'

Conor considers the lump in the floor. On his hands and knees, he presses its centre. His hands work back along the boards.

'I'd say it was weight distribution,' says Innes Quinn, as if to save Conor the bother.

Conor doesn't say a word. He removes the kick-plate from the front of the larder cupboard, lies down so that his head is almost under it.

'I thought so,' he says, his arm reaching into the far corner, right under the cupboard. He pulls hard at something that won't give way.

'I have it,' he holds up a small block of wood.

One of the blocks which defined the expansion gap, left in by mistake.

'My error,' says Keane. 'There would be no movement possible on the corner there, with this wedge in the gap.'

'Not the cupboard?' Moss and Innes Quinn don't look so sure.

'Leave it awhile,' says Keane. 'We've caught it soon enough. No harm done. The floor will ease back.'

Relief spreads around them all. All except Conor. He's tense. Not looking at Amy.

'Mountain out of a molehill,' says Innes Quinn.

Nothing more serious than a wedge of wood in the expansion gap, removed with no more difficulty than taking a splinter from a finger. Like a splinter, a small problem, a large irritation. The house is still standing. The kitchen firmly fitted. The floor will float again.

'I'll call later to see how it is. I must go now.' He leaves with barely a glance towards Amy.

'I hope Keane's right,' says Innes Quinn.

'It could be a few days, before it settles down again,' says Moss.

'I'll be keeping an eye on it. I'll speak to Keane, have him back next week to check it. Don't worry, Amy.'

'Not like Keane to miss a detail,' says Innes Quinn.

* * *

'Amy.'

'Conor?' He calls only moments after Innes Quinn and Moss have left.

'I'm sorry about the floor.' It was a silly mistake. Not like him. He had wanted to do a good job for her, but he also wanted the job finished, to be out of her house.

'It will be fine, Amy.' The line breaks up. She can't hear what he's saying, every other word is deleted by gaps in transmission. He has to say it three times before she has the full sentence.

'About your friend's house. Us meeting there. I'm sorry, Amy . . .'

'It's OK, Conor, if you're not . . .'

'It's not that. I have to go to Ireland.'

'When?'

'Next week. I have to go. Caitlin has a date for her operation, I heard today, just before I came round. I couldn't say anything with everyone there.'

'How long for?'

'A week at most. I have to see her.'

He wants to arrive the night before she's admitted. He'll take her to the hospital in Dublin, then stay for as long as he can. Once she's discharged, she'll go down to the family in Cork.

'Of course, you must go.'

'Come with me, Amy.'

'What?'

'Come with me.'

'Conor, what are you saying?'

'Be with me in Dublin.' He's talking fast, he's upset. He's not clear about any of it. He will see how things are when he gets there, see what's possible. If it's halfway possible he will phone her.

'I need to see you, be with you. Away. Away from the Quinns, the house and all. Out of London.' A rare chance, he's seizing it.

'You will come, won't you?'

32

Flight

Amy turns the souvenir tin tray round. *Dublin's best loved meeting place for over a century: lovers, poets, politicians from near and far*, say the white words printed on its rim. She studies the picture: the mosaic façade with BEWLEY'S ORIENTAL CAFE in gold letters; a woman, in a cloche hat and fur-trimmed coat, leads a child through the wide entrance; a man on a bicycle, wearing a bowler hat, is frozen in the moment he rides past. No furtive lovers in this idealised scene. She puts the tray back on the shelf. She can't take home a souvenir from somewhere she's not supposed to have been.

A group of nuns passes behind Amy, taking the dark wooden stairs to a function on one of the upper floors. The place is packed; the height of lunchtime busyness. Conor had said to find a table on the mezzanine. She turns away from the smiling nuns, looks again at the stacks of tea and coffee in red, yellow and green packets, as if she is like any other visitor. Conor will be collecting the car, calling in on Caitlin. The mingling smells of fresh coffee, buttery pastries, melting cheese are hard to ignore. She looks up to the mezzanine. She could sit there and see him coming, but she couldn't eat a thing even though she's light-headed. It's more from lack of sleep than hunger.

At 2.00 a.m. as she had sat at her desk, tracing her finger back and forth along the spiral curve of Conor's bowl, wishing she had a photograph of him, the telephone had rung. A shocking sound. She had let it ring, afraid to answer. Bad news. Imogen or Alice. Imogen had called from Barcelona only the day before.

She and Maxine were having a great time. Was this the Spanish
authorities? Surely at this time of night Alice would be fast asleep;
safe as houses in Yorkshire. Amy had driven Alice and Jane up
there on Sunday.

Somebody, somewhere wants this to come right. Why else
would she be here in the heart of Dublin. It is meant to be. This
is what she's told herself ever since she answered the phone in
the early hours and heard Conor's voice.

'Did I wake you?'

'Conor?'

'I'm sorry to call at this ungodly hour. I had to talk to you.'

'No, no, I was awake, couldn't sleep.'

'Me neither.'

'How's Caitlin. Is Caitlin all right?'

'She's grand. Putting the world to rights from her hospital bed.'

'Are you all right?'

'I'll feel better for seeing you, Amy. Could you get a flight here
tomorrow sometime, or the next day?'

Caitlin had been delighted to have Conor take her into hospital,
to sit with her the day she was admitted. They had talked all
afternoon. She was scared. She wanted it over with. She might
never have planned to have children, but not having a choice
now felt too final. She had wept. Conor had never seen her
that way. The operation had been straightforward, with none
of the possible complications. Once she'd come round from the
anaesthetic she was ordering everyone around as only Caitlin
could. Conor has been at the hospital each day. It didn't take
Caitlin long to see how preoccupied her brother was.

'Can't hide anything from her,' he laughed. 'She reads my
mind.' He'd tried to brush it off, said it was pressure of work,
business worries. He knew she wasn't buying that, so he'd told
her about making the bowl, making things again the way he used
to, how he wished he had more time for that kind of work. Caitlin
kept on digging. In the end he told her about Amy.

He has the keys to Caitlin's cottage. They could have two days
at most.

'Amy, I want you to come more than anything, but . . .'

'What?'

'It's hard to say.'

'Try.'
'I'm scared, Amy.'
'I know.'
'Scared.'
'What of?'
'Most of it. All of it.'

Amy could not think of getting back into bed. She had packed a few things: jeans, a sweater, a dress, the new underwear. *Two days at the most.* A light bag, she didn't want to be weighed down. It was bound to rain; she found her folding umbrella. She looked up the telephone numbers of the airlines. She had even called one; an answering machine told her that the lines opened at 7.30 a.m. for bookings on all flights, subject to availability. Please let there be a seat. If she was going, it would have to be on the first flight. If she stopped for a moment, if she slept on it, gave it any rational thought she would lose her nerve. Two days with Conor. Alone.

It was after three when she ran a bath, shaved her legs. *A temporary psychosis.* 'I must be certifiable,' she'd said out loud to the fish on the bathroom tiles as they gaped up at the lily pads. She ran the water as hot as she could stand it and in the steamy heat she calmed down. Afterwards, down in the kitchen in the dark, with only the light of the fridge, she heated milk, laced it with brandy. Two days with Conor, she couldn't believe it would happen. She thought of the things that might yet delay her. A call from one of the girls, no seats on the Dublin flight. Touch wood. She wiped milk from the wooden surface. Conor was in the fabric of her house, the roof timbers, the floor, this work surface, the iron handles, the etched glass in the cupboard above her head. Conor was in the details. In the half-light she thought she saw the floor rising again. A fine crack had appeared in the wall. 'Settling will occur.' So they keep telling her, Moss and the Quinns; a house is never still, there are stresses and strains. The new plaster will crack.

Around four she lay on the bed, dozed. It was six when she stirred, the sun was strong; another hot day. She ordered a taxi. She was in no state to drive and anyway there wasn't time. She would be in Ireland before lunchtime. She would phone Conor from Heathrow, let him sleep.

Inside the terminal she had queued for her ticket in a line of men with laptops and mobile phones. She wandered round the shops, bought a packet of tissues, a morning paper, changed money at the bank. She found a phone. She had two calls to make.

'Liz.'

'Amy? What time is it?'

'Sorry to wake you. I'm at Heathrow.'

'What?'

'I won't be able to collect your keys tomorrow. I won't be able to house sit. I'm waiting to board the Dublin flight.' And wondering if she wasn't making a dreadful mistake. Amy spoke quickly, filling Liz in on Conor's call, Caitlin, the cottage.

'Amy, you've got this far. Get on that plane. But don't expect anything beyond two days in Ireland. Think stars rather than moon. Don't even consider the possibility of a sunset.'

With the next call she had to dial twice before she made a connection. He had given her the number of his hotel, but she preferred to call the mobile. She didn't want to go through a receptionist. This is how it is. She, Amy, cannot exist, must remain invisible. Conor and Amy exist only in the pockets of time and space which can be slipped into, unnoticed. Forgotten places. The voids beneath the floor boards, under the stairs, the expansion gap around the wooden floor, eking out the moments, tucking in time together wherever it will fit.

'Conor.'

'Amy?' his voice thick with sleep.

'I'm at Heathrow.'

He had said nothing for what seemed like days. He hadn't meant it. An aberration in the small hours. Drunk. He doesn't know what she's talking about. She imagined it; he hadn't rung her. What does it matter, the price of a flight to Dublin. Her pride.

'What time do you land?' He would hire a car. He couldn't say how long it would take and he would need to call in on Caitlin at the hospital. Amy must take a taxi from the airport, meet him at Bewley's in Grafton Street. The taxi would drop her by the gates of Trinity College. Grafton Street was pedestrian only, if she walked on for a few hundred yards, it was on the right.

'Be sure to say the Bewley's in Grafton Street.'

Amy has never been to Ireland before. Bewley's. Grafton Street. Trinity College. A litany of names she's only known in fiction, history or the songs of Van Morrison. Perhaps this isn't really happening; somehow she's got caught up in the lyrics.

She had expected grey clouds and rain, but the sky remained clear all the way. The midday sun was fierce; it might have been Athens. Had she caught the right plane. To make sure, she read the letters on the terminal building: DUBLIN. *BAILE ÁTHA CLIATH*.

'The heat. You'd not be expecting it,' said the taxi driver. A drought in London, so they say. He had lived there himself, five years. Putney. Bar work. Did she live near Putney? North London. Nice. Holiday was it or business? It could break any day now. They're giving rain by Thursday. He didn't require answers. She handed him a twenty-punt note, not waiting for the change. Conor would not be at Bewley's yet. The journey from the airport had been quicker than she'd expected. She might have to wait an hour or so. She had walked through the arch into the cobbled quad of Trinity, Caitlin's world. This is where she spends her days. Somewhere close by is Caitlin's study. If Amy had known where, she would have taken a look, peeped into the life of this woman who was elsewhere in the city today. This woman who was annoyed because she hadn't quite finished her fourth book before she'd been called to the hospital. Contemporary Irish women poets. The cobbled quad was busy with American tourists, the odd bicycle resting against the chain fence round Library Square. In term time, it would look different. Busier, messier, filled with intense young people.

Amy puts the change in her purse. Irish money mingling with English. She will sort it out later. She has bought the green packet of coffee, medium roast. They will need coffee.

'Amy,' she jumps at the sound of her name.

They face each other. Say nothing, do nothing.

What have we done?

He touches her arm, kisses her cheek gently.

'Let's get out of here,' he says. The car is by the bus station. They walk across the Liffey, traffic streaming up O'Connell Street, the pavements are crowded with tourists. It's a bonus for everyone to see Dublin sun-soaked. He walks fractionally ahead of her, his back stiff with tension.

She wants to say: I thought you didn't know anyone in Dublin. This couldn't have happened if Caitlin had had her operation in Cork. Cork city is full of his relatives, friends, friends of friends. It wouldn't be possible to walk through the streets of Cork with Conor. Of course he would be uncomfortable, tense, but his distance unnerves her.

'Guilt. Do not underestimate it. He may triumph occasionally but he will never quite make it.' The awful accuracy of Liz's words.

'If you've had second thoughts, say so.' She manages this much as he puts her bag into the boot of the hire car.

He says nothing.

'Let's get on the road.'

He's all concentration as they work their way out of Dublin, past Phoenix Park, the zoo, till they join the road to Limerick. Clear of the city they are on a stretch of fast road. Conor drives steadily.

'Relax,' says Amy.

'Yes,' it's more of a sigh than a whole word.

Ahead the sky is thickening. Further on, clouds hang lower still. The other side of Portlaoise the rain starts. A soft, fine rain that covers the landscape. She could be anywhere. They stop at a roadside pub, newly whitewashed, its window frames bright blue. They order cheese and soda bread and a half pint of Guinness each. The thick black liquid fills her; she won't need to eat for days.

'I'll feel better once we're there,' says Conor. 'I'm glad you're here, but I can't pretend it's easy.'

Most of the journey passes in a grey haze of rain and the silence they have settled on. They travel through villages where the houses are the colour of sugared almonds: pink, green, yellow, lilac. Conor is deep in his own thoughts. He wants and he does not want. They might be away from London with a stretch of water between them, but Maureen is here, in every blade of grass, every bare rock, every drop of rain on the wind-screen.

At the last small town before taking the coast road to Caitlin's place they stop at a general store.

'Milk,' says Conor. Amy watches him through the open door as he pays for bread, milk, eggs, cheese, four bottles of wine.

They take the road along the peninsula. There are fewer and fewer houses: the ruin of a stone cottage, the occasional new bungalow, a barn stacked with hay, more hay outside wrapped in black plastic. Then nothing but rocks, scant grass, heather, hills on one side, water on the other. In the middle of nowhere a pile of freshly cut peat. Rich brown blocks, like giant squares of chocolate. The rain has stopped, the sky clears. A lowering sun streaks what is left of the clouds, pink and yellow, as they hug the bald hills.

'Almost there,' he says, and smiles properly for the first time. On either side of the road the hedgerows are thick: fuchsia, honeysuckle, blackberries. Further on, the road rises and nar-rows, hedgerows give way to steep rock on either side. Once they are through this short gorge, the rock falls away, and the road starts to dip again. Amy sees the bay spread below. Conor pulls over to let her take in the view. A ragged coastline gives way, at the farthest end, to a crescent of sand. Beyond the beach, a rise of rocky hills. Directly below there are green fields, dotted with the yellow of gorse. A lone white horse nibbles grass. There is a small white house with a grey roof. Washing blows on the line; children play in the field.

'Holiday let,' says Conor. 'That's Caitlin's place, over there.' Another small, whitewashed house on a rise. It faces the sea. Nothing but green fields around it. It must be still half a mile away. Amy can't imagine how they will get there. They sweep past the field with the horse; the road becomes a track as it curves along the rocky shore. Ahead there is the ruin of a stone cottage and just beyond it, the track forks, one arm of it bends inland. The track to Caitlin's house. Poles march back the way they have come, carrying a slack wire between them.

Gravel surrounds the house, the tyres crunch to a halt. Amy opens the car door on stillness. The warm stillness of early evening. The smell of the sea.

33

The White House

Eyes heavy, her head more in sleep than out, Amy slides her arm across the bed. She knows that he's not there. The heat of him has gone. It could be any morning because Amy's first thought on waking is always of Conor. Before she starts each day, she conjures him. A real moment recalled slowly, turning over a phrase of his, magnifying the way his lips part when he kisses her. Some days she makes things up, how it will be. She invents moments that may or may not happen.

The muffled sound of a radio travels up from below. The smell of coffee and toast reaches her, coaxes her to wakefulness. She is hungry, hungry, hungry. Today, she could call Conor's name and he would come. He is here with her, in a white house with a blue door, miles from anywhere, by the sea. He is downstairs in the kitchen, she can hear the rattle of cups; the blue-and-white cups that hang from hooks on the dresser. It is him, really him, not the usual morning phantom. She can feel the fullness of him deep inside her.

Yesterday they had brought their bags in from the car, awkward, falling over each other in the square entrance, treading clumsily on Caitlin's post. Conor had gathered the letters into a neat pile, placed them on the foot of the stairs that rose straight behind them, cutting the house in two. To one side of the stairs was a sitting room, to the other a kitchen. Amy had wandered into the sitting room. There was a window at each end. The front window had a clear view across the fields and down to the bay.

The back window was filled with the rocky hills. Inside, it was more lived-in, more like a home than she'd imagined. Caitlin's books lined the walls and sat in piles where she left them on the wooden floor: poetry, criticism, philosophy. A thick rug, patterned with bright abstract shapes, filled the centre of the room. A large wooden bowl sat in the hearth of the stone fireplace and two smaller wooden bowls on the windowsill; all of them carved from green timber, the cracks producing subtle shifts in the rim or the sides. Conor's work.

'Here, give me that,' Conor had taken the bag she was still holding. She could hear his tread on the stairs, then above her head. How many times have they been together in the company of Moss, the Quinns, Desmond, Liam, with no other thought than to reach out and touch one another. Now, here they were, alone. Yet when Conor had come back down, they faced each other in silence. She had felt the heat in her neck. Conor's colour heightened, and he looked away as if watching for someone out of the window. A bashful turn of the head while his face burned. She knew her neck would be covered in blotches. She waited for him to face her again, wishing it were later, darker, and that she were ten pounds lighter. She cannot pretend to have the body of a twenty-year-old.

'You look tired,' she had said, to break the silence.

'It's a long drive.'

Amy was suddenly tired, too; the lack of sleep, the early start, the drive through an unfamiliar landscape.

'Here, make yourself comfortable.' She sat on the far end of the sofa and picked up books from a pile on the floor. Though she read the title on its spine she could not say what it was.

'Drink?'

'Please.'

She heard the pock of the cork from the kitchen across the hall. A room she had not been in, though she'd noticed its stone floor.

Conor joined her, sitting at the other end of the sofa. They sipped the red wine.

'Where's the bathroom?' She was crumpled from sitting on the plane, in the car; sweaty from the morning heat. He led her up the steep stairs. The bathroom was above the kitchen.

'Your bag is in there,' he pointed to the bedroom opposite.

She relaxed in the warm flow of the shower, washing herself with Caitlin's soap and shampoo. In the bedroom, she used Caitlin's hair dryer, sitting on the double bed. There were more books, mainly fiction: classics, thrillers, new hardbacks. Caitlin's clothes hung on a metal rail in the corner, a jumble of thick, colourful sweaters and a handful of summer frocks; a strong, not unwelcome, presence.

Conor had been busy down below. The table in the kitchen was set for two, he was breaking eggs into a glass bowl.

'The best I can do in the circumstances.' He was easier, smiling, another glass of wine inside him. A buttery smell rose from the pan, the tap, tap, tap of the fork on the bowl. He filled her glass.

'You'll have to imagine the salad,' he laughed, placing the omelette before her. She was weak from the lack of food, the wine made her hungrier. She wanted to say: tell me a story, tell me who you are. Reading her thoughts, not for the first time, he obliged. This was very like the house that his grandmother had lived in, further on from here, the other side of Bantry. He'd spent each summer there until he was twelve. He, Caitlin and another brother and sister were sent for the school holidays. Gran shooed them out of the house most days. They would climb up to the standing stones, Caitlin making offerings to the fairies. When they were older, that's where they hid their cigarettes. When Gran shouted them in Caitlin would make them all hide in the fuchsia listening to her call, Conor ready to give them up, not wanting to make the old woman cross. Caitlin shushing him. 'Wait, now, Conor. Wait.' Longer and longer she would leave it, timing it to the split second, knowing the moment when they would have gone too far. 'Here, Gran. We're coming.'

Along the track from the standing stones a new property was being built, a bungalow that would have a wide sheet of glass for a window. When the men didn't turn up one day, Caitlin picked her way through the heaps of bricks. She found a ladder and set it against the new timbers. There was half a roof on, no ceilings. They could climb right up to the roof timbers, sit astride the apex.

'What is it?' Conor had stopped mid tale, shrugged.

'You don't want to hear all this.'

'Yes I do. Go on.'

Caitlin had gone tearing ahead, agile, legs swinging over the beams, up she went, no fear.

'I froze at the foot of the ladder, totally lost it.' Caitlin called to him. 'Look at me Conor. Keep looking at me.' She had willed him up there, her eyes never blinking, never letting go of him. Always the strong one. It had shocked him to see her weep the day before the operation. 'I've never seen her like that.'

In her day-dreams, Amy had imagined Conor's naked body many times. She had spent hours thinking about it, piecing the bits together from clues, glimpses through garments: the thigh muscle tight against denim as he sat in the car, the strong back, stretching to measure, the freckles seen on a hot day, shirt neck open. How many times has she unbuttoned Conor's shirt in her head. She can't remember how they got there. They had left the kitchen, taken the wine up to the bedroom and she had peeled back his shirt. The utter joy of seeing him naked for the first time, of feeling skin on skin, the length of their bodies, her breasts dissolving into him, toe touching toe. To know every inch of his skin, if this is all the time she has with him, she wants to know his skin, how it feels on hers, what it tastes like.

'Coffee?'

Conor stands in the doorway wearing only his jeans.

'This may be breakfast, it may be lunch. You decide.'

'What time is it?'

'Never mind. Here, move over.'

Casting off his jeans, he climbs in beside her. They pile up pillows, drink coffee and eat toast. Amy could eat the duvet. So hungry.

'Hungry? I could take you for lunch at Casey's,' he laughs. Gran would take them once each summer to Casey's Hotel where the tables were set with white linen and silver plate.

'Soup spoons the size of ladles. We used to put them to our faces, you could magnify your eye.' They always sat at the same table. Conor and Caitlin faced the kitchen door where the girl in a black dress and white apron brought out the greasy slices of beef or pork. Conor and Caitlin watched the door as it swung back; there was just time to see the twist of yellow fly paper stuck with corpses. They would pick carefully at the currant pudding. Casey's was long gone. There's a new restaurant there now, an hour's drive from here, and at this time of year it's booked up a week ahead with tourists.

In the shower, Amy soaps Conor's back; thousands of freckles. She must remember them all.

'Wait,' she says as he tries to turn around. 'I'm learning your back.'

It's late afternoon when they leave the cottage to walk down to the sandy bay.

Amy kicks off her shoes and puts a toe in the water.

'It's warmer than it looks.'

'Gulf stream, want to swim?'

'Tomorrow maybe,' she laughs. They walk along the bay, easy, arm in arm. There is no sound other than the breeze in her hair, the lapping of water on stones.

Up on the headland Amy scans the view, tries to see how far they have come. Caitlin's house is a white dot amongst green. She cannot have come all this way for nothing. They cannot have come this far only to return, slip back into their other lives. There must be a way out of here, a road they can take, a place where these other selves could live a life that is surely meant to be.

Waking in the night, Amy had watched Conor breathe, his chest rising and falling, the warm weight of him next to her. Talking, laughing, making love all afternoon. It makes perfect sense. How can they go back and live the wrong lives?

The Atlantic swells and lifts, spray flying high from the rocks. They could take a boat across the water. *Your floor will float.* Make a raft of her new beech floor.

Over the headland is an old mine shaft, fenced off. A young sheep, caught behind the wire, can't find its way back to its mother.

'Let's go,' says Amy. She doesn't want to hear the anxious bleats of mother to child, child to mother.

*   *   *

Amy has produced a meal from what she found in Caitlin's freezer, and cupboard.

'Ready,' she calls Conor. 'Hors d'oeuvre.' She offers him smoked oysters that came from a can. She's arranged them on water biscuits.

'Not quite the real thing.'

'No R in the month, anyway.'

Amy lights a candle that she found in the table drawer.

'Better than Casey's hotel produced in three generations.' Conor laughs.

In the oven, parcels of tin foil contain fish from the freezer. For dessert there is ice cream to go with the blackberries they picked from the hedge along the lane.

'Conor,' she doesn't want to say this, to break the spell, but she wants to prepare herself. 'How long have we got tomorrow?'

He's quiet, head down. That look passes over his face. A look she has seen before: in the meeting with Moss, in the boat at Dungeness, as they walked along the shore earlier. Now, in the candlelight, it seems more intense, as if, in the flickering half-light he's safe to give it the fullest expression. If only she could transcribe that look, write the full detail of what he says with his face, she would have it, to keep.

'We must leave early.' There's family arriving from Cork. Conor will have to put an appearance in at the hospital by the end of the day.

'An early start, then.'

'Tomorrow's another day. Here, fill your glass.'

'Conor, whatever happens . . .'

'Sh. Here and now. Don't let's waste it.'

'Sorry.'

'Here and now, Amy. I've never felt so good.'

34

Appointments

Conor drives around the block again hoping there'll be a meter free the next time round.

He had tried not to let it happen. God knows he had tried. The genie will not go back in the bottle.

'There's no going back once some things are done,' he had said to Caitlin in her hospital bed.

'What's stopping you. What are you afraid of – that you might be happy?'

'It's not that easy.'

'Most things worth having don't come easy. Sounds to me like you've held back long enough.' When she offered him the cottage keys she said: 'For Jesus's sake, get it out of your system, or move on to the next step.'

Back in London for over a week now, Conor had seen Amy briefly, a hurried half hour in a crowded café and neither of them could say what the next step might be. He's telephoned her every day. He doesn't even have to see her; her voice on the phone for five minutes can do it. She's certainly not out of his system. Stores of energy lying dormant within him; think what he'll have to produce to spend the energy she's tapped. He imagines all the wood he will have to cut, carve, shape, to fill up the space that will be left if he can't have Amy in his life.

'Whoever she is, she knows who you are.' He didn't have long with Caitlin once Amy had left, but it was long enough.

'What do you mean?'

'You look like you. More like you than I've seen in a long while. She knows what's in you, sees your potential. Not to find out what you're capable of, not to know what you have in you, Conor, isn't that approaching the level of sin? What do you think keeps me teaching year in year out?'

'To put that before my children?'

'You'll still be their father.'

'It won't be the same.'

'Yours won't be the first marriage to end, nor the last.'

'Think of the pain it will cause.'

'Think of what a better father you might be, living a life that's true to yourself. What kind of message are they getting anyway, watching you in this emotional neutral you call living. It's not a rehearsal, Conor.'

He's missed that one. A woman in a Volvo is already reversing into the space by the time he sees it. Round the block again. He will be late.

'Maureen is good. A good person, a good friend.'

'Is friend enough?' He would have said yes, before Amy. He wouldn't expect Caitlin to understand about companionship, compromise. Caitlin and compromise don't go easily together. And Caitlin had said things she'd said before in many ways but never so starkly, so head on: Maureen is safe. Maureen confirms what you already know about yourself. Maureen is where you came from. With Amy, where might he go? This makes it hard. He knows that with Amy he would move on, do what he's ready to do. This is why it is so strong between them. They each know who they are, it's not as if they have fallen for some youthful imagining of what they might become. How he is with her is not the dream of a twenty-year-old.

Barely half an hour he's been in Amy's company since they returned from Ireland but it's enough to know that he's not ready to say he'll never see her again.

'A complete break Conor,' Amy had said, as they discussed the possibilities. To live the rest of his life unable ever again to touch her hair, the soft waves that lift and surround her face. Never again to watch the fine lines gather around her eyes as she smiles. Never again to reach between the sheets, feel her toes and the warm press of her thigh.

'I'm confused, Amy.'

'There's no hurry.'

He was hoping she would have an answer. Maybe she has looked at the tangle and seen a way to unravel it that he, in his confusion, has missed.

'There aren't many choices are there?' She had been calm: end it now, agree never to see each other again, ever, or, run off into the sunset and bring the house down. Neither of these will do. Isn't there somewhere between the two extremes?

'Conor, the only thing we could do right away would be to end it. To say there's no way through.'

'That's not what I want.'

'No, but it may be what you decide you have to live with. And anything else will need time.'

Today they will meet to decide if this is the end. If it is to end it would have to be soon, swift. No more contact. What scares him most is that either would be an appropriate choice. A low-key life with Maureen, loving his children. Would living with Maureen be the wrong life? Not so much the wrong life as not quite the right one. He's more certain of his feelings for Amy than anything, but certainty of feelings doesn't bring with it the certainty of how to act. Four young lives that he and Maureen created. All the love in the world that he feels for Amy cannot alter that fact. If he walked out tomorrow to be with Amy that fact would remain. He can't fault Maureen, he can't be angry with her. A good person. Maureen preparing lessons for her classes; Maureen gripping his arm in the night, the cramps and the stain on the sheet for a second, third time; the pure joy on her face when Kevin was born.

'Is Aunt Caitlin going to die?' It had been late when he arrived back from Dublin. Maura had stayed awake, determined to see him.

'What makes you think such a thing?'

'Because you went away without us for all those days.'

'Caitlin's grand.'

'Are you going away again?' He kissed the warm softness of her cheek, pulled the cover to her chin.

'Say good night to Teddy.' She offered him the stained, crumpled bear.

'Good night. Sleep now, it's late.'

In five years Kevin would be at university, but Michael, Clare and Maura would still be at school. If he waited until Maura was sixteen, that's thirteen years.

'There's no hurry,' he hangs on to Amy's words. The only thing they could do in a hurry, she said, was to end it. Anything else would take time. Thirteen years. He couldn't ask that of her. Thirteen years of snatched phone calls, a lunch here and very few nights together. It's not enough.

He drives past Oscar's to see if Amy has arrived. It's hot again. The glass panels have been folded back, tables spill onto the pavement. She's not there. He'll maybe risk parking on the single yellow line.

If it wasn't the end, that meant carrying on in some way. A double life. What could he manage? For now, Maureen was still putting down his preoccupied state to Caitlin.

'You know Conor, she would never have had children, not now, not at her age,' Maureen had said, as Conor sat lost in himself, watching some New York cop series which he could barely follow because running through his head was the thought of leaving his own children. It's not like the quarterly figures, the VAT return, which come right in the end. Four young lives, changed. And Maureen had carried on, not really looking at Conor because she was concentrating on sewing name tapes into Michael's new PE kit.

'It's not what she wanted from life. Though, I'll grant her this, it must be hard to know you never will.' And he could tell by the way her mouth tightened, she was remembering the time when it looked as if she would have none. The sudden bleeds. Lying in bed for three weeks and still not holding it. She's said many times: they are a gift. She could never take them for granted because she nearly didn't have them. And that's what he would be doing. Taking them for granted. Taking as read that they would be all right if he no longer lived under the same roof; taking it for granted that their lives would not be the worse for it.

*   *   *

He's reversing into the space when the phone rings.

'Conor?'

'Maureen, what is it?'

'The letter came in the second post.'

He's no idea what she's talking about.

'The appointment.'

He turns the wheel full lock, eases out the clutch, touches the bumper of the car behind.

'Conor are you there? Can you hear me.' The line breaks up.

'I'm parking the car. I'll call you back' A black cab toots its horn. Conor's front end is still in the road. He'll have to go out and come in again. The angle is all wrong. And he's wracking his brains to think what appointment Maureen is referring to. He knows he should know.

Since Ireland he's felt a strange distance from Maureen but he can't think ill of her. He wants to be more helpful, more reasonable, to listen to what she's saying. Maureen is a loyal friend.

'Sorry, I was parking the car.'

'Gerry said you were out for the afternoon.' Conor says nothing. He won't answer the question implied by her statement. He won't lie unless forced to.

'The appointment, you said it had come.'

'The orthodontist, for Michael.'

'Good, good.'

'Well it clashes with Clare's dancing exam. I can't be in two places at once. It's late afternoon so Kevin could have Maura, but really Conor could you go with Michael?'

'When did you say it was?'

'Monday.'

'That'll be OK. I'll take him, don't worry. I must go now.' Taking the children for granted would hurt Maureen as much, more maybe, than her own sense of betrayal. Five, seven, ten years, what was the most he could ask? If he saw Maura into secondary school that would still be eight years.

He feeds the greedy meter, two hours. Not enough. He fills it up for the full four.

35

Oysters

Amy doesn't want to arrive at Oscar's before Conor. She looks in each shop window: delicatessen, exclusive furnishing fabrics, second-hand books. In amongst these recent enterprises there survives an old-fashioned hardware store. The pavement is stacked with goods. A dustbin. A barrel of galvanised zinc with ribbed sides and a tight-fitting rubber lid. She needs a dustbin now that the skip has gone. Amy has grown accustomed to the giant litter bin outside her house. Whatever household rubbish she had soon disappeared, crushed beneath rubble and clay. Getting rid of things, up to now, has been simply a matter of opening the front gate and aiming well.

Inside the shop it is cool, dark, a refuge. A small electric kettle catches her eye. Perfect for Imogen to use in her own room. She can't buy a dustbin and a kettle and turn up for lunch with Conor. It comes upon her suddenly. An alien thought: she doesn't want to meet him. She's hanging back. She wants to go home. She doesn't want to sit across the table, eating lunch, drinking and then. Then what? One last frantic grope in the car. Or will it be dignified, shake hands, say goodbye standing on the pavement, walking to their own cars, to cry quietly before returning to their real lives.

Further back in the shop, amongst the cleaning materials, she finds firelighters. A black box with an illustration showing yellow flames rising from beneath the coals. *Keep away from children. If swallowed seek medical advice.* On the back, another illustration shows three easy steps to light a fire. *When not in use, store away from direct heat and all other sources of ignition.*

Why not leave it as it is. She saw him briefly last week. She saw how it was for him, the confusion. She could go home now. She would like to buy the kettle for Imogen. Amy's happy for Imogen to create her own world up in her new room. Since coming back from her travels, Imogen is altogether a nicer person; still keeping her distance but easier to be with. She's planning a party. Amy's never seen Imogen so enthusiastic.

'And Desmond? Is he coming?'

'He's history.'

Nothing can touch the memory of those hours at Caitlin's house, their day at Dungeness, their meetings here and there in cafés. Perfectly formed, blissful moments. She's hoarding the memories, preserving them, like jam, for the winter. She will go home now. It will be best for everyone. They will recover.

There is something about his stride that is unmistakable. She sees him as he's almost at Oscar's. A black cab with its one yellow eye, comes into view, blocking Conor for a moment. If she raises her hand now, now, it will scoop her up, take her away from here. A young waiter in black jeans and T-shirt directs Conor to a table. The waiter points. Inside or out? Conor is speaking. He will be saying her name. He will be telling the man that there is a table booked in her name. She telephoned yesterday. She asked for a table inside. And though it is unlikely that Maureen will be in this part of London, at this time of day (Amy has assumed this, she has not confirmed it with Conor), and though it would be lovely to sit outside in the sun, she asked for a table inside, in the far corner. And as she watches Conor with the waiter she thinks: he's better than I remember. The shock of seeing him quickens her pace.

The same waiter leads Amy to the table in the corner. A small, round table. She doesn't want to sit opposite Conor, she wants them to sit side by side, to feel the heat of him. The waiter rearranges the settings. When he's done this, he places a small dish of olives in the centre; shiny black olives lifted from a herb-soaked brine. He brings a basket of fresh bread rolls.

Conor squeezes her arm. A light kiss, not quite on the mouth.

'Sorry I'm late,' says Amy

'I'm only just here myself. Drink?'

'Are we celebrating?'

Conor says nothing. A look passes over his face. The look she has seen before, the one she is trying to transcribe. If she could do that, she would have it all in words. She has seen it before: in the boat at Dungeness, on the beach in Ireland, in the candlelight of Caitlin's kitchen and again, as he helped her into a taxi on a busy Dublin street. The eyes are deep, knowing. It's as if he is standing further away, regarding her from a distance, even though he is inches from her. The set of his mouth is not tight, but closed, resigned. There is a pulling in of the brow. Different levels of tension in the facial muscles. These words do not say the same things as his face. It's extraordinary how much knowledge is beyond language. Still she tries. The eyes tell her that his connection to her is at the deepest level. It baffles him. Connected in every sense: physical, emotional, intellectual. Who could say which came first and which is the strongest. An unbreakable bond, even if they never meet again. The eyes, the brow, the set of the mouth. It cannot be put into words. None of these words say exactly what his face says. She will have to commit that look to memory, learn how to conjure it when she needs to know it again, remember what it says.

'Sorry,' she says. It was a silly remark, because either way it was hardly a cause for celebration.

The young man in black brings the day's menu.

'Look,' says Conor, 'they have Irish Oysters.'

'Lovely.'

'Will I ask to see their passports?' They try to laugh. Their knees touch underneath the white linen. Conor's hand finds her thigh, a gentle squeeze.

Unbreakable.

She tells him about the contract that came from the museum. She'll be travelling around the country between now and Christmas. The exhibition is scheduled for this time next year. The carpets are confirmed for the week after next. Roy and his men will deliver her possessions from storage shortly after.

This is better than nothing. They could do this once a month, twice a year. She wants to say: don't say never again, don't doubt me. *I'm afraid your passion for me will soon die. I'm afraid I can't offer you enough.* Fears he revealed when they met last week.

Don't be afraid. This is enough. This meal, the table, a drink, an island in the middle of a day. Even as she enjoys the present, a part of her is preparing for the future. The moment when she will have to step out of the car and not know if she will ever see him again. If they agree today to stop this, there will always be the possibility of a chance meeting. It could happen. Shopping with Maureen and the children. Or maybe, like her, he will go sometimes to the places they have been together.

'Conor, I need to . . .'

'Later,' he refills her glass, brushes her cheek. Conor talks easily about most things, the flow of his words, the sound of his voice, isn't this what enchants her? But saying 'never again' is not a thing that will come easily nor will arranging a double life. He responds intuitively, the brush of his hand on her cheek, the tenderness of his body next to her. To put it into words, to name it and talk of practicalities of meetings and times and futures is perhaps more than she can reasonably expect of him.

You're not twenty. Eke it out.

She thinks of living with the burden of his guilt. Another kind of look on his face, the pain of hurting Maureen, of walking away from his responsibilities. Amy would like to say: is there not also a responsibility to act on the truth of these feelings? They are not twenty, they know who they are. Each knows their own strengths and weaknesses. This makes it worse. They know who they are and she could spend the rest of her life with this man.

In Ireland there had been enough space, all the space they could ever need. A cavernous space. Here, there is no real space. What they have is like the space between the floorboards, under the stairs, the expansion gap around the beech floor. Tucking in time together wherever they can make it fit. She wants to ask him what he thinks will be the hardest thing. It's silly to do this, to spend the time she has with him preparing to be apart.

The waiter is on his way over with their order. She doesn't want the meal to start. As long as the meal doesn't start then neither can it end. He straightens the silver cutlery, smooths the white linen and lays before her a cool porcelain plate, rippling with oysters. She plucks one from its pearl grey fan. The sea fills her mouth. The salt-clean breeze in the boat at Dungeness. *I'm sorry.* Along the headland in Ireland and she hears the anxious bleat of mother to child, child to mother. She lifts the last shell to her lips, drains the juice. The Atlantic swell, an unbiddable force, sucks out all sense of direction. The next wave crest, another tug of a current, might lift her high above the whole ocean or slap her onto firm, ridged sand.

Acknowledgements ∫

From the reading which helped me to develop this book, I would particularly like to mention: Warren Colman's article 'Love, Desire and Infatuation: encountering the erotic spirit', in the *Journal of Analytical Psychology*; Julia Kristeva's 'In Praise of Love', from *Tales of Love*; Derek Jarman's notes and Howard Sooley's photographs in *Derek Jarman's Garden*; Alison Carter's *Underwear: the fashion history*.

Many contemporary artists, craftspeople and designers have influenced my thinking about the significance of objects. Works in this book owe a debt to Steve Armitage, Eileen Cooper, Kate Malone, Jim Partridge.

I am indebted to the MA Writing Programme at the University of Glamorgan, especially to Helen Dunmore for her generous support and perceptive criticism. My thanks also to Amanda Dalton, Anatol Orient and Mary Stacey for their comments on various drafts, good talk about writing and unfailing support throughout; to Pennina Barnett, Jane Kirwan and Frankie Wynne for their thoughtful comments on the final draft; to Lisa Eveleigh, my agent; to David, Jacob and Isabelle for their love and patience.